When I Was

When I Was

Miranda Miller

BARBICAN PRESS

Published by Barbican Press

Copyright © Miranda Miller, 2025

This book is copyright under the Berne Convention. No reproduction without permission. All rights reserved.

The right of Miranda Miller to be identified as the author of this book has been asserted by her in accordance with sections 77 and 78 of the Copyright, Designs and Patents Act, 1988.

Some names have been changed and characters have occasionally been conflated in order to protect others' privacy.

Registered office: 1 Ashenden Road, London E5 0DP

www.barbicanpress.com

@barbicanpress1

A CIP catalogue for this book is available from the British Library

ISBN: 978-1-917352-00-0
eISBN: 978-1-917352-01-7

Born in London in 1950, to an Anglo-Indian mother and writer father, Miranda Miller has written eight novels, stretching from the eighteenth century to outer space. As well as the life of the artist Angelica Kauffman narrated in the first person, Miranda has given us the voices of London's homeless women. A former Royal Literary Fund Fellow at London's Courtauld Institute, visual art is a key ingredient in Miranda's work, as is her ear for dialogue which stems from a love for theatre. While London is the heartland of her life and work, her writing also takes in experiences from her years living in Saudi Arabia, Libya, Japan and her much-loved Rome. Married with one daughter, she lives and writes in London.

By the same author

NOVELS
Angelica: Paintress of Minds
Under the Rainbow
Nina in Utopia
The Fairy Visions of Richard Dadd
Loving Mephistopheles
Smiles and the Millennium
Before Natasha
Family

SHORT STORIES
A Thousand and One Coffee Mornings

NON-FICTION
Bed and Breakfast: Women and Homelessness

Memories have huge staying power, but like dreams, they thrive in the dark, surviving for decades in the deep waters of our minds like shipwrecks on the seabed.

~ J.G. BALLARD

Remembrance of things past is not necessarily the remembrance of things as they were.

~ MARCEL PROUST

For my family, alive and dead.

One

Colleen knows this is *her* party; the new young queen on this her coronation day couldn't be feeling more triumphant than Colleen does now. She has put on weight after four children but she knows the architecture of her black satin dress contains it. The skirt's short enough to show off her slim legs and her huge dark eyes can still command a room. Her smile is radiant, far more eloquent than anything she says.

The polished walnut torso and brown wire netting stomach of the Samuells' television set presides squatly over the drawing room, an altar to the new reign they are celebrating and to the Samuells' prosperity. Some of the guests haven't seen a television before, they stare into its grey cave-like depths, trying to extract the brilliant colours of pageantry. A row of children sit cross legged in front of it, waiting to be entertained. Colleen glances over at the sofa where her old mother sits, wearing a dreary brown suit and a prim expression that is infuriating but also makes Colleen's own success more delicious. She can't be right unless miserable old Edie is proved wrong.

Colleen turns back to her best friend, Sally Wilmott, who still looks as young and lovely as she did during the war. Sally's wavy blonde hair is swept up above the harmonious lines of her face and she glows like alabaster with the sun behind it. Her pale blue silk dress, like all her clothes, moulds her slim figure obediently. Sally's beauty would be hateful if she wasn't so sweet, and if Billy didn't have a roving eye.

'It won't catch on,' Maurice says to the group around him. 'I'm an old film man myself, nobody's going to bother watching these flickering black and white ants when they can go down the road to the cinema and see Technicolor gods and goddesses ten feet high.'

As if to confirm his shrewdness, the picture on the television leaps and disappears upwards like the eyeballs of a madman. Westminster Abbey and its congregation of medieval robes self-destruct into jagged abstract patterns. The children wander out into the garden or up to the nursery as the adults laugh and Maurice and Colleen stand helpless, waiting for someone else to fix it. Jim Bates, a photographer, finds some tools in the cellar, switches off the television and opens up the back of it. He's never seen one before, but he patiently settles down to understand it.

'What a practical chap you are, Jim,' Maurice says with admiring condescension.

Jacob Mannheim, a theatrical and film agent, has been staring at Ben as he leaves the room. 'Is that one of yours, Maurice?'

'Ben? Yes. Why?'

'We're looking for a child to play Jimmy Mason's son in that new film. He's perfect. Looks like a little Outer Mongolian Prince.'

Colleen overhears this and glares at Jacob, vowing not to invite him again. Jacob is conferring with his wife, Trish, who efficiently runs the business with him. 'Could you bring him down for a film test next week?' he asks Maurice, who is thrilled at the thought of a son in show business.

'We can have lunch now!' Colleen announces to the assembled friends and neighbours. 'Just a picnic, really.'

It's all laid out on a white lace tablecloth on the long mahogany table in the dining room at the back of the house: lobster flans, quiches, smoked salmon, pâtés, éclairs, marrons glacés and meringues from Fortnum's; chickens and ham from Henry, Colleen's pet black market butcher; salads and fruit salad made by Mrs Hunt, who Colleen thinks is a very unadventurous cook. She's planning to sack her as soon as her wages have been paid. Mrs Hunt stands beside the laden table in a white apron, waiting to help serve.

'Mummy! What do you think you're doing?' Colleen hisses at Edie who's on her knees beside the table, taking curry puffs out of a dark blue hatbox and shoving them onto pink plates which don't match the Meissen plates and all too obviously come from Epsom. Come from another world in fact, like the rich smell of cardamom, cumin, coriander, turmeric, mince, onions, and fresh puff pastry. 'Get up!'

'Just trying to help, dear.'

Edie scrambles to her feet as the stampede for food begins and her curry puffs, she notices, disappear as rapidly as the rest. She's a slim woman who never eats much but most people here are ravenous, as if rationing has ended this morning. Edie can't quite get used to the enormous woman her skinny little daughter has become. She thinks she looks like the queen of the gypsies, in her Chelsea palace with her noisy children and her smiling husband who never does a day's work.

Maurice beams hospitably as he opens more wine. He really is handsome, thinks Gertrude Roxenbrist, who's meeting him for the first time. So tall in his well-cut dark suit, with wavy black hair, clear green eyes and noble features. Rex Gubbins has finally brought her along after boasting for months about his friends the Samuells. Gertrude, a connoisseur of both good looks and money, is vetting them. Maurice looks at her directly for the first time and is struck by her elegance and power. She isn't beautiful but carries herself as if she still was, with a ruthless confidence that reminds him of his mother.

'Any connection to…'

'I was married to Armand Roxenbrist.' In more bohemian company she usually adds, *and I've got the rocks to show for it*, but she isn't sure how this will go down with Maurice. He has already noticed the massive diamond bracelet and necklace she wears with her well-tailored grey suit.

'She has a fabulous story, Maurice,' says Rex, who has agreed he will get ten percent if a deal is struck. 'You really should hear it some time.'

'I'd love to.'

'Rex has told me you're a writer. I'm looking for someone to help me write my memoirs.'

'Are you German?' Alex, Colleen and Maurice's eldest boy, has emerged from the crowd around the table, his mouth full of quiche. Gertrude, who loathes children, thinks there are far too many at this party.

'No, darling. I'm British like you. My husband was Austrian, but we lived in Geneva.'

Alex thinks she looks like a spy. Colleen thinks she looks like an old tart and makes her way anxiously across the crowded room to protect her husband.

'What did you do in the war?' Alex asks Gertrude insistently.

Maurice is proud of his clever son but worries he doesn't always know when to stop. 'Now that's enough. Go and see what the twins are doing.'

Alex, who considers himself a grown-up, is bored by his younger siblings. The twins, Ben and Will, don't even look alike, like proper twins in books. 'I know what they're doing. Martin locked them in the shed and they're crying again.' He doesn't mention that he helped Martin, Sally's son, to find the padlock.

Sally and Colleen rush off to rescue the little boys whose grey flannel suits and white shirts are full of wood shavings.

'And is the little girl yours, as well?' Gertrude asks Maurice pityingly. Viola, a fat toddler in a smocked red dress, sits on the floor between Edie and her nanny.

'Yes, four children,' he admits, with a baffled air. Maurice wants to collude with the contempt for family life he senses in this attractive woman although, really, he's proud of his dynamic wife and confident children. But Maurice always becomes the person he is expected to be and he's willing to play the family martyr for Gertrude.

People begin to trickle back into the drawing room where Jim's still mending the television, a glass of wine and a plate of lobster flan and salad beside him on the Aubusson carpet. Jim's in his mid-thirties, a small, balding, blunt-featured man who lives with his widowed mother in a small house in Ealing and is deeply impressed by the Samuells, who seem to live a charmed life. Jim's struggling to build up his own photographic company—this is the first day off he's had for months—and Maurice's benign idleness is his ideal. One day, he thinks, I'll do bugger all and live in a bloody great house with a bloody great family.

Jim turns on the television again and the young queen, even more loaded with jewellery than Gertrude, floats down the aisle to marry her country. They all cheer and gasp. There are about thirty people in the room now, including neighbours who have come to watch what is still the only television in the street. The children think of it as a pantomime without the jokes but for most of the adults in the room the coronation is moving. The war that dominated their youth, that pickled it in excitement and danger, has finally ended and now they can move on. The newness of the queen and the technology they are watching her on are thrilling glimpses of the future.

Maurice, who had a hostile meeting with his fellow trustees yesterday, isn't in any hurry for things to change. He hears his mother's witty brutal voice: If you're ever going to be successful, Maurice, you'll have to do it by the time you're forty. This invisible barrier was passed two years ago and he's still not sure what he's going to do. The jobs in journalism and films he had in the thirties wouldn't pay for the boys' school fees, the cause of the arguments at the meeting yesterday. He reaches out for Colleen, who's crying, her tears clogging her powder and mascara. Her emotional fertility still bewilders him; she seems to feel so much, so often. She turns to him with her Strength-through-Joy smile and he realises she's happy. Gertrude stares in distaste and Colleen runs off to repair her face, followed by Sally, who is also deeply moved but too poised to cry in public.

At Colleen's kidney shaped dressing table, with its triple mirror and turquoise glass bottles and jars, they feel like girls again. The dark face and the fair one stare at themselves in the mirror and then at each other. Sally allows herself to cry and

Colleen hugs her. She feels boosted, as always, by her big, sunny bedroom and sprays herself generously with *Femme*, inhaling the musky sophistication she longs for.

'Lovely house.'

'So is yours.'

'Yes, but it's miles away. Billy says he's sick to death of Sussex. No sex, he calls it.'

Colleen looks embarrassed, remembering Billy's rampant bisexuality when she first met him, during the war. 'You know you can stay here whenever you like.'

'I'd better take him back tonight so he can sober up before that audition on Friday.'

'Terence Rattigan! Oh, my dear! Wouldn't it be wonderful if he gets it?'

'Yes, but he won't. It's the boozing, it makes his face all puffy and then he drinks even more because he can't get the parts.'

'But he used to be so successful. I thought he was brilliant in that musical about sailors and Wrens.' Colleen wants Sally to be happy again, like her. She hums tunelessly, thinking of all the dancing the four of them used to do together at the Gargoyle, dancing the Blitz away. She wants to go back to the party where she can keep an eye on Maurice, who hardly drinks at all and whose devotion to her is as solid as this house—but that Gertrude woman is obviously after him.

On the landing they hear screams and roars coming from the nursery, up the next flight of wide red carpeted stairs. Colleen and Sally were both obedient only daughters and are pleased that their children are so rowdy. As Colleen comes into the drawing room, she sees Edie sitting alone on a sofa, maddeningly erect and prissy. My children will be free to do as they like, she thinks ferociously, and then forgets all about them as she throws herself into her party.

Maurice is standing with Billy (who really is very squiffy), Gertrude and Rex, who is determined to leave with her at the end of the party. Rex always wears spectacular clothes to make it clear he's an artist and today he's wearing a red and yellow spotted bow tie, a yellow and black check waistcoat, green jacket, and yellow corduroy trousers. Short, tubby, and quick witted, he knows his place as jester to his richer friends.

'Are you still being an angel, Maurice?'

'Awfully risky, backing plays.'

'Did you lose some money?' Rex can't keep the glee out of his voice.

'It wasn't his fault,' Colleen says defensively, coming up and putting her arm through Maurice's. '*Murder at the Vicarage* was much better than *The Mousetrap*, yet that's still running.'

'I thought Agatha Christie was gilt-edged,' Maurice admits. 'How about you, Rex? Still doing the clinches?'

Rex clutches his head in mock despair. 'Don't remind me! The deadline's tomorrow. He ripped her flimsy frock and cried: I cannot let you go like this. Full colour. Part three of *The Doctor's Daydream*, a passionate drama about hospital life.'

They all laugh. Encouraged, Rex wonders if he should tell them about the pornographic drawings that pay so much better than the women's magazines. Collectors' pieces. No, he'll wait until he's got Gertrude on her own.

Billy's smiling, but Sally's watching for the moment when the whisky hits his self-pity and he lashes out, either verbally or physically. Her mother, who lives with them, says she must stop Billy drinking but Sally has no idea how. Billy stares back at his wife, dreading the moment when he's packed into the car and driven back to captivity. He's so envious of Colleen and Maurice that he can hardly look them in the eye and was secretly pleased when his son Martin locked their spoilt brats in the garden shed. Sally's niceness, her refusal to get blotto with him or complain, bring out the worst in him, which is much worse than he ever suspected. On the way here they had another row about Marie, Sally's widowed mother, who looks after Martin and has paid the household expenses since Billy's acting career dried up. At Gatwick Billy announced dramatically that Sally would have to choose between them and by Roehampton he realised, from the quiet determination of her profile behind the driving wheel, who she would choose. Sally knows the row will continue all the way home and Martin will hear lots of words she doesn't want him to know. She would willingly bribe a producer to give Billy a part, just to coax him back into the gentle, playful mood he always seemed to be in a few years ago. His face is bloated, his fair hair is receding but she can still see the big pink handsome charmer she fell in love with. His smile hasn't changed, he shouldn't smile like that. Then she realises she's smiling too. It's what you do at parties.

Colleen and Maurice are tired now and the food and drink are running out. Richard Dimbleby has rumbled his last blessing on the new age, the chart has appeared on the screen, neighbours and fractious children are trickling home. It's a funny time for a party to end but most of them are parents now and nannies aren't what they used to be. They expect time off and walk out after a few months and children are all too audible and visible. Edie's still on the sofa, where Viola has fallen asleep in her lap, her fat little body crushing her grandmother's delicate knees. Colleen's ayah spirited her away so that you would hardly have known there was a child in the bungalow. Then Edie remembers she isn't allowed to talk about India, she purses her lips in case her thoughts burst out and disgrace her. When Sally politely asks if she's enjoyed the party Edie replies with irreproachable dullness that it was very nice. She looks forward to tomorrow morning when she can get the train back to Epsom, to her dear little house, Quetta, and her uncensored memories.

Rex has manoeuvred Gertrude into accepting a lift in his vintage Rolls Royce. Maurice can't resist a few jokes about Mr Toad, but Rex is happy as he sets off with her: a woman of the world, a gay divorcee. Billy's too drunk to drive and Sally wants to get home before darkness makes the unlit Sussex roads dangerous. They're going to give Jim a lift to Ealing.

Arm in arm at their front door, Maurice and Colleen watch their friends leave. Glancing at her face Maurice sees that she's still happy and kisses her, shamelessly washing his clean linen in public.

Two

Viola's alone in the huge nursery. She's heard the grown-ups say it used to be a ballroom, she imagines balls rolling all over the cold polished floor. At least they would move and make a noise, she hates the silence in here. She knows she's meant to do things with all these objects, but they don't do anything back.

Standing up, she can see and smell Mr and Mrs Bear's shop. They are elderly bears who ignore her. Mr Bear wears corduroy trousers, a brown leather waistcoat and looks worried. Mrs Bear wears a headscarf and a green apron and a fat stuffed tummy. They don't look happy in their shop, and they don't sell anything you'd want to buy. The roof of their shop bangs down on your fingers when you try to touch it. Viola gazes at the counter and the rows of dusty shelves behind it, stacked with little rolls of fabric, cups, teapots, vases, jars, boxes, pans and pots. The bears stare back. Viola rubs them against her cheek, sniffs their sour clothes, licks them, whispers to encourage them to be more interesting. As she gives up and tries to put them back in their shop, she knocks over a row of miniature jars and boxes that fall to the wooden floor with a clatter. Above the shop, on the wall, Rex's paintings of a clown and Pinocchio watch her. Viola knows Rex put them there because every time she sees him he kisses her, pinches her cheek and asks if she likes them.

She doesn't, and doesn't think they like her, either. The clown looks down at her spitefully.

Viola tries Nelly the engine, who is red and yellow and blue and rolls around the floor when you push her. She pushes Nelly over to Bronco, a blue tin horse with a red saddle and pedals. If you climb on his back and push the pedals very hard, he jerks around the floor. Near the window the rocking horse looms over her; if you climb up and put your arms around his neck and smell his grey witchy mane he really moves, the gardens lurching below you. But even the rocking horse doesn't go anywhere; Viola knows she isn't allowed to climb up there alone because she will fall off, or perhaps she did fall and hurt herself and cried. Somebody fell. The friendliest part of the room is Gulliver, a teddy bear bigger than Viola who lets her hug him. He's dirty yellow with buttons pretending to be eyes and doesn't know how to talk.

The voices come from the table under the window, but she can't make them happen on her own. The voices go round and round when a grown-up comes: there once was an ugly duckling with feathers all muddy and brown the other birds in so many words said cluck cluck get out of town plop plop plop little April showers I'm getting wet but I don't care at all. Viola loves the ugly duckling man, who's funny and has a voice that whips the air. And wheee, he was a swan. Her heart sings with the hopefulness of it. The April showers lady sounds silly, she ought to wear her raincoat. She loves the boy who points out the Emperor hasn't got any clothes on and wonders if she'd be brave enough to say it. Then there's the teddy bears' picnic man, who sounds like one of those grown-ups who pat your head and pretend they like children. Picnic sounds nice but she doesn't like the idea of teddy bears having a secret life. She looks at Gulliver suspiciously.

Wanting voices, Viola goes to the gate at the top of the stairs and shakes it. She hates the gate; they say it's there to stop her falling downstairs but it's really just to stop her joining them. Daddy's working, the boys are at school, Mummy's shopping again. Her voice comes from the telephone in her bedroom: 'That's Samuell, with two 'l's. Can you deliver it tomorrow afternoon?' Unlike Mrs Bear, Mummy loves being in shops. She disappears into them all the time and even sits in her bedroom to talk to people in shops instead of to Viola.

'Mummy! I want you!'

Sitting on her bed with a list of phone calls to make, Colleen feels a familiar surge of guilt and rage. The little accident. When the twins were two, and she was worn out by looking after three little boys under the age of five, Colleen became pregnant again and had an abortion. It was all done properly in a private nursing home but it hurt her down there and for a while ruined her sex life with Maurice, which had always been marvellous. When she became pregnant yet again four years ago, she thought, what the hell, one more won't make any difference in a house this size.

But when the nurse handed her the bundle it did feel different. Not ecstatic, like when Alex was born, and not clever, like the day she produced twins.

She looked nervously at Sally, who was visiting her in the nursing home, and said, 'I'm not sure I know what to do with a girl.'

Sally said, 'She's lovely.'

Edie also came to see her in the nursing home and stared

at the dark baby with the same grim, pinched expression she'd worn when she first saw Ben. Later, she lavished more affection on those two than on the others, calling them 'my Ben' and 'my little girlie'.

Now Viola's always following her, clinging, sucking her in with those huge dark eyes. Nannies aren't like ayahs; they lose their tempers and flounce away. The Samuells have got through three nannies in two years and a new one is due to arrive next week. Meanwhile Colleen can't understand why Viola isn't happy in her wonderful nursery. She remembers her own delight as she strode around the toy departments in Harrods and Fortnum's, choosing the biggest and best toys for her children. In Karachi all she had was a broken pottery doll and the little black sambo doll that Daddy threw on the fire, glaring at his daughter, *We don't need any more darkies in the family*—but Colleen doesn't want to think about the past. She has made a perfect nursery for them upstairs and Viola should be able to play there on her own. She has a charming little pink and white bedroom next to the nursery yet every night there are tantrums because she says she wants to sleep downstairs with the rest of them. The boys don't want to play with her, being so much older, and she can't be expected to spend all day with a three-year-old. When she does take Viola around the shops with her the child gets tired or demands presents. The gate at the top of the stairs has come to seem a good idea, not just for Viola's safety but for her own.

'Mummy!'

Wearily, Colleen climbs the stairs to the nursery. When she unlatches the gate, the little girl almost knocks her over, hugging her and clutching her hands. She's far too intense, Colleen has confided to Maurice.

'Can I come too?'

'Where?'

'Everywhere.'

'I'm only going to pick the boys up from school.'

'When can I go to school?'

'When you're five.' Thank God. Sally says that now Martin's at school she feels ten years younger.

'Can I sleep downstairs tonight?' Sometimes, if she makes enough fuss, she's allowed to sleep in Daddy's dressing room.

'Not tonight. We're going out, so Mrs Hunt will look after you and put you to bed.'

'Where are you going?'

'We're having dinner with Jim and his girlfriend at the Ox on the Roof.'

They often go there. Viola knows an ox is like a cow and imagines them all on the roof, the cow and the big fat grown-ups with their tables and chairs. It sounds dangerous, she's worried they'll fall off or go floating away.

Colleen's worried too, because the dinner has been set up to ask Jim to help Maurice find a job. He hasn't worked since he was in the navy during the war but somehow the money Florence left is running out, trustees are getting nasty—it's all very unfair and has made Maurice, who used to be so sweet, petulant.

Colleen doesn't like walking. In India it was too hot to walk so you got tongas or rickshaws. In London it's usually cold or wet and so, as she can't drive, she gets taxis. When Maurice says she's spending too much, Colleen asks sharply if he expects her to stay at home all the time? She puts on her camel coat with the lynx collar and buttons up Viola's cherry red coat.

Colleen sets off with economic intentions but she's late and Viola's little legs will get tired and there isn't a bus that goes all the way there and a beautifully free taxi appears in the Fulham Road—so she hails it. She and Viola smile at each other in the dark purring interior as they swoop over to Queensgate. It's a nice little school, Colleen thinks, full of boys who would be suitable friends. Her faith in her sons is boundless although she does wish Will would learn more tact. Last week when each boy had to stand up in class and describe his family Will said, my mother's Indian and my father doesn't do anything.

Viola is amazed there are so many boys in the world. Big boys in blue caps and blazers and short grey trousers come pouring down the street, yelling and fighting. She stares at the other side of Queensgate, near Kensington Gardens, where the school she will go to one day looms. Boys and girls can't go to the same school. On the pavement outside their school stand her three brothers, looking angry. Colleen would like to keep the taxi to go home but if Maurice hears about it, he'll lecture her, so she pays the driver and walks towards the three boys, wanting to hug them but knowing they'll be embarrassed if she does. They stare at her with various degrees of indignation. She's always late.

Alex has just been told he's been entered for the Townsend Warner History Prize, and he doesn't think anyone is sufficiently impressed. His teacher, Batty, mentioned it casually at the end of the day and his brothers don't seem to understand this means he is one of the cleverest boys in the whole country, although he has just told them so several times.

Will is in tears because of his utter humiliation in the gym just now. Like Viola, he's fat, and gyms are designed with thin children in mind. He can just about lumber up the wall bars but swinging on ropes and jumping over the horse are impossible feats and anyway he can't see the point. He explained this to Sergeant Taylor who roared in front of the whole class that Samuell Minor was a spastic and made him run at the horse, thighs and breasts wobbling while they all giggled and then roared with laughter as Will flung himself at the horse and got stuck there, flailing and gasping. Even his friends laughed. Will hated the rows of skinny little boys and the smell of dusty leather in his nostrils before he clambered down. He almost suffocated, trying not to cry for the rest of the afternoon. Now he wants to let the scalding tears run down his face and explain how horrible it was, but he can't do both at once and nobody's listening.

Ben used to be sympathetic to his twin's problems but he's sulking again. Dark and compact, the most handsome of the brothers, he walks apart from the others and behind them, as if he'd like to lose them. Ben doesn't cry but broods on injustice. Although he's half an hour older than Will he has been put in a lower class and they all think he's stupid. The words they can all see dance and tease him, his exercise books come back to him slashed with red ink and just now, when it was his turn to read aloud in class, he had to guess at the words that came out all jumbled.

Viola drops her mother's hand, sensing that she's lost her attention. As they walk past the bombed-out church she looks up and notices that Will's crying. She's shocked that even when you're eight things are still so bad that you have to cry. She knows how awful it is when you can't stop, when the hiccups and shudders come. Viola takes Will's hand, which is small and thin and doesn't make her feel safe like her mother's big hand with its fierce red nails and fingers bulging with rings. Will lets her hold his hand until he remembers that holding hands with a girl in the street is even worse than blubbing and drops it.

Alex dances between the twins. 'When was the battle of Waterloo?' Ben glares at him in silence. Will knows, he struggles to speak. The tears swill around inside him, later they will curdle and cause another attack of catarrh and he'll have to go to bed. He can't speak.

'1815, stupid!'

'I knew that, anyway.'

Colleen's overwhelmed by their insistent egos. It's wonderful to have so many children, she can feel the pain of her lonely childhood receding; yet when she's with all four of them she sometimes feels as if she's being eaten alive. Reminded of food, she stops at the baker's shop on the Fulham Road where she lets them choose doughnuts, chocolate cake and crumpets for tea.

Three

Viola's alone in the nursery again. The gate at the top of the stairs is shut, Mummy's busy shopping, Mr and Mrs Bear have failed to entertain her again and she has flung them on the floor in revenge. She crouches beside the table by the window, trying to make the songs happen. It's something to do with the thing called the needle, which goes round and round—she tries to force it and it snaps. She cries, then yells, directing her noise at the clown smirking on the wall and the silence in the vast shadowy room. Far below a door slams. Her brothers have come back from school and her heart beats with excitement.

Feet come thumping up the stairs and she holds her breath. Sometimes they come up to the nursery but more often they go to their rooms or have meetings in the garden shed which is their clubhouse, where girls aren't allowed.

Will comes into the nursery. He's alone, brothers are nicer on their own. He sits importantly on the wicker chair opposite her and asks if she can read yet. He takes a book from a shelf and hands it to her. Viola is entranced by a wonderful picture of a thin child man with pointed ears running through steep cobbled streets where little houses are squashed so close together that their windows almost touch across the street. Two women stand at their windows, chatting to each other. Viola wants to go there, to live in a house so small that you can open your window and talk to someone. Will points to the black specks around the picture and asks if she can read them. She shakes her head impatiently and turns the page, looking for more pictures. An old woman in black is holding an apple. Inside it are the streets and houses and people, mysteriously shrunk: a little world, another world that Viola longs to enter.

'Read it to me.'

Will sighs because people ought to be able to read. It's silly that Ben can't read but Viola is quite young. Perhaps she will learn if he teaches her.

Will reads the story. Viola isn't sure if it comes out of the book or out of Will's head. Is this town somewhere she can really go to and meet the apple woman? There are words she doesn't know, details she doesn't understand, but this doesn't destroy her excitement that these things can happen. She runs over to the shelves where there's a toy called a snowstorm. When you shake it snow falls on tiny houses inside a glass ball. She shakes it vigorously at Will, who doesn't make the same connection. But he agrees to read it again, flattered by his sister's passionate attention.

Of course, she isn't really his sister. He's a Prince of Atlantis, lost at birth and adopted by these coarse people who pretend to be his parents. One day they will admit the truth and he will return to his kingdom, where his subjects will recognise his true worth and adore him. Meanwhile his sister's admiration makes him feel like a magician. But it's boring to read the same thing twice, so about halfway through he closes the book.

'I'm going downstairs. Don't you want to watch Children's Hour?'

'No. Read it again!' She needs to hear it again, to see if

all the words come out the same, like songs, or if they change each time.

'Oh, read it yourself.'

'I can't.' She stares angrily at the swirling black marks in the book he hands her. He stands up to go. She knows that tears, which usually work on grown-ups, just annoy big children like Will. He cries too, sometimes, but they never seem to cry together. She follows him through the gate at the top of the stairs because at least there will be people down there.

The television's been demoted from the drawing room to a small dark room behind the kitchen where the children usually eat. The boys have disappeared into their rooms and Mrs Hunt is in the kitchen, rolling out pastry and talking to Johnny, who has a big glass of beer. He often talks to Viola and lets her sit with him in the dark cellar where the boiler is. He gives her sips of his beer, which she thinks tastes disgusting but is somehow comforting and friendly like a horse's breath and laughs when she spits it out. Mrs Hunt's as old as Grandma, with grey hair and a face so full of paths and mounds sprouting with hair that she looks like a park; when Viola told her so a few weeks ago she was cross. She's usually cross, Viola knows Mrs Hunt doesn't like her or her family. They stop talking as soon as Viola comes into the kitchen. Johnny looks like a walnut but doesn't mind being told so.

'What you up to then, sunshine?' She likes talking to Johnny. He laughs a lot and says, 'funny old world,' which seems to cover everything.

Viola goes to the big wooden table where there's a huge red tin of biscuits.

'You'll spoil your supper,' Mrs Hunt says grimly.

'Can I have some? Please?'

'They're not mine. Help yourself.'

Johnny opens the tin for her, and she takes a fistful, cramming them into her mouth until the hard wall melts against her gums into mushy sweetness. She wanders through to the back room where Johnny switches on the television, which hisses and splutters and dances wildly until he touches something at the back and the chart appears. This is a sort of grey chessboard with a picture of a girl in the centre and is supposed to be fascinating, although Viola would much rather look at the pictures in the books upstairs. Some days children from other houses in the street knock on her door to ask if they can watch television, but today Viola's alone in this grey cave. The chart flickers and grown-ups appear, smiling too much and putting on soppy voices like the April Showers lady. Mummy and Daddy Woodentop appear with their jerky walk and Viola's embarrassed for them because some grown-up obviously thinks this is what children want.

'Ah, the spastic family.' Alex is standing in the doorway, smiling in his superior way.

'I think they're silly.'

'What kind of stories do you like?'

She wants to tell him about the ugly duckling and the town in the apple and her long boring day in the nursery, but the words can't get out of her head. She stares up at her huge brother, who remembers she's shy and wanders out of the room. The flowerpot men appear, Bill and Ben (who isn't her brother of course). They're always saying boddle up, which is very rude, to Little Weed, who's some kind of girl and has a silly voice. She sways and the flowerpot men move in jerky slow motion, you can see their strings. Viola feels sorry for them because they can't walk or talk properly and the garden they live in is drab and grey.

When Colleen climbs down from the taxi, loaded with bags, and opens the front door she feels exhilarated that this is her household. Then Viola runs to her, and Alex doesn't. She remembers how he used to, how he adored her, then she meets Mrs Hunt's disapproving gaze from the kitchen. Colleen needs a gin and tonic and time to do her hair and make-up before Maurice comes home—but there aren't any Indian servants to anticipate her wishes, so she has to calm Viola, who seems to think her mother has abandoned her forever every time she leaves the house. Over her daughter's head Colleen stares at her eldest son, who stares back coldly from the stairs.

'What's the matter, Alex?' She takes off her coat and puts it in the cloakroom, while Viola clings to her like a limpet. When Colleen goes back to the hall Alex is still on the stairs. She holds out the arm that isn't wrapped around Viola. 'Darling? I'm sorry I couldn't pick you up from school, I had to meet Sally for lunch. I'll pick you up tomorrow.'

'I don't want you to.'

She remembers that children don't mean to be rude and says, 'Was it fun coming back all by yourselves?'

'What's chee-chee?' He watches her face and sees that tense, hard expression under all the powder she wears.

'Do you mean chichi, darling? It means fussy and a bit pretentious, like a restaurant that's expensive but not very good.'

'You're not a restaurant.'

'Of course not. I think you've got a bit mixed up. Have you done your prep?'

'Harris Major said you were chee-chee. I want to know what it means.'

'It doesn't mean anything. Just a silly word children use.'

Colleen loosens Viola's arms and runs past the kitchen, where Mrs Hunt and Johnny are staring at her, past Alex who steps aside much too politely. In her bedroom she locks the door and bites her lips, allowing herself a few sobs and tears. Outside the door Viola wails. She cries too much, Will does too, it's no use being too thin skinned. Colleen stares at the pink satin bed, at the Persian rug and the pink satin pelmet and curtains. Maurice doesn't understand. Touch of the tar brush, darling? Never mind. But she does mind, she can't escape. The girls at school in India sneering at her, giggling at her chee-chee accent that Mummy said was Welsh; the English ladies at the Club on the cantonment in Quetta ostracising Mummy. After that Edie refused to go to the Club and her parents' marriage became even more silent and miserable.

Colleen sees herself in the triple mirror of her dressing table, her face a mess of smudged powder, crimson lipstick and mascara. Sitting on her stool, she cleans her face with cotton wool and astringent lotion, reassembles herself. This is the face Maurice loves, the children love, the face that lives in the house she loves.

'Mummy!'

'I'm just coming.'

She sprays her brown hair with lacquer and squirts on her favourite perfume, *Femme*. An expensive, sophisticated scent; Florence gave her the first bottle and she has used it ever since. It guarantees that she will be a Florence woman, not an Edie one.

'Mummy! I want you!'

Colleen unlocks the door and lets Viola adore her. Small children are so easy. Alex became critical early on. One evening when he was four, she came into his room to say goodnight before she went out and Alex stared at her and told her she looked like a sofa in her new dress. She never wore it again. Viola and Will are the most temperamental of her children but also the easiest to talk to. From Will's absolute certainty that he will be an artist he commiserates with her about what his brothers are to do. What if you need Maths to be a prime minister? What if Ben never does learn to read? Into Viola's wide dark eyes Colleen pours her thoughts, secure that the little girl can't understand or judge her.

It's nearly time for Maurice to come back from looking for the job he has so heroically agreed to do to save them all. Colleen hurries to the twins' bedroom to remind Ben to get ready for his lesson and then goes down to the kitchen to remind Mrs Hunt to have the Stilton and biscuits ready for Maurice when he comes in.

Maurice looks exhausted and baffled as he opens the front door. Viola watches the two vast shambolic figures embrace. Daddy smells of fog and coal and the cold night outside, Mummy smells of dressing table. Viola loves being with them in the firelit green drawing room with the curtains safely drawn. Johnny goes down to the cellar to stoke the boiler and Mrs Hunt makes dinner. Daddy's smelly cheese and whisky, Mummy's gin and Viola's sharp lime juice are all together on the little round table in front of Daddy's green velvet chair. She climbs onto his knee and Maurice, between yawns, sings: Joggety, joggety, joggety, joggety, goes the galloping major. Then he sees Ben, the little major, sulking in the doorway.

Maurice beams at him, hoping there won't be trouble this evening. Ben is the best looking of all his children and in many ways his favourite. Alex is often too clever for his own good, Will hardly seems like a boy at all and Viola doesn't really have a personality yet. But Ben is a little man, compact and dignified. When he was a toddler he used to fly into rages all the time and, when told he had to apologise, would mutter, 'I say I'm sorry but I only ickle bit.' His failure to read has already cost him that film part and how can he possibly get through his Common Entrance in a few years—Maurice sighs and shudders, unable to imagine the appalling fate of a boy who can't go to a public school. Ben catches his sigh and glares at them all.

He hates every moment of his nightly humiliation: being dragged out of his room when he's playing with Will (who is always quite happy to do his beastly prep for him) and having to read for Daddy like a seal doing tricks in a circus. They all think he's stupid, he knows they do, and it's not fair. Words on the page dance and go blurry and he says silly things, the wrong things. He learned that boring book about the cat and the rat by heart and recited it last night, but Daddy caught him out and now there's a new book and he can't even read the bloody cover.

Watching Ben cry is awful. Colleen looks away, clutches her gin and tonic and hums as Viola starts to cry in sympathy and is told to leave the room.

The children usually eat in the dark little television room behind the kitchen, where Mrs Hunt eats. There's beef stew with jacket potatoes and bread and butter pudding. Alex says they ought to have a talking prize at supper, and an eating prize. Will tells him to shut up. Ben comes in late, looking furious, and says he isn't hungry. Alex takes the Jacket potato off Ben's plate and eats it. Viola's very quiet, hoping nobody will notice she's still there. Bedtime is ages away, perhaps it will never happen; she will stay down here forever with all of them and never have to go up into the darkness with the bad dreams.

Four

'Wonderful, darling!'

'Can I have some more?'

'I want thirds. I won, didn't I Daddy? I always win.'

Colleen bustles happily between the dining room and the kitchen, humming tunelessly as she makes more sweetcorn fritters and takes the second chicken out of the oven. She enjoys Sunday lunches, when Mrs Hunt goes off to visit her so-called husband (who Colleen suspects is in prison) and she can feed her family.

Maurice inhales the delicate smell of sage and onion stuffing as he carves the second roast chicken with a flourish, singing under his breath: *There was I waiting at the church*. He's disappointed that none of his children can sing, they all seem to have inherited Colleen's flat voice. When Maurice was a little boy, he won prizes for singing and before they left Hampstead the rabbi told his mother he had such a beautiful voice he should become a cantor. Mother looked very unenthusiastic. She always used to say religion was for the old, the poor and the ugly. At that time, they wanted Maurice to be a stockbroker, like his father Aubrey. No, they can't sing, and they don't seem to be athletic, either, although last term Ben delighted him by winning a boxing prize. He looks fondly at the dark, pugnacious little boy.

'How's the boxing coming along?'

'I knocked Chesham out.'

'Splendid.'

Ben loves dancing around with big gloves on, lashing out. He has tried it on Alex and Will when they tease him about not being able to read. Will was terrified but Alex just kicked him. When Ben pointed out that was against the rules Alex said he didn't care about rules. There he is again.

'I did win this week, didn't I?'

'Now pipe down, Alex. Wait until we've had pudding and then I'll decide. Will, you're very quiet. What's the matter?'

Will is quivering with indignation. 'It's not fair if he wins. I made my speech about Michelangelo, that was really interesting, all Alex did was go on and on about Napoleon again.'

'Napoleon was the most famous man in the world. All Michelangelo did was paint pictures.'

'He was a sculptor.'

'And he painted too. He painted the Sixteen Chapel. See, you don't know anything about it.'

'It was the Sistine Chapel. And I do know, I know far more than you, so there. Anyway, all Napoleon did was fight battles and kill millions of people, what's so great about that?'

Maurice sighs. When he's sitting at the top of his family table like this, he's haunted by those other family meals, Friday nights at Rose's in Bishop's Avenue. His powerful grandmother ruled them all, even Florence, who seemed like a schoolgirl again at her mother's table. In the warm light of the big silver menorah Rose had brought from Warsaw Maurice used to listen to his aunts and uncles tease each other and boast about how much money they'd made. Jokes flew in Yiddish and Rose always invited some broken down old émigré who chatted to her in Polish or Russian.

Alex and Will are kicking each other viciously under the table. 'Maurice! Do something!' Colleen mutters.

Sunday lunches always end like this, with Alex and Will arguing and Ben sulking and Viola daydreaming. To her it seems that these meals go on forever, she longs to run away from the table but knows that isn't allowed.

'Wonderful meal, darling,' Maurice says to Colleen as she brings in the golden apple pie, fragrant with cinnamon and cloves. Then she fetches a blue and white striped bowl of cream with a ladle in it and puts it down proudly on the long table.

'Real cream! No more sympathetic cream.' She smiles fondly, remembering how sweet her little boys were when she knew more than them.

Alex pours half the bowl over his apple pie and the twins squabble over the rest. Maurice, who likes cream too, finally gets annoyed. 'You'd think they'd never seen food before!'

'They've just got healthy appetites. There's more cream in the fridge. It's marvellous now there's so much food in the shops. Poor Henry's going out of business.'

The Samuells didn't suffer much from rationing. Florence had American colonels billeted at Erlwood, her big house near Ascot, and she was generous with the extra food and coupons they gave her. After Florence died Colleen became the favourite customer of Henry, a black-market butcher in World's End. Colleen remembers a bleaker war, before she met Maurice, when she lived in the cold Epsom house and Mummy was ill and Daddy was dying, and she was expected to concoct meals for them all out of powdered eggs and spam and pilchards in that nasty little kitchen. That draught from the front door blew up her skirt as she carried yet another tray up to the freezing bedroom where Daddy lay dying. Mummy was always dying, she'd been at it as long as Colleen could remember. But Daddy used to be strong and energetic, it was heartbreaking to see him lying there. Even when he was so weak she had to feed him with a spoon he wouldn't speak to his wife, he flirted with the nurse until he had no more voice to flirt with. But he was always nice to me, Colleen thinks, and I wish he was still here, and she'd died instead—but that's all in the boring old past.

Colleen smiles radiantly and stoops to kiss Maurice, who responds tenderly. He wishes they could go to bed but the house is full of children and anyway there's all that palaver with rubbers or Dutch caps nowadays.

Alex is furious that they're being soppy when they should be admiring him. One day Will might win the talking prize and if that happens Alex thinks he will commit suicide or possibly murder his brother. He hurries to finish his second helping of apple pie and stands up. 'Pudding's over. I've won, haven't I, Daddy?'

Maurice stares at his eldest child in perplexity. He really is a clever boy, wonderfully articulate with a retentive memory. He argues all the time—but if he becomes a politician that will be an asset. When he was tiny Alex used to lie in his cot making up songs and poems while his parents listened adoringly. His favourite was: a lorry and a van called me; Maurice often thinks he seems to be crooning it still, over and over. He doesn't get on with the younger ones, doesn't even try. Then Maurice remembers his own violent jealousy when Benjamin was born. He smiles benevolently and hands Alex the shilling for the talking prize, as he does every Sunday.

Will screams with rage and falls on Alex, biting and scratching his hand to get the prize. Ben helps Will, because he's his twin and Will's no good at fighting and Alex is their natural enemy. Alex, who has already hidden the shilling in his pocket, yells, 'They're ganging up on me!' and looks at his parents for help.

Colleen ignores them, clearing the table before they break everything on it. Boys fight, that's what they're supposed to do. Maurice tries feebly to break up the fight, which has moved over to the French windows that lead to the small paved garden. Then he decides he's had enough of family life and announces he's going to the Embankment for a bit of exercise.

As he puts on his coat in the hall Viola runs up with her coat on, clutching some bread she's saved from lunch. She looks a mess, with her cherry red coat all crooked and her dark greasy hair in tangles around her sallow moon face. Another nanny has just left, and Colleen doesn't seem to have time to do much washing and brushing. Viola's covered with crumbs from the thick white slices of bread she clutches as her passport to the walk she desperately wants.

Maurice, who is fastidious about appearances, straightens her coat, washes her hands at the basin in the cloakroom, wipes lunch away from her mouth with a flannel, pulls up her white socks and puts the bread in a paper bag. Then he accepts her hand and they walk together down Beaufort Street. For Viola, this walk is her weekly prize. She knows she can't talk as much as her brothers. His hand feels dry and warm, completely safe. Maurice enjoys her quiet company and wonders if the talking prize was such a good idea after all. He started it when Alex was four to encourage the twins, who were not as precocious as Alex, to talk more. Also, he remembers, he wanted his children to be self-assured, not crushed by rules and strict governesses as he was when he was small. He hardly ever ate with Florence and Aubrey, by the time he was Alex's age he'd been packed off to prep school. Well, they're certainly confident, even cocky; perhaps it's time to stop the prize. But then there will be sulks and fuss—he decides to leave it and beams down at Viola, who is skipping with excitement as the river opens up in front of them, a vivid blue streak beneath the wide sky.

Seagulls like the paper aeroplanes her brothers throw scream with joy and swoop on the bread she flings over the wall, down at the muddy beach. The lucky people who live on the houseboats wake up every morning to water and sky and freedom. In summer guttersnipes swim in the river, Daddy says, and Viola wishes she was a guttersnipe. They're boys, he says, and they take off all their clothes, jump off the bridge and get typhoid.

Viola looks up at the looming blur on her left. 'Are they doing it now?' she asks hopefully.

'Not today. It's only March. It's Spring.'

Grown-ups don't like it when you ask questions all the time. March and Spring have an atmosphere of sun and light and walking into this wonderful surprise where the houses end and the water dances with the sky. Every Sunday after lunch it's amazingly still here.

Maurice looks down at the tubby little girl who laughs as she throws bread at the wall. He wonders if she'll be pretty and who she will marry. They'll all have money of their own—he sighs as he thinks of the complications that's already caused.

All very well to tie the money up in trusts for the children but how is he supposed to live on his piddling income while he brings them up? Sydney is their family solicitor, Maurice has known him all his life and would never have expected him to be so tough. Next week he starts the new job Jim has helped him to get with a big oil company. Public Relations, whatever that means. Lots of lunches with clients, Jim assured him. You'll be good at it, Maurice, you're so affable.

But he's a writer. He thinks of his study, where he hasn't sat for months, the desk piled with unpaid bills and toys. Not a real writer perhaps, like Boris, whose early novels were heralded with rapture and fanfares of praise. But where's Boris now? Drinking himself to death in a poky flat in North London, still writing that great novel he started before the war. Maurice doesn't want to be that sort of writer. He would like to write film scripts again but when he sent *Babs Knows Best* to the studios where he used to work in the thirties, they sent it back with a very chilly note. He thinks of Gertrude, of her marvellously colourful past as a chorus girl who married and divorced one of the richest men in the world. He thinks of her present, too, of her wit and charm and her elegant, bejewelled figure sitting alone (so she says) in her luxurious flat near Regents Park. We must get together and talk about my book, she always says, implying that getting together will be a memorable experience.

Viola has run out of bread and turns from the ducks and seagulls to her father, sighing heavily above her. He's slow and sad, like most grown-ups, she gives him her hand again to cheer him up. On the way home she lists her requests for the week, knowing that if she says Daddy says she can, it will happen:

'Can I sleep downstairs tonight?'

Maurice knows she will cry and scream for hours if she has to sleep alone on the top floor. He has almost resigned himself to giving up his dressing room to her.

'Just for tonight, then.'

'You're the nicest daddy in the world. Can I go to Emma's house tomorrow?'

As soon as the gate at the top of the stairs was taken away, Viola left the house and went out to the communal gardens where the children play, watched over by their nannies. High brick walls topped with shards of broken glass keep out nasty boys. Viola thinks most of the children in the gardens are quite nasty enough, she hates their noisy games but she loves Emma, who is just like her and has the same fairy godmother.

'I don't see why not.' Maurice looks down affectionately at her chubby beaming face.

Five

The children have chicken pox. The quarantine period is two weeks, when they can't go to school or play with other children. Each night they have to be bathed in a special pink solution that smells like disinfectant.

Susie, the new nanny, sighs with exhaustion as she chases Viola, who's running squealing and naked round the bathroom, to envelop her in a big pink towel. It has taken an hour to get the three boys into their pyjamas and pack them off to the twins' room, where they're allowed to read until bedtime. Susie remembers her own childhood, in a bombed-out cellar in Rotterdam with her tubercular mother and her baby brother who died because her mother didn't have enough milk. These people have so much food that at the end of every meal they throw away enough to feed another family: milk, cream, butter, bacon, cheese, pork, chicken… rich Jews, according to Mrs Hunt.

Susie's pale with the strain of pretending to like children. She's chained to these four spoilt overfed brats and the only men she ever meets are Mr Samuell, who is handsome but old and blinks at her short sightedly through his glasses as if he doesn't even see her, and Johnny, who stokes the boiler and does the garden and must be at least sixty. On Wednesday afternoons she goes to her English lessons in a school on Tottenham Court Road and on Sundays, her free day, she wonders what to do.

'You're hurting me. Ow!' She has finished drying the wriggling child and is pulling a comb through her dark hair, which is fine and tangles easily. Every night bedtime is a war. If she lets down her defences for one minute and shows Viola how much she longs to slap her the child will go down to the drawing room and complain to her mother.

Viola has the most beautiful nursery and bedroom Susie has ever seen, like something in a movie. Even Susie's room behind the nursery is twice the size of the cellar where she spent most of her childhood. Yet every night Viola storms and rages about having to sleep up there 'all alone'. So is Susie nobody, then? She has to listen to Viola's tantrums, all night she wakes up complaining about her bad dreams and whines for her mother, who doesn't hear. Susie is getting very good at not hearing.

'I don't want to go to bed. The boys don't have to go yet.'

'They are big boys.'

'I'm a big girl.' She is, tall and fat, covered with chicken pox sores. 'I'm not tired. Tell me a story.'

'What sort of story? My English is not so good.'

They have got as far as her pink nightdress and dressing gown and the landing; now Viola will either agree to go upstairs or go rushing downstairs to Mrs Samuell, who is one of those mothers who thinks all her piglets are swans. Tonight the Samuells have guests, so it will be particularly bad for Susie if Viola bursts in with tales of being ill-treated. Firmly, Susie takes the child's hand, leads her up to her bedroom and tucks her in, wishing she could tie her to the bed she wriggles and whines in.

'I want a story. A fairy story.'

'I don't know such stories.'

Downstairs in the twins' room the three boys are reading *Greenmantle* for the second time. While they're ill they are allowed to read aloud in their pyjamas until they're sleepy, they've already got through four Biggles books and *King Solomon's Mines*. Alex discovers books, reads them himself and then dispenses them to his brothers, sure that they won't understand them properly. Will mispronounces words, he doesn't seem to know what the First World War was, and Ben always pretends to have a sore throat so he doesn't have to read aloud. Alex sits on the floor between their twin beds (even their beds are twins, excluding him) and reads in a rapid, fluent voice.

Colleen pauses outside their door to check that they're all right. She's wearing her Norman Hartnell black satin dress with the diamond necklace Florence left Alex. There's no point in letting it moulder in some bank vault. The diamonds are Cartier but not as good as the ones Gertrude's wearing downstairs. Poor Sally has come to dinner, too, and Rex and Jim and Jacob and Trish. Colleen has forgiven Jacob for his Outer Mongolian crack, Maurice says these things don't matter anymore.

Greenmantle. When she was a child, her father wanted her to read it but there were no women until page 166 and she preferred *The Secret Garden*. Mary Lennox, lonely and unhappy, was as close to herself as a child in a book could be, thrust from India to the cold grey strangeness of Yorkshire. Like Mary, Colleen couldn't dress herself or understand what people said to her in their broad Yorkshire accents. She read the book again and again, even now she can remember phrases that seemed unbearably near the bone. *A little thin face and a little thin body, thin light hair and a sour expression; a sickly, fretful, ugly little baby; a plain little piece of goods; a disagreeable child; she could scarcely be expected to love her or to miss her very much when she was gone.* Mary's mother had died, hers hadn't but she'd often wished she would, so that she could be adopted by the real Mary's parents or her warm-hearted Yorkshire relations. When she eventually fell in love with her cousin Robin it had been because he reminded her of Dickon.

But Colleen knew *Greenmantle* had some special meaning for her father, that he was trying to tell her something about his years in Persia, the lost period he ranted about when he had bouts of malaria. Ben reminds Colleen of her father, Edie thinks so too and has just given him the Russian enamelled cashbox full of her dead husband's medals. Ben keeps it under his bed and saves up his pocket money in it.

Colleen smiles, full of love for all her children, for Maurice and this house. On the top floor Viola, who should have been asleep hours ago, is crying. Colleen pants as she climbs the stairs to the nursery. These nannies are useless. When she was Viola's age her Ayah slept across the threshold of her room and leapt up if Colleen so much as whimpered in her sleep. Viola is sitting up in bed, sobbing and screaming hysterically. Susie stands by the window in a white nightdress looking sullen and helpless.

Viola wraps herself like a boa constrictor around her mother. She tries to tell her about the horrible things that have just happened to her, about being all alone in the burning city and running down steep streets to the black sea. But the words can't get past the raging storm of her feelings.

'What's the matter, darling?' Colleen wants to get back to her dinner party and Viola's tears and slobber are not doing her dress any favours.

'I want to sleep downstairs!' the child finally gasps between sobs and Colleen decides it's going to be less bother to let her sleep on the camp bed in Maurice's dressing room.

During a lull in the reading the boys hear their sister's voice.

'Why is she crying?' Ben asks.

'She's a girl, girls cry all the time,' Will explains.

'So do you,' Alex sneers. 'Waterworks.'

Colleen, in the abrupt voice she always uses with servants, tells Susie to take Viola downstairs to the room next to her bedroom. Susie doesn't understand all her words but is irritated by her intonation. She speaks like a queen giving orders to a slave, Susie hates her fat arms bulging out of her black dress.

Downstairs, over coffee and liqueurs, Jacob is trying to persuade Maurice to back another play and Rex is teasing Gertrude. Maurice, at the top of the long mahogany table, watches the sparks between these two and wonders if they're still lovers. Now that he's married his friends no longer confide in him about their love affairs, as if he has moved to a different continent. Gertrude literally sparkles, in those vulgar but covetable diamonds, and her alert face (not beautiful, Maurice reminds himself) is hungry for amusement. Rex, sitting opposite her, is deliberately casual, the only man who isn't wearing a dinner jacket. His red bow tie and green waistcoat announce he's an artist, although he spends more time talking and drinking than painting. 'Let's face it, Gertrude, you and I are just too selfish for family life.'

'You speak for yourself. I'd love to settle down, I adore the things children say. I think I'd make a marvellous mother.'

A bit late, Rex thinks. The Artist's Daydream. Clinch with Gertrude and her alimony.

Jim, who always says the nice but obvious thing, raises his

glass as Colleen totters back into the room: 'Well, here comes the best mother in London.'

Sally, who is too miserable to talk much, wishes she'd just put her son to bed. Then she remembers Martin will be fine with her mother.

Colleen tells them all about her daughter's sleeping dramas. Gertrude, a bit squiffy, stands up, determined to prove her talent for motherhood.

'I'm going up to say goodnight to her. I just love little children,' she says to nobody, although it's clear this remark is aimed at Rex, who has evaded marriage and children for forty-five years and has no intention of giving in now. He smiles and turns towards Sally, who is younger and prettier and looks lonely.

Ten minutes later Gertrude comes back, convulsed with laughter. 'Viola said—aren't children wonderful—she said, now can you send the men up, please.'

They all roar with laughter and upstairs the children, lying awake, hear them and wonder how it feels to be old.

Six

Sally has come to stay because Billy's being very silly. Silly-billy, Viola says, and gets a laugh from her assembled family. Viola adores Sally and hopes she will stay forever. This is partly because, while Sally's sleeping in her room, Viola gets to sleep in Maurice's dressing room which she's filling with her toys to claim her territory. Also, Sally looks like a Princess, with her long fair wavy hair, blue eyes and golden skin. Viola, who has no idea how she looks, intends to look like Sally when she grows up. Every morning, as soon as she wakes up, Viola climbs the stairs to make sure she's still there.

Sally, who has come to escape from family life and think about her marriage, pretends to be asleep as the door creaks open and the child stands over her, breathing heavily as she pushes a large toy spaniel into her arms. Poked in the eye by a velvety paw, Sally sits up, resisting the urge to stay in bed and cry all day. 'Your mummy will be worried about you.'

'No, she won't. She's still asleep.'

'I can hear children playing in the gardens. Why don't you go down and play with them?'

'I don't like children. I like you.'

'I expect you want your room back again.'

'I hate my room.'

'But it's so nice. I'm not staying long, just until Tuesday.'

'How long is that?'

'Today's Saturday. What's the time?'

The child looks blank and Sally realises she lives in a timeless world. Live for the moment, Billy's always telling her, annoyed by what he calls her bourgeois obsession with order. Drunk and disorderly. He has actually been arrested twice by the village policeman and his latest affair is with a widow called Cynthia Peters who lives in Brighton.

Last Wednesday at midnight, after another row, Billy drove off to see Cynthia and Sally ransacked their bathroom cabinet for sleeping pills because if Billy didn't love her any more she didn't want to live. Her mother, who was supposed to be asleep, came into the bathroom, flushed all the pills down the toilet and turned to her angrily. She has lived in England since before Sally was born but still sounds very French.

'Don't be so idiot. What about your son? You think Martin wants a dead mother?'

Sally, who needed sympathy, stared into her mother's leathery old face. Seen through tears it looked even worse, as if the big nose was melting into the obstinate chin. What about me? She wanted to ask. Why shouldn't I have some fun and love before I look like you? But her mother was getting ready for her sacrifice speech—'You have a child, you have to make sacrifices for him. Billy is cretin, but you choose this cretin, you must live with him now.'

After Viola goes down to breakfast Sally lies on her bed and misses her little boy. Colleen and Maurice have said she can stay as long as she likes, she wants to hold out until she hears from Billy. She has left so that he will realise how much he misses her and now she's terrified he won't. Sally remembers how happy she and Billy were in the war and even after Martin was born. Her English friends all think she's crazy to live with her mother, they don't realise that Maman's pension and savings are what they live on. They bought the house out of the money Billy earned during his brief stardom and it's full of beautiful French furniture Sally's mother brought with her before the First World War. Sally's English father died on the Somme, she can't remember a time when she didn't depend on Maman, who looks after her grandson and cooks wonderful food for them all.

Sally thinks of Gertrude, of her husky voice and watchful eyes, the way men look at her. Divorced. Divorcée sounds even worse. It must be Gertrude's fault; Maman says no decent woman would divorce her husband. Sally enjoyed Rex's flirtatiousness last night, but she knows she can't have an affair and there's no question of divorcing Billy, whatever happens. Catholics can't divorce and he had to become one to marry her; Sally wants her boy to be brought up as a Catholic. One of the strange things about staying here is that there's no religion whatsoever in the air. Maurice and Colleen look bored and embarrassed at any mention of it, Viola thought Sally's rosary was a toy and Alex asked her yesterday how she could possibly believe all that rubbish. Yet Sally likes it here, she envies Colleen, her big house and sober devoted husband.

Sally remembers the war: Billy was a star, she was a glamour puss, Maurice was the handsome son of rich parents and Colleen was desperately shy. When the four of them used to go out together she and Billy were always the centre of attention and the other two were their admiring sidekicks. Once, in the ladies' room at some nightclub, Sally remembers giving Colleen a make-up lesson, for which she was abjectly grateful.

Colleen knocks on her door. 'Darling! He's on the phone!'

Sally rushes down to Colleen's unmade bed where the warmth and smells of another couple's intimacy surround her as she picks up the black receiver and asks suspiciously, 'Billy? Where are you?'

'I'm at home, of course. Missing you dreadfully, old girl.'

His voice is so seductive when he wants it to be. She tries not to capitulate too easily. 'I'm having a marvellous time in London. There was a dinner party last night and today Colleen and I are going shopping.'

'I see. Martin cried all night for you.'

Guilt chokes her. 'I want to talk to him.'

'He's still asleep. He was quite ill, we were worried about him. Your mother wants a word with you.'

Maman and Billy have always detested each other. Sally tries to imagine this alliance that has sprung up in her absence, more evidence of her husband's treacherous charm. Her mother speaks in rapid French, their private language, and tells her daughter she must come home at once, this gallivanting in London is no use at all. She sounds indignant, as if she has quite forgotten it was her idea that her daughter should disappear for a few days.

Colleen is delighted that Sally's marital crisis has been resolved. 'How could Billy be such a bastard?' she asks Maurice in the bathroom as he shaves and she lies in a bath perfumed with jewel coloured eggs she keeps in a turquoise jar beside the basin.

Maurice, who is six years older than his wife and has seen more marriages, is cautious about taking sides. He stares at his soapy beard in the mirror and whistles melodically. Colleen's father used to whistle too; Maurice doesn't know his whistling is one of the reasons she married him. His irrepressible pleasure in life, in himself, expands from pursed lips into full throated singing:

Pop, pop, poppety pop, in the pop pop popular sweet stuff shop.

The population all about,
They all pop in and they all pop out…

In the mirror Maurice can see her big, desirable breasts and shoulders rising from the foam. If they lock the bedroom door, they can have a quick fuck before domesticity takes over again. Colleen lies back and wallows in warmth and security. Outside the bathroom door, Viola bathes her rabbit, sprinkles him and the red carpet with talcum powder and smiles to hear her father's light tenor voice, the sound of happiness. Daddy likes bathtime.

So pop in and see pretty Poppy one day
In the pop pop popular sweet stuff shop.

Just pop into the bedroom, pop up her, Colleen climbs out of the bath and he wraps her in a vast pink towel. Viola looks up as the wet two-headed monster slithers into the bedroom.

Warm and fragrant, they fall together onto the bed. They're both at least twice the size they were when they met but the balance is still perfect, Maurice thinks as he slides inside her. Colleen remembers she hasn't put her Dutch cap in. It's in her dressing table drawer, surrounded by curlers and gathering fluff because she hates using it, doesn't want to feel her body invaded by anything except—thoughts dissolve in groans and gasps of pleasure. They both come, they always do, and lie in each other's arms, laughing, almost sobbing.

Sally, walking downstairs, hears them and wishes she and Billy could make love like that, simply, as they used to. There's always an obstacle: Martin, Maman, her period, fear of another pregnancy, his drunkenness. These two bellow like a pair of mating rhinoceroses and Sally's shocked to see Viola calmly playing outside their door. She takes the child's hand and leads her downstairs, hoping she won't refer to her parents' sexual antics. You never know what these Samuell children will say.

In the dining room Mrs Hunt and Susie serve eggs, bacon, sweetcorn and toast. The children eat and eat, then their parents come down and devour more breakfast. Sally, who worries about her figure, has a cup of coffee and a boiled egg. Will and Alex are squabbling again; she's surprised they're allowed to behave so badly at the table, yelling and kicking and roaring insults at each other. Viola expected to be heartbroken by Sally's departure, but she's been distracted by Ben, who has said she can go to the post office with him.

Ben saves up all his pocket money, locking it in a red tin post box which is then hidden inside his grandfather's padlocked Russian cashbox under his bed. The other children spend any money they get immediately on toys, sweets or books, they're puzzled by Ben's thrift and so are their parents, who have never saved any money. Last month Ben began to suspect Alex of plotting to steal his cashbox, so he insisted on opening a post office savings account.

After waving vigorously to Sally as she sets off in her blue Renault to rebuild her marriage, Viola and Ben walk up to the post office on the King's Road. Children playing in the communal gardens try to follow them, but Ben won't allow them to.

He explains the theory of interest to Viola, who can't count. At the counter he hands over twelve shillings and fourpence farthing, with a sense of power. He loves it when the man stamps his brown book and gives it back to him with TOTAL satisfyingly added to. Numbers don't dance and play tricks the way words do. By the time he's big enough to run away and have adventures he will be richer than his brothers.

In the pocket of her green dungarees Viola feels the rust coloured ten shilling note her fairy godmother gave her. She doesn't tell Ben about it because she's afraid he'll make her lock it up and she wants to spend it. Next week she'll go to the toyshop with Mummy, they pass it on the way home and she gazes at the window display of soldiers, ragdolls, cars and boats, bright and clean and unplayed with. She wants them all and wonders how much ten shillings is.

Seven

Viola walks down Beaufort Street between her mother and grandmother. Every few steps they swing her between them with a 'wheee!' and a gust of laughter. She feels utterly safe, held by these two hands, loved by these two. Behind her is the cinema where she had to be taken out of *The Wizard of Oz* because she was so upset by the witch; the shop, Tulley's, where she visits Father Christmas every year; the greengrocers where the man gives her free walnuts. On her left is her house and behind that glass topped wall is her fairy godmother's house. On her right is Emma's house, where she will go tomorrow. She wants everyone to look out of their windows and see her now.

She longs to run ahead of Mummy and Grandma, who are slow because they're old. Viola charges to the corner and then looks back, terrified that they won't be there. They are, still smiling at her, they give her one last swing before the bus stop.

'All girls,' Viola says with complete satisfaction as they wait for the bus.

Colleen doesn't feel like a girl. She hated being a girl, anyway, until Maurice bound up the wounds of her raging discontent. Edie has come to stay for a week, the longest the two women have spent together since Edie opposed her marriage eleven years ago. This is the second morning and

Colleen feels she's winning. Her mother's old now, frail and lonely and eager to please. She knows what will happen if she starts talking about India or utters the slightest criticism of her daughter's perfect life: she will never see her grandchildren again.

Edie is discovering that being a grandmother is far easier than being a mother. You don't need servants, all you need is kindness and a full purse. Also, she's discovering London, that monster that defeated her when she first arrived from India twenty years ago.

They go to Peter Jones where Colleen stalks through the departments on her high heels. This is her shop; she knows and loves every inch of it and wants to show her mother how magnificently she possesses her city. Edie trails behind. She likes her little house in Epsom but thinks paradise is probably a London department store. As a young bride she enjoyed ordering from the Army and Navy catalogue, ticking a dozen dinner plates or a serge liberty bodice which miraculously materialised in Karachi a few months later. Now she's inside the wonderful pictures in the catalogue, it has come to life and so has she.

The two women try on dresses and gloves. When Viola gets bored, they take her to the toy department to buy her a yoyo. Edie remembers when they were popular in the twenties, she tries to show Viola how to make it gracefully rise and fall but Viola can't get the knack and is furious with this uncooperative toy.

They have lunch in the restaurant at the top of the shop where an orchestra plays dance music and Viola runs from window to window, entranced by the rooftops. Edie eats a toasted sandwich, nibbling it fastidiously. Her birdlike appetite is one of the grudges held against her by Colleen, who tucks into steak and kidney pudding while Viola stands up so that she can enjoy the knickerbocker glory she has ordered. In the tall triangular glass layers of whipped cream, tinned fruit, jelly and ice cream luridly wait to be demolished by her long spoon. It never tastes quite as wonderful as it looks but Viola removes the pink paper parasol from the top and sets to work.

In Selfridges Colleen tries on a red cashmere coat with a big lynx collar. She loves the way her head rises from the long fur and the folds of heavy material hang above her legs which are still slim although the rest of her has inflated.

'You shall have it,' Edie says grandly.

'Are you sure?' Colleen's hesitation isn't convincing. She feels her mother owes her far more than a coat.

'Are you rich, Grandma?'

'Ernie has been good to me.'

'Who's Ernie?'

Edie tries to explain premium bonds to her granddaughter, who imagines a room above the post office where Ben's money is stored. A machine like a boiler stretches out its arms to her grandmother, its hands heaped with ten-shilling notes. Edie buys a coat too, a solid brown tweed. Her daughter tries to persuade her to try on a bright green one.

'No. I've only worn green twice in my life and both times I went to a funeral the following month.'

'But Mummy—'

'No, Colleen, green's unlucky, I don't care what you say, and anyway I'm too old for garish colours.'

This is friendly arguing. Both women are energised by spending money on clothes. Edie was once a beauty and Colleen feels she still could be, given the right mirrors. They stride across the carpeted acres tirelessly. Colleen observes that her mother, after spending thirty years in bed, seems to have been revitalised since her husband's death. Edie knows that she's free for the first time in her life, with good dividends from those oil shares Maurice recommended. Jews understand money, not that she's going to say a word.

Viola is bought a coat too, blue with velvet buttons and collar. She submits, longing for the toy department that is her bribe for being good.

They visit the ladies' toilet which Edie calls spending a penny. Locked in her cubicle, she's suddenly overwhelmed by a sense of how it felt to be Viola's age, being accompanied to the toilet by her big sister Daisy, poor Daisy who died of typhoid just after the First World War. How she and her big sister used to sing.

Viola and Colleen, waiting in the queue of women, are startled by her croaky voice: *Daisy, Daisy, give me your answer do...* Viola's enchanted by her naughty grandma, she giggles while Colleen puts on more crimson lipstick and ignores her mother's antics. She likes men who whistle but women who sing in public lavatories are just embarrassing; she tries to remember if her mother had any sherry before lunch. She feels the other women staring, that terrible sense she had all the time after they arrived in England that they looked and sounded wrong, that Home wasn't home at all.

But Edie's irrepressible, determined to share this vision of her happy childhood, and she starts to teach Viola Daisy's song: *It won't be a stylish marriage, 'Cause we can't afford a carriage...* Viola bellows the words happily, amazed that all this noise can come out of her quiet grandma, out of her papery white skin, her brown hat impaled to her blueish hair with a vicious hatpin. She takes one of her gloved hands and leads Edie, almost dancing, into the glorious toy department. Colleen follows, wanting to put a stop to this Daisy nonsense.

One of the lovely things about having Grandma to stay is that she, like Sally, sleeps in Viola's room, so Viola can't. In Maurice's dressing room, which is now full of her toys, the nightmare about the burning city doesn't come so often, and when it does, they hear her screams. Every morning as soon as she wakes, she goes upstairs to check Grandma's still there and finds her sitting on the edge of the bed, already dressed, her handbag firmly clutched on her lap. She looks nervous, as if she's been invited to a party she doesn't want to go to.

On Sunday, Colleen's birthday, Grandma takes them all to Veeraswamy's for lunch. There are too many of them to fit in a taxi, too many huge Samuells, and Maurice's Humber never seems to be working. So they get the 19 bus to Piccadilly and walk through to the little patch of India Edie is still allowed.

Her heart surges at the sight of those tall, handsome men in tunics as white as the tablecloths and scarlet turbans. They could be the sons of the men on the North West Frontier, the wild Pathans who her husband Carr admired even while he policed them. Fine men, he used to admit. The frisson of excitement that ran through all the women in the cantonment when stories were told about English ladies being kidnapped; sometimes in her bitterest moments Edie used to think it would be a relief to be carried off by a man who was interested in her.

Edie exchanges a few words of Hindi with the old manager and Colleen frowns. But she's in a good mood, her nostrils are full of the perfume of hot syrup from the Indian sweet shop downstairs, cardamom and saffron and frying poppadoms. The carved wooden screens and fans, hardly needed in an English October, make her homesick. Not home, she reminds herself, but she's pleased by her children's delight in the exotic decor. Viola sits proudly on a small golden elephant with a crimson velvet cushion and the boys are arguing over the enormous menu.

'I'll have the least hot thing.' Maurice is amused by Colleen's passion for strange food. When they first met, she insisted on taking him to the Hong Kong restaurant in Shaftesbury Avenue, then almost the only Chinese restaurant in London. Simpsons is his favourite restaurant; he loves English food but also has fond memories of his grandmother's gefilte fish. All this oriental cuisine seems to be an awful lot of fuss about rice. There's a separate English menu for people like Maurice; he orders a steak and Viola orders prawn cocktail and scampi. Ben tells her they're the same thing, but she doesn't believe him.

Alex is studying the menu for the most difficult, the most impressive dish. 'What's Vindaloo?' he asks the turbaned waiter.

'Dynamite, Sir. Exceedingly hot.'

Alex orders Chicken Vindaloo, the grown-ups titter and Will's furious because Alex is showing off again. Will hates these outings with his family. He has accepted now that the royal family of Atlantis seem to have abandoned him, he's here on his own, apart from Ben, who's loyal but inarticulate. Will looks over at other tables and wonders if the people sitting there are having interesting conversations.

The banquet arrives, wheeled on trolleys and served in silvery dishes. They all eat with relish except Edie, who is still proud of her slender figure. She gets vicarious pleasure from watching her daughter's enormous family guzzle and swill. Edie watches her daughter's large face grow pink, then red with heat and pleasure. Colleen knows she's sweating profusely but she can't stop eating, she loves this food, it fills and comforts and assaults her senses like… Maurice, watching her, knows she will want sex tonight.

The other children watch as Alex confronts his dynamite. A waiter hovers with a jug of iced water as the boy bites on a chilli, smiles, and carries on. Daddy has said there won't be a talking prize today, so Alex is concentrating on his food.

'I don't suppose it's really that hot,' Will says, reaching over to take a forkful. A bonfire leaps down his throat, his eyes water and he spits out the ferocious chicken. They all laugh, Alex loudest of all. Will swallows two glasses of iced water. Even Ben laughed, Will looks at him reproachfully.

Suddenly Alex's face goes redder than Colleen's and he looks astonished. Like a fish, Will thinks. They all stop eating and stare as the jolly birthday feast lurches into horror. Alex is gasping and stabbing his finger at his throat as panicky advice is yelled:

'Slap his back!'

'Stick a finger down your throat, Alex!'

'Drink some water!'

One of the elegant turbaned men, who always seem more like agents of fate than waiters, whisks the boy behind a screen. The adults glance at each other, afraid to voice the seriousness of the situation to the younger children. Will picks up this fear, he feels sick and somehow guilty, as if he has choked his brother on the bones of the hatred he so often feels. He and Ben look pale and dismayed, Viola cries, not understanding what's happening but sensing danger.

Alex emerges from behind the screens, looking ill and shaken. A little boy, his sister and brothers suddenly realise, and his parents also see him as a child again, their firstborn. Colleen's in shock, Edie twitters and reaches for her smelling salts, Maurice is bewildered, as he always is when tragedy pollutes the smooth pool his life is meant to be. The elegant waiter produces the chicken bone that nearly killed Alex, with a flourish.

Hands reach out to touch Alex, to make sure he's still there.

'Nearly lost our future prime minister,' Maurice says.

Will and Ben are annoyed that Alex has made himself the centre of attention yet again. 'If he's going to be prime minister I'm leaving the country,' Will mutters.

Eight

Viola and Emma sit together stolidly at a long table in a room at the top of Emma's house. Emma's small and fair and light, Viola's large and dark and heavy, but they're alike in temperament: quiet and sedentary. They talk, draw, paint, play Pelmanism and Snakes and Ladders. They don't like games that involve running or shouting and prefer the company of grown-ups to most children of their own age. Emma's brother Thomas is almost a grown-up, a vast figure who has to stoop when he comes into the attic room. To Viola it seems amazing that a brother should quietly guard her. In fact, he's being paid to babysit in his summer vacation from Oxford, and his polite silence is depression. His mother's second marriage is breaking up and he doesn't know if he'll have a home to go to at Christmas.

Emma's mummy wants to meet Viola, who's rather alarmed. She hasn't heard of Emma having parents before and had assumed Thomas and Jean, her Scottish nanny, looked after her all the time. Thomas leads her down the dark stairs to the threshold of an even darker bedroom where a figure lies in bed smoking. Viola thinks it's odd to go to bed in the middle of the day. The room smells ancient and stuffy, the horizontal mummy looks old and sick, smoke in the room adds to the gloom.

'I'm so glad Emma has found a friend.'

Viola isn't sure if she's the friend or if there's another one she doesn't know about. She loves Emma and is suddenly afraid there's some mysterious test she has to pass to become her friend. She holds Thomas's familiar hand and hopes he'll lead her back upstairs to Emma. Instead, he leads her downstairs and crosses the busy road with her, leaving her at her front door.

'Can I come and play again soon?'

'Of course. Tomorrow morning.' He smiles and crosses the road.

Time is still unfathomable; Viola has no idea how to impose herself on it. In this now she misses Emma and doesn't want to go home because she knows her parents and Susie are out. She wants her other friend, so instead of going home she wanders into the communal gardens and stares up at Charlotte's window.

For as long as she can remember, falling over has been the signal for her fairy godmother to appear at her door and take her into her wonderful house. So, although she's able to walk perfectly well now, Viola pretends to fall over and then looks up hopefully.

Charlotte stands, as she so often does, at her bedroom window. She has picked at the breakfast her maid brought up on a tray and holds a silk shawl around her shoulders against the chill she feels, even in her centrally heated house. Since her last illness her body has faded, she has lost weight and, she sometimes thinks, substance. It's as if she floats through the empty days, and when she looks in the mirror in her bathroom she sees a transparency in her pale face, like a sheet of tissue paper with a very weak flame behind it. The visits of dutiful—or hopeful— younger relatives and friends her own age don't seem real.

She knows her remote manner is seen as senility; perhaps I am gaga, she thinks indifferently. Her husband, who was twenty years older than her, used to say that the past was far more convincing than the present. At the time this irritated her, and certainly didn't make the silences between them less oppressive. But now that it's too late to tell him she agrees with him, she does: her childhood is almost unbearably vivid and tidal waves of it break on the walls of her empty rooms.

She was the youngest and her sympathy has always been with the youngest and smallest, whether bullied children or hunted fox cubs. Watching the dramas played out by these children in the communal gardens, she relives it all and fervently hopes none of these nannies is as sadistic as Mrs Bream, who used to lock five-year-old Charlotte in a dark cupboard full of rats and spiders for hours. Modern parents seem to spend more time with their children, they don't go off travelling for months as hers did.

Two years ago, when she moved here and started to watch the children, Charlotte saw at once that Emma and Viola were too young and vulnerable to be out there. She started to go down to the gardens to talk to them, giving them sweets and toys. She likes Emma because she's so ethereal and Viola because she's so clumsy, although she soon realised that all this falling over was a ploy. She spoke to their nannies and arranged for them to play in each other's houses. The other children resent her favouritism and call her a witch.

It's quite obvious to Viola that Charlotte belongs in a fairy tale, probably the one about the old apple woman. Charlotte ignores the New Look and wears long skirts in soft colours. Today she's all in lilac. The atmosphere in her house is calm, the rooms smell of polish and lavender and Charlotte herself smells of flowers, unlike Grandma, who smells of mothballs. Viola always comes to this house as a sanctuary.

Upstairs in the bathroom Charlotte puts a plaster on the fictitious wound. They smile at each other.

'Better?'

'Yes. Can I stay?'

'I don't see why not.'

Their arrangements are always vague, like this.

'Can I see your pictures?'

In a small room on the ground floor there's a cabinet full of miniatures of Charlotte's ancestors. These tiny faces surrounded by wigs and bonnets fascinate Viola. The cabinet's protected by a leather curtain you have to draw back. Charlotte switches on the light and watches as Viola presses her nose against the glass and stares, enthralled, at her great-grandmother, who was famous for flogging servants. My rogues' gallery, Charlotte calls it to friends her own age; generation after generation drinking and gambling away the estate until by the time the Fenians burnt the house down there was nothing left.

'They can't all have been in your family?' Viola tries to imagine a table as long as a bus, a house as big as Selfridges.

'Different generations. I mean most of them died before I was born.'

'They don't look dead. Is there one of you?'

'We had photographs. Miniatures were old-fashioned by then.'

Charlotte laughs as she sees the child struggling to imagine anything more old-fashioned than her.

'Can I see the photographs?'

'Next time. My cousin's coming to luncheon, I'm afraid you'll have to go home now.'

'I don't want to.'

'Why not?'

'There's nothing to do at home. We've got a new puppy, a poodle called Dandy, he's lovely but he doesn't like playing with me and my brothers won't let me play.'

The gentle, dreamy, pale blue eyes suddenly look as hard as the enamel ones Viola has been staring at. Charlotte pulls on her long black coat and pushes Viola out into the street.

'Are you cross?' She's frightened. Charlotte has never been angry with her before.

'I'm coming home with you. We'll soon see about those boys.'

Colleen and Maurice have gone out to lunch and Susie and Mrs Hunt have a day off. Alex is in charge of the house, with strict instructions not to let anyone in. When the bell rings imperiously the boys come downstairs from their rooms and stand in the hall. They peer through the glass door inside the front door and see the old witch who lives down the road standing there with their sister. Alex says they shouldn't let them in, Will thinks they should and Ben isn't sure. While they squabble Charlotte grows visibly angrier and when they finally open the glass door she bursts into the hall like a vengeful old crow, squawking at them. They're taller than her but back away in alarm while Viola shelters in the dark folds of her coat.

'What's all this about not playing with your sister? Do you think you're too good for her?'

'She's a girl,' Alex says defensively.

'Oh, did you think I hadn't noticed? And what's wrong with girls?'

She glares at them all while they giggle and shuffle.

Alex, who is harder to squash than the twins, says defiantly, 'Boys are stronger.'

'Ha! When you get to my age you'll know better.' He stares at her, not sure if this preposterous suggestion is meant to be a joke. She's older than Grandma, older than he could ever possibly be. 'Where are your parents, young man?'

'They've gone out to lunch, old woman.' Alex knows as soon as he says this it's a mistake.

'Shall I tell you why I prefer little girls? They're kinder, politer, and altogether nicer to be with.' It's not true, even as she roars at him, she remembers her brother Edward, who she adored, and her son, who she still adores but who has gone to live in New Zealand. This cocky little boy infuriates her and the moulten rage that has ruined and enlivened her life comes pouring out. 'And if I ever hear again that you're being unkind to your sister I shall come and see your parents and make quite sure they know all about it. I shall speak to your father.' She glares at the three boys, then looks over her shoulder, sees that her cousin's car has drawn up, and sweeps off.

She doesn't realise that she herself, not the vague and liberal Samuell parents, is the threat. In addition to being a fairy godmother and a witch she's a Lady. One way and another it's better not to get on the wrong side of her. The boys stare at their sister. It has never occurred to them to play with her. They've never bullied her; they've been too busy bullying each other. They've simply ignored her. The boys confer while Viola fiddles with the toggles on her red duffel coat and wishes Charlotte hadn't started this. To be played with as a punishment is worse than not being played with at all.

They usher her into the cloakroom. She hesitates. There aren't any grown-ups in the house and for a moment she thinks they're going to play some horrible trick on her. But they're smiling as she looks up at them solemnly.

'Now this is what we're going to do,' Alex announces with his usual air of importance. 'The cloakroom is a magic place.' Viola looks doubtfully at the grubby toilet and basin and the hooks piled high with familiar coats and jackets. 'When we come in here, we change. This is the gateway to Good Dog Land and Bad Dog Land. I become the bad dog, Boney.'

'And I'm Towser,' Will says. 'I'm a bit cowardly but I'm good really.'

'I'm a good dog too,' Ben says. 'I'm the Galloping Major and I'm really brave.'

'What about me? What am I like?'

'You're the little girl who comes to our country and has adventures,' Alex explains.

'But what am I like?'

'You're a little girl.'

Viola holds her breath and shuts her eyes. She knows her brothers are standing there and the cloakroom's a cloakroom and this is a game. But it isn't like hide and seek or grandmother's footsteps when you all run and shout and chase and your heart thumps in case you get caught. If she believes enough, she can make something happen and then it will happen to all of them. Eyes tightly shut, she walks into the dark cloakroom.

Yes, the air has changed. There are voices and a rushing wind, she stands frowning with concentration in the middle of some kind of battle. A dogfight or a boyfight. Viola is whirled around and pushed and pulled and suddenly, happily, is at the centre of things.

'We must rescue her from Boney!'

'I'm coming to conquer London and I eat little girls.'

'Towser, quick, untie her!'

Viola, freed from non-existent ropes, smiles, shutting her eyes again to see what's really in the cloakroom: a prison, a high wall, dogs with swords. They're all excited, talking loudly and laughing, it feels as if a warm cloud has wrapped her up and floated with her to a world she hasn't reached before. A place that will always be there now, waiting for her to make the door that will let her in.

Nine

Colleen and Maurice sit at the long polished mahogany table in the dining room over cheese and biscuits and coffee. The French doors are open onto the tiny garden and through them come the sounds of a hot London Saturday night: traffic, drunken yells, a foxtrot on someone's radio. Until half an hour ago there were bedtime squeals but now the children are finally in bed and can be discussed.

'But I don't want them to board!'

'They'll come back every weekend.'

'They're still so little!'

'Darling, by the time I was Alex's age I'd been a boarder for two years. And I never went home at weekends.'

Colleen stares back at him tearfully. Until now she has never questioned Maurice's values. She has disapproved of, and got rid of, some of his friends but has otherwise accepted the package she has married. Public school, that peculiar English mountain that has to be climbed, suddenly looms over her.

She was pleased when Maurice put the boys' names down for a famous school as soon as they were born. Her father complained all his life that promotion in the army went to men who had been to public school and university, that he hadn't a chance—at this point his face used to twitch with anger and his daughter knew he was thinking of his wife, her mother. Edie was the real problem, somehow her Irish mother and brown brothers and sisters had destroyed the career of Colleen's daddy. Anyway, "public school" was a concept familiar to Colleen from early childhood, something desirable and expensive that people like them couldn't have. So of course she wants her boys to have it; but she'd expected them to be taken away from her later, when they were almost grown up.

The prospect of being parted from them now, for most of the week, hurts so viscerally that she can't speak. Maurice shifts uneasily in his chair as her tears soak her biscuits and her face becomes red and puffy. He thinks, but doesn't say, that the folly of being over-emotional is the first lesson they will learn. Will and Viola seem to have inherited Colleen's tendency to weep and wail at the drop of a hat. In a girl this is just about acceptable, but Will needs discipline and so does Alex, who's too cocky by half, and Ben needs hours of coaching if he's to pass his Common Entrance exam.

Colleen knows that Sally has already gone through all this. Martin was sent to a Catholic prep school from which he promptly ran away. He walked and hitchhiked two hundred miles to get home, where his mother and grandmother welcomed him—and Billy sent him straight back. To be beaten into submission.

'But the house will seem so empty without them,' Colleen sobs when she can speak again.

Maurice sighs and decides he'd better not tell her that they won't be here. Sending the boys to be weekly boarders at a school in Hampstead is the first stage of his master plan to reduce expenses so that he can finally manage to live on his salary plus his income from the trusts.

'What did that beastly old man say yesterday?' Colleen snarls, her sadness giving way to anger.

'Oh, just a lot of legal waffle, I won't bore you with it.' Maurice is shocked by Sydney's toughness and his insistence that his brother Benjamin might still return, ten years after the end of the war. Yesterday he read Maurice a story in the Daily Telegraph about a Japanese soldier who has just emerged from the jungle in Borneo, convinced that the war is still being fought. Maurice looks nervously at the dark trees rustling behind Colleen's head. He remembers the nasal solemnity in Sydney's voice as he read from Aubrey's will: 'Whereas my dear son Benjamin George lately serving with His Majesty's Forces is missing and I am unaware whether he is a prisoner or not or if he is alive. In the event of my son Benjamin George being alive at the date of my death then I make the following provision for him…' Maurice feels the familiar twinge of jealousy. He has never told anyone, not even Colleen, that he was pleased when Benjamin disappeared. And the death of Aubrey, whom Maurice loved even if he wasn't his real father, seemed to be the punishment for his silent hatred. Poor dead Benjamin was much easier to deal with than live Benjamin, with his vile temper and his habit of doing all the things Maurice couldn't do—standing up to Florence and getting into Cambridge and saying witty, cutting things. In fact, it's quite absurd to suggest that such a sophisticated young man would turn into Tarzan and then emerge years later to claim his inheritance. And now Colleen is being difficult.

Maurice fell in love with her partly because of her naivety and the assurance it seemed to give that his life, and his children, would be his own. He grew up surrounded by powerful women, notably his mother, and doesn't want to end up as mincemeat the way most of their husbands did. Florence parked Aubrey at their country house and did exactly as she liked in London, spending his money and flirting—was it more than flirtation?—with dozens of men. Maurice's formidable Polish grandmother, Rose, who spoke five languages and produced ten ambitious children with upwardly mobile, non-Jewish names, taught them to despise the elderly pawnbroker she'd married. Florence always said that when her father Abraham died it was several days before anyone noticed. Maurice wants to be a real man.

'Maurice, stop dithering. Tell me what's going on.'

'Darling, there's no need for you to worry about all this. Let's go to bed.'

'No! You're hiding something.'

'Nonsense. I'm sorry you're upset about the boys, but they'll never get anywhere without a decent education.'

'All right,' she says with a quivering sob. 'As long as they come home at weekends. But not Viola, I'm not letting go of her.'

'For heaven's sake, Colleen, she's only four. Anyway, she can go to some little day school, we don't want her to be a bluestocking.' Maurice gets up and goes to her chair. He knows he hasn't been exactly honest, but he hasn't exactly lied, either. It would be cruel to tell her about the house, he can't bear it when she cries. He touches her hair, she reaches up to take his hand and puts it to her lips. Colleen still feels she's being shut out but perhaps it's all right as long as they're here, now, together.

Much later, after they've made love, they talk again in bed. Colleen has been hiding the bills as they arrive and is worried he might have found out. She wishes he was really rich, like Florence. 'Are you asleep?'

Maurice sprawls in the warmth of her soft curves. 'Not quite.'

'Won't that beastly old solicitor let us have any more money?'

'He certainly enjoys saying no. I must do some more work on Gertrude's book, I'm sure there's a market for it.'

'I don't like that woman.'

'Still, she's had a fascinating life. Growing up in the Middle East—'

'East End, more like.'

'And starting in the chorus when she was thirteen and then marrying one of the richest men in the world. You have to take your hat off to her.'

'As long as you don't take off anything else.'

'Now then, Colleen! Rose and Crown!'

It's a running joke between them to pretend that Colleen used to work as a barmaid. She doesn't mind because she knows he enjoys her dirtier jokes. Chuckling, they fall asleep in each other's arms.

Ten

Colleen buys a very expensive sewing machine so that she can save money on the children's clothes. She and her friend Mary used to make their own clothes in India when they were young; she sets to work confidently and presents Alex with a pair of trousers he refuses to wear because one leg's shorter than the other. His uniform for the new school near Swiss Cottage cost a fortune but Viola's school, fortunately, doesn't have a uniform. Colleen makes her a red corduroy pinafore dress with a lopsided hem which Viola doesn't notice. She's anxious about going to school for the first time, so Colleen gives her a small teddy bear as a mascot and makes a little sailor suit for it. She tells Viola that as long as she holds onto her mascot nothing bad will happen.

One afternoon as she's sewing in her bedroom and Viola's sitting on the floor looking at picture books Colleen hears the telephone ring above the noise of the machine and abandons her sewing with relief. 'Mary!'

'Colleen! I was thinking of you, I just had to phone.'

'I was thinking of you, too. Do you remember those dresses we made for the Colonel's ball? Hang on a minute. Viola, go and play in the nursery, will you, please.'

'I don't want to.'

But eventually she goes; Colleen sits on the bed, dropping

back happily into a younger self. 'How's the farm?'

'Hard work, but we love it. Pete says he's so glad to be back in England, he's had enough of the army. Just think, Colleen, if you'd married your cousin Robin.'

'I don't think I was cut out to be a farmer's wife. But I'm glad you're happy,' she says politely, shuddering at the thought of cows and hens and bleak early mornings. If Robin had once seemed like Dickon in *The Secret Garden*, by the time Colleen was grown up she thought of his farm as *Cold Comfort Farm* and had no intention of experiencing something nasty in the woodshed.

'Still enjoying London?'

'It's wonderful.' Colleen can't resist boasting about their house, the children's expensive schools and the parties she has been to. Mary listens for the invitation that never comes.

'Now we're back in England, I want to see you. I've missed you, Colleen. Why don't you all come to stay one weekend?'

'It would be far too much of an invasion.'

'No, it would be lovely. Come during the school holidays so that my children can get to know yours. And I want Maurice and Pete to be friends. Now, I've got my diary out, let's fix a date.' But Colleen's still evasive, although she asks with genuine warmth about Mary's parents. 'Oh, they're fine, they've settled in a little bungalow ten miles away, just outside York, so we can see a lot of them.'

'They were so kind to me.'

'They were very fond of you, Colleen. They'd love to see you.'

When Colleen and Mary were ten Edie, in one of many deathbed scenes, had asked Mary's parents to adopt her daughter, who had been quite disappointed when her mother recovered. She felt safe in the affectionate atmosphere of Mary's home.

'And how's Edie?'

'Much better. Being a widow seems to agree with her.'

'Well—' Mary remembers the misery in that bungalow on the cantonment in Quetta. The first time she went there, when she was seven, she just cried because it was so awful. Colleen's mother never spoke to Colleen's father and Colleen herself seemed to shrink as soon as she stepped onto her veranda. After that the two girls always played at Mary's bungalow, which was exactly the same only bigger (because Mary's father was Carr's commanding officer) and infinitely happier. 'Well, I suppose she might prefer the climate here. Does she keep in touch with her family?'

'What family?'

'Oh, you know, all those people who saw you off at the station when your father retired and you went back to England. My father said it was lovely to see Indians and Irish and Welsh all united in one family. My parents were never prejudiced, you know, although some of those memsahibs were dreadful, weren't they? Anyway, who cares nowadays. Colleen? Are you there?' Mary's longing to see her almost-sister pours down the phone as she says, 'Let's meet, Colleen. Just you and me. We can talk about India.'

'Sorry, my dear, I've got to go. A domestic emergency.'

'But Colleen…'

Mary feels rejected in her farmhouse kitchen while Colleen, in her sunny pink bedroom, chokes with rage. At her mother, at Mary for wanting to talk about the past, at herself for still caring about all that.

Both Alex and Viola dread their new schools. Alex feels he's being pushed away, out of the family circle he despises but needs. He has done a practice run of the endless bus journey across London he will have to perform twice a day in his embarrassing pink uniform. It's only for a term, his parents say, after that he will board. He will be bored, crucified on some kind of board, forced to eat meals out there where you never get enough to eat. While he's away the twins will take over his room and his books and complete the coup d'état of his parents' affections that started when they were born.

One morning in late September Colleen walks with all her children to the 31 bus stop behind Beaufort Street. It's a terminal so there are lots of buses here, awkward red monsters who look as if they don't know where to go. The other children watch as Alex, tall and aloof, gets on the bus. Viola wonders who will be Boney in Bad Dog Land now. Colleen wants to kiss Alex, but he doesn't want to touch her scarlet lips. There might be spies from his new school on the bus, waiting to laugh at his ridiculous family. They all wave but Alex refuses to look back at them as the bus leaves. Colleen feels as if he's being torn away from her, her clever wonderful boy. She asks Will what the time is (she never wears a watch).

'Eight o'clock. I'm starving.' He feels liberated by Alex's disappearance. Although Ben's half an hour older than him, Will is bigger and better at most things except gym and fighting. Already, without Alex, there's more oxygen.

They go to a café in the Fulham Road where the twins order a second breakfast. Viola's too nervous to eat and Colleen's trying to diet. She can no longer fit into the clothes she bought before Viola was born and a puffy face she doesn't like stares back at her out of the mirror. Although she'd love a piece of that chocolate cake, she restricts herself to a cup of coffee, watching with pleasure as her sons devour their bacon and eggs and sausages. After she's paid for breakfast, there isn't enough money for a cab so, reluctantly, she walks with them to Queensgate. The twins run ahead in giggling squabbling intimacy while Viola holds her mother's hand, clutching Lionel, the sailor bear who is to protect her, and a green linen shoe bag. The twins join the river of blue boys that flows into the big pale house, then she and Colleen cross the road.

Almost at the top, near Kensington Gardens, there's a girl river. Colleen takes Viola inside another creamy building and delivers her to a scratchy looking woman called Miss Smythe. Viola watches in horror as her mother disappears and she's taken down to the brown basement smelling of old shoes and toilets, where she's told to leave her coat, Lionel and shoe bag on a hook, take off her shoes and put on her indoor shoes. She obeys these complicated instructions but tries to explain that she can't leave Lionel.

'No toys in the classroom,' Miss Smythe announces and Viola, who isn't used to being told not to do things, watches indignantly while Lionel's strung up on the hook like dead meat in a butcher's window. Lionel isn't dead, he's very much alive and her only friend here. She refuses to leave her hook until Miss Smythe pulls the troublesome new girl upstairs into a big room seething with girls to hand Viola over to another Miss.

The morning passes in a blur of noise and smells and bewilderment. Viola knows a morning is only part of a day but this one has gone wrong; it lasts forever and she's lost in its wrongness. It would be less horrible if she had Lionel with her—she glares at the bossy Miss who has imprisoned him in the basement.

A bell rings. Mummies and nannies appear, Viola searches the foggy shapes for the coat with the big fur collar and thin legs like stalks beneath it. They all pair off, each big cloud attached to a small one and she's left alone. She thinks Colleen has probably forgotten where she left her, just as she's forgotten where she left Lionel. She'll have to stay here with the Misses, mummyless, teddyless.

'Now why are you crying?' The voice is so brusque that even Viola, an Olympic crybaby, stops in surprise. 'Are you a new girl?'

'Yes, she started today. Viola Samuell. Her mother's late.'

The hard voices bark above her head. She finds herself holding two hands, neither of them reassuring, being pulled through a new maze of stairs and corridors. They stop in a room full of voices and long tables and food and Viola's told to wait for her mother. She sits on a bench between two big girls, so vast that she can't believe they still go to school. They loom down to talk to her, kindly, and she perks up, telling them all about herself and making them laugh. They're eating long pink things, worms in blood sauce, they tell her. They keep offering her some and she keeps refusing with giggles and extravagant disgust. She sings a song: There's a worm at the bottom of the garden and his name is Wiggly Woo. Colleen stands in the doorway watching her youngest scream with laughter and is pleased she's settled in so well.

But down in the basement cloakroom there is no Lionel. Viola makes Colleen move all the lockers and benches, searches all the hooks as she works herself up into a hurricane of grief. It's the most public scene she's ever made and Colleen is abashed, surrounded by these cool sensible women who are her natural enemies. Not the end of the world, we'll buy you another one, I expect it'll turn up. But Viola's been robbed and betrayed and has no intention of suffering in silence. Her suffering is deafening, it continues all the way home.

'I felt as if I'd sat through the whole of Hamlet,' Colleen tells Maurice that night in bed.

'I'm afraid Viola and Will are just going to have to toughen up.'

'Poor Alex didn't get back until six, he looked so washed out.'

'He'll get used to it.'

Maurice has just had a humiliating interview with Sydney and has no sympathy to spare. He tries to find words to explain to Colleen that those vast sums of money Aubrey and Florence left aren't really theirs, they're in trust for their children and can't be spent. But he knows that if he raises the subject now, she'll make a scene and he won't get any sleep tonight. He's exhausted, he has to get up at seven to go to work and be charming all day.

'What did that old bastard say?' Colleen has decided that Sydney is holding onto the money out of sheer malice because he's jealous of their happy marriage and lovely house. She has never met him—Maurice is terrified of what she'd say if she did—she imagines a miserable old gnome sitting on the pile of treasure he has stolen from them.

'Oh, nothing much.' Maurice yawns exaggeratedly and pretends to drift off into sleep.

Behind his closed eyes the meeting with Sydney replays itself and he wishes he'd been more heroic, wishes he understood those rows of figures Sydney brandished at him. Maths has always been his downfall; it was the reason he failed the entrance exam to Cambridge when Benjamin so mortifyingly passed and now his fatal weakness is victimising him again. Sydney said he and Colleen have been irresponsible and extravagant. Maurice pointed out that compared to Florence, with her flat in Grosvenor Square, her country house and footmen and borzois and jewellery, they live very simply. You don't live within your income, Sydney retorted, firing numbers at him to prove it. Maurice remarked that the income was simply inadequate, that poor old Aubrey and Florence hadn't realised how much the cost of living would go up after the war. At this Sydney turned from old family friend to hanging judge and announced that enough was enough, he must cut his coat according to his cloth, the wishes of his clients must be observed: death by cliché. Maurice feels sick as he realises that all those bills on his desk—the outstanding rent and ground rent on this house, the accounts at department stores, the children's school fees—are not going to be paid. The letters from the bank have also taken on a very unpleasant tone, almost as if he was some kind of criminal. In fact, he has stopped opening most of his post.

Eleven

One morning, when Maurice is at work and the children are at school, Colleen takes delivery of a large, official looking envelope addressed to both of them. She opens it because she thinks one of the department stores is going to sue and instead reads a menacing letter from their landlords: they're six months in arrears and must leave the house by December the fifteenth. She stands in the hall holding the letter, staring at the house where she's been so happy, her house. It must be a mistake. She wants to rage at the landlords, wants Maurice to rage for her, she's furious with him because he isn't here. She considers phoning him at work but she'll have to speak to a secretary who will offer to give him a message: Come home immediately, murder Sydney and give me back the life I've become accustomed to. She sees Mrs Hunt staring at her from the kitchen, glares back at her and runs up to her bedroom.

Colleen doesn't want to go to bed in the middle of the day; she knows it's the Edie thing to do, but her legs have turned to cotton wool. The letter she's still clutching feels heavier and horribly convincing. Colleen throws it across the room.

At lunchtime Susie comes back with Viola who has reluctantly accepted captivity. Susie dresses her like clockwork every morning and isn't interested in discussing the injustice of going to school. Viola has made friends with a girl called Annie and at twelve-thirty, when their nannies come, they hold hands and escape together, gasping and laughing. They run until the ends of the earth, which is the first road, and by the time they cross it they've forgotten about school which might never happen again.

Viola has lunch in the kitchen with Susie and Mrs Hunt and Johnnie.

'Where's Mummy?'

'She's in her bedroom.'

'Can I see her?'

'She's resting.'

Viola is aware of a lot of nodding going on, a silence that's waiting for her to leave the room. 'Can I go and play with Emma?'

Susie takes her across the road and delivers her to Emma's nanny, a kind elderly Scotswoman called Jean. Colleen says Jean's a treasure and Viola thinks this means she's rich. On the dark stairs they pass an open door where Emma's mummy can be seen, lying down. Now that her own mother has started going to bed in the day Viola thinks perhaps it's all right, it's what mummies do. At the top of the house Emma stands alone in the middle of the room, looking very small, and Viola sees she's been crying. They don't play their usual games but sit cross legged by the open fire that burns their knees and flushes Emma's pale, tiny face. Jean brings them mugs of cocoa.

'Thomas has gone away; he's cross with Mummy. She's ill again. And soon Jean will have to leave. And we've got to go and live miles away in a little house and I don't want to.'

'Just you and your mummy?'

'I think so. I don't know, they won't tell me.'

Viola looks round and sees Jean sitting in a wicker armchair, sewing, looking as comfortable and solid as ever. 'But Jean shouldn't leave you.'

'They haven't paid her, she says.'

'But she's rich.'

'No, she isn't. I don't know. Anyway, we're poor. Will you still be my friend?'

They're shivering despite the heat and whispering. 'Of course I will. You can come and live at my house.'

Emma looks delighted and turns to Jean. 'It's all right. I can go and live with Viola. Can Jean come too?'

'I'll have to ask my mummy.'

Jean laughs and then sighs.

'It's not funny,' Emma shouts.

'I didn't mean to hurt your feelings, dear.' Suddenly Jean picks up her sewing and runs out of the room.

'Let's go and ask your mummy now.'

'We can't today. She's in bed. You can come home with me now if you like. I'm not sure about Jean. She's a bit big.'

Emma gives a wobbly smile, and they sit at their usual places, on either side of the table under the window, to play Snakes and Ladders. Her heart surges and lurches with the dice. Up the rungs, climbing to happy freedom; then a steady plod along a straight line before the delicious terror of the plunge down the slimy snake, right back to the beginning of the story. Emma's winning but Viola knows there's still just a chance she could leap up all the ladders and overtake her, so she shakes the dice. Jean comes back into the room and sits quietly. It feels almost but not quite right.

When Susie rings the bell to collect Viola Jean says, 'Now, you two wee girls must kiss and say goodbye.'

They've never kissed before. They bend towards each other and peck cautiously, then giggle and start to sing 'goodbye' in silly voices: a baby voice, a grown-up voice, a lady singing on the radio voice.

That evening Maurice knows as soon as he opens the front door that Colleen has found out. She isn't in the drawing room, which feels neglected and still smells of last night's fire. He can hear the children talking and arguing as they have their supper in the little room next to the kitchen. Nobody comes to meet him; he feels as if he's back at his prep school in the headmaster's study waiting to see Flip, his terrifying wife. Maurice was only sent there twice because he was a well-behaved boy and his parents' money protected him. He has always had money to protect him and has certainly behaved well: Maurice has a noble nature, his mother Florence used to say, as he smiled through Benjamin's tantrums. But other people have vile tempers and suddenly Colleen is another person, no longer an extension of himself. She's up there thinking of hurtful things to say, she'll scream and cry, the children will hear. He helps himself to a whisky and soda, eats a handful of stale cheese footballs and starts to prepare his defence.

Colleen hears him come in and wills him upstairs to comfort her and tell her that it isn't true. Her mouth tastes sour, her hair's a mess and her purple dress is crumpled. She doesn't want him to see her like this so she goes into the bathroom to wash and stares into her red eyes. As she opens the bathroom cabinet behind the mirror and takes out Maurice's Optrex and blue eye bath she sees his silver razor and Trumpers shaving cream and longs for his comforting presence, standing here in his wine-red paisley silk dressing gown, shaving, whistling.

Her anger dissolves into sobs again because it really is him she wants, not just his money. But the money was after all part of the deal. She asks herself if she would have fallen in love with Maurice if he hadn't had such a dazzling setting: the flat in Grosvenor Square; all those well-known people he casually referred to; his magnificently stylish mother. I don't know, she mouths back at herself in the mirror. But the face that stares back at her is firmer now, her eyes have regained their blue whites and her mouth strengthens as she applies a slash of scarlet lipstick. He didn't love me for my money because I never had any, just determination and good looks; amazingly, he loved me for myself. Nobody else ever did, not really.

When she comes into the drawing room Maurice is sitting back in his green armchair as usual, wearing his dark suit, striped shirt and the red silk tie she gave him for Christmas. His wavy hair looks as crisp and black as usual but pouches have appeared under his green eyes, spotlighted by the standard lamp beside his chair. He looks older and as he stares up at her with an expression that is both furtive and nervous something shifts between them.

'You should have told me we had to leave this house.'

She has her back to him, pouring herself a large gin and tonic and hasn't asked him, as she usually does, if he wants another drink. Maurice has prepared himself for hysteria and her dignity wrongfoots him.

'I thought perhaps—Sydney said—I didn't want to upset you.'

Colleen sits opposite him and cradles the heavy glass in both hands. Tears sting again but she forces them back down. 'I'll start looking tomorrow. Where shall we go?'

'I thought we'd try North London. It's a bit cheaper and near the boys' new school and very pleasant, you know.'

'Near the Heath? We'll need at least six bedrooms; the children all need their own rooms now and we must have a maid to live in.'

'Well, not exactly. I thought a bit lower down, around Swiss Cottage, and perhaps a flat, just for the time being.'

'But where will we put all our lovely things?' She gazes at the curved Boulle chest of drawers, the inlaid glass fronted cabinets full of Meissen china, the enormous Persian carpet, Florence's Chinese cocktail cabinet. Not Florence's. Ours, mine, she remembers.

'We'll put it all into storage until we find somewhere permanent.' Maurice tries to sound casual, as if he knows what he's doing.

'How do you find somewhere to live?' All the other places have been found for her, by the army or her parents or by Maurice.

'Oh, there are agencies. And advertisements in the Sunday papers. We've got over two months, that's plenty of time. I'll just—this is what Sydney says we have to restrict ourselves to for rent.'

He writes a figure on a piece of paper and hands it to her. Colleen thinks it seems a lot and nods. She doesn't understand, Maurice realises, and is relieved when Ben and Will burst into the room because Alex is chasing them, and Susie comes in to complain that Viola won't get into the bath.

Twelve

'Funny old world.'

Susie's English is good enough now to understand most of what Johnnie and Mrs Hunt say. The three of them sit around the kitchen table over tea and biscuits and discuss the Samuells.

'Same as happened to the last lot here. Got through money like nobody's business and had to leave. I used to look after their boiler and all. Frankenheim they was called, they was foreign too, Jewish or sommat.'

'They are not British?' Susie asks.

Mrs Hunt pours her another cup of tea from the big blue and white striped teapot. 'They're not foreign the way you are. They speak English proper. *He* was born here, he's a gent even if he is a Jew, but *she's* from one of them oriental places. China, innit?'

'India. She's in perjure, see. That's why she don't hardly never go out. It's against their religion to go out, for the women that is.'

'She does go out, goes shopping all the time.'

'If she was in her own country, they wouldn't even allow her to go out the door on her own. She'd have to wear a veil and that.'

'She is not Jewish?' Susie is totally confused.

Johnnie takes a deep puff on the pipe that sticks out of his mouth like a root in his vegetable face. Susie thinks he looks like Mr Potato Head, a game Viola has that involves sticking a plastic nose and moustache and spectacles onto a potato to make it look comical. Johnnie looks naturally comical but he's kind and tries to explain things to her. Mrs Hunt tells Susie she's stupid when she doesn't understand and then shouts the same words at her again so that she can be stupid twice. Sometimes Susie feels they're her parents or grandparents, there's a ghastly intimacy in these hours they spend together in the kitchen.

'They're Hindoo or Muslin over there, aren't they Johnnie? Gawd knows why they called her Colleen, that's an Irish name. And *they're* mostly Catholic when they're not murdering each other.'

'Never mind,' Johnnie says tolerantly. 'Takes all sorts. What'll you do, then, when this lot leave?'

'*She* wants me to go with them. Suppose I might as well.' Mrs Hunt sighs. Steve will be in prison at least another two years and she can get to the Scrubs from anywhere in London. One of her grudges against Colleen is that Steve was done for black marketeering and Colleen used to spend a fortune at that black market butcher down the road but it's one law for the rich. Looks like the Samuells aren't rich anymore; still, wherever they go next it'll be better than what she can get on her own. Mrs Hunt has no prospect of having a home of her own again until Steve gets out. One good thing about him is he always makes a bit of money before he gets caught; she doesn't like other people knowing her business, so she asks, 'How about you then, what'll you do next?'

'I'll just work for the next lot.'

'What if they don't want you?'

'They'll have to. Can't do without me, nobody understands this old boiler like what I do.'

Their two crumpled old ugly faces stare at Susie, who stirs her tea and gazes into the ripples. Mrs Hunt says you can see your future in tea leaves. Just like the British to make a religion out of a cup of tea. She has been here two years now and is used to the Samuells. There are times when she enjoys the children, even the naughty little one. Susie remembers the feel of Viola's hand as she dragged her across the road to Emma's house, unable to believe that her friend had really moved, that the house where she'd played so happily was really empty. Susie knows this sense of loss well, she lost her home and toys and friends during the war, so she hugged and comforted the child. Now she kicks the leg of the big wooden table that has also been pretending to be reliable.

'And what'll you do, love? I expect you'll find yourself a nice young man.' Mrs Hunt leers at her.

Susie is fed up with this fiction about nice young men. It seems to her that there aren't any men between eleven and forty in London; perhaps they all died in the war.

The front door bangs and they see Colleen standing in the hall. Instead of the usual shopping bags she holds her brown crocodile handbag and a bundle of misleading descriptions of flats; her demands have fallen from six bedrooms to three and even so she can't find anywhere.

This afternoon she looked at a damp basement in Primrose Hill, a gloomy third floor flat overlooking Marylebone Station and a much-partitioned ground floor near Golder's Green. None of them was cheap and they all filled her with that terrible sense of helpless gloom she associates with her first years in

London, with traipsing round Herne Hill and Tooting with her bickering parents. Now she's back in her wonderful house but it doesn't feel solid anymore; the magic carpet trip with Maurice is over and they have to be out of here in five weeks.

She sees them all staring at her from the kitchen. The twins and Viola come charging downstairs to make more demands on her. There's hysteria in Colleen's voice as she barks at Mrs Hunt, 'I'll have a large gin and tonic.' She kicks off her shoes and almost collapses onto the green Parker Knoll sofa as the children surge into the drawing room.

So, I'm a barmaid now, Mrs Hunt thinks resentfully as she stands over the prostrate figure with the drink on a tray. I've been on my feet since six and you didn't get up till nine. She watches Colleen gulp her drink and smiles grimly, thinking of what Tessa, the char, has told her about the empty gin bottles in Colleen's wardrobe.

By the time Maurice comes home the house smells of burnt food and bad temper. The smile he's been wearing all day with his dark three-piece suit and striped tie takes on a petulant and furtive air as he tries to get into the study to open his post before he's seen.

'Maurice!'

'Daddy!'

'Mr Samuell!'

He turns instead into the drawing room, where Colleen's tragic dark eyes in her puffy globe of a face no longer light up at the sight of him. He sits down on the green armchair opposite her and is immediately surrounded by: Viola, who doesn't want to go to bed; the twins, who say Alex has taken some soldiers from their toy fort; Johnnie, who hasn't been paid for a month; Mrs Hunt, who says she's sorry she's burnt the steak and kidney pie but better eat it now before it gets any worse. Colleen mutters that she's too tired to be hungry and Maurice looks at her glass suspiciously.

They sit at either end of the long mahogany table in silence. The friends who have sat here at so many convivial parties and the children who have chattered at Sunday lunches are invisible witnesses. Colleen is swallowing the row she wants to have until they're alone and Mrs Hunt's appearances with awful food (Maurice thinks she does it on purpose because she hasn't been paid, either) punctuate the joyless meal.

Maurice keeps asking for more coffee to keep Mrs Hunt downstairs. He's terrified of Colleen's rage, it reminds him of Flip, the headmaster's wife at his prep school, and his mother and grandmother, a long line of formidable women who make him feel small.

'You can go to bed now,' she barks at Mrs Hunt with that memsahib intonation that sounds so odd in Chelsea.

'I wouldn't mind another cup of coffee, darling.'

'It'll keep you awake.'

As if there's any chance of sleeping, with Colleen's misery hanging over the bed like a bomb.

Suddenly she detonates: 'I never would have married you if I'd known we were going to have to go and live in some hovel.'

He gapes, remembering her desperation to marry him. Perhaps this isn't the moment to remind her. He says sadly, 'When I met you, darling, butter wouldn't melt in your mouth.'

'Well, it will now. I'm not putting up with it, Maurice. I'm not being dragged off to the northern wastes. I hate North London!'

'Perhaps you'd rather go and live with your mother in Epsom?'

She bursts into tears, making him feel brutal. Epsom is in a lower circle of hell than North London. 'I just want to stay here!'

'So do I. But we have no choice and it really won't be for long, just until I can move the trusts to another solicitor.'

'And how long is that going to take?'

'I wish I knew.'

'Well, you bloody well ought to know. It's your money, isn't it? That beastly old man just does what he likes, you ought to stand up to him.'

'Mother's will…'

'Your mother never would have wanted us to suffer.'

'We're not suffering…'

'Scrimping and counting every penny…'

'I'm sorry I had to shut down the Fortnum's account, but they were threatening to sue. You really have been rather extravagant, Colleen.'

She has been safely at the other end of the table but suddenly she runs towards him; he ducks just in time as she throws a silver candlestick.

Mrs Hunt hears the thump from the kitchen. Four gins and that Colleen's not such a lady of the manor. I've never thrown anything at Steve. Nothing that heavy, anyway.

Alex hears it, as he sits up in bed trying to learn Latin verbs for the test tomorrow. Lessons at his new school are much harder and nobody seems to be interested in whether he likes it or not. Downstairs something has been thrown or someone has fallen or perhaps it is just up here, in his heart, that the thump happened.

The twins hear it in their room as they lie in their twin beds, not quite asleep. Are they dancing? Ben whispers. But there isn't any music. Will knows they're fighting but he doesn't say anything because he's afraid.

Viola, tucked up in the camp bed in Maurice's dressing room, is dreaming again of the fiery port. The sky and the sea are red with fire or blood and the streets are melting around her as she runs past ruins and finds herself in another deserted building. Everyone's dead, the city's dying, she can't escape.

Then she opens her eyes and realises she has escaped after all, she's safe in bed and soon Mummy and Daddy will come up and she will hear their comforting going to bed noises.

Thirteen

Suddenly Maurice announces that from next week Alex and the twins will be weekly boarders. The twins are stunned; they knew they had to change schools but not now, not in the middle of term. The three boys stare at each other and then at their parents where they sit like exiled royalty on the green sofa. Several pieces of furniture have disappeared, as if the move has already started.

Will realises he will miss the Art Competition, which he's sure to win, and being a pirate in the Christmas production of *Treasure Island*. Ben's glad he'll miss the end of term exams and wonders if they will have exams at his new school. He doesn't want to be a boarder, but it will be all right if Will is there. Alex is relieved he won't have to spend hours every day shivering at bus stops, lumbering through the dark city. His brothers will threaten the place he has fought for at school, especially Will, but Alex wants them to see how hard it is out there. The worst thing about going to the bus stop at seven-thirty each morning is knowing that the younger children are still in bed, waiting to be given breakfast and made a fuss of.

Maurice dispenses their future while Colleen sits beside him, smiling and supporting his fatherly wisdom. It doesn't occur to any of the boys that they can challenge the decision or that their parents might not agree with each other.

'It's a bit funny changing schools before the end of term,' Will says.

'It's because we're moving,' Maurice explains blandly.

As the door closes behind them Colleen spits angrily, 'They're too young to board.'

'After Christmas they can be day boys again. When we're in the new flat, wherever that is.'

'Promise me you won't make them board again?' She stares at him with huge dark eyes brimming with tears, making him feel like Jack the Ripper.

'Not until they go to public school. I promise, darling.'

He doesn't bother explaining that there's no money to pay for their fees as boarders for more than a few weeks. In his pocket is the letter he hasn't shown Colleen from the boys' present school, saying that the twins will have to leave unless the fees owed are paid immediately. The new school, on the other hand, offers a generous reduction for siblings and hasn't insisted on fees being paid in advance.

'It seems to be a very good school,' he says to Colleen, who submits to his superior knowledge of the mysteries of English education. Maurice wishes she wouldn't get so emotional about everything. But she's cut down on her drinking and has been more reasonable this week. When they first met, he used to say he was going to educate her but somehow it hasn't happened. An educated Colleen, he's sure, would be less likely to cry and throw things and become hysterical. Of course, he often says with a patronising air, Colleen and I come from very different backgrounds. But now all his energy goes into educating his children—and there's also, in an ill-lit corner of his mind, the suspicion that Colleen might turn out to be quicker and brighter than him. Maurice has never liked intellectual women and certainly wouldn't want to be married to one.

On Monday morning Colleen gets on the bus with her three sons. The twins sit together in front in their pink uniforms, whispering and giggling. She sits beside Alex, who stares out of the window, then takes Macaulay's *History of England* out of his leather satchel and reads it all the way to Swiss Cottage. Colleen is aware that Alex has already moved away from her, into school and books and friends she has never even met. In the aloof profile beside her she searches for the brilliant, volatile child who used to delight her with his funny remarks and passionate affection. All gone, cut out of him like fins and skin and bones lying on a fishmonger's block. Now she's afraid that the twins are about to suffer the same filleting process and she will lose them too.

Her own home life was so awful that all those schools she went to as her parents moved around India were a welcome relief. Seventeen, she counted them the other day. But these boys, who are so much loved and wanted, shouldn't be torn away from her so soon. She wants them to appreciate her—but Alex turns away from her to his book and the twins are sealed together in their private bubble. When they all get off the bus at Swiss Cottage the boys are struggling with their suitcases full of gym shoes, football socks, pencil cases, geometry sets and uniforms festooned with name tapes. She was up until one sewing them all on. Colleen wants to gather her boys to her one last time, to hug them and be hugged, to confirm that their family life until now has been just about perfect. In the kind of musical Billy used to star in, the kind she loves, the mother would burst into song at this point and her children would tap dance around her appreciatively, in a Technicolor garden. But the Finchley Road is very grey and anyway she can't sing.

So many boys in pink caps and blazers; those scarred and vulnerable knees between the tops of the grey socks and the grey shorts where naked flesh hasn't yet been controlled. Alex strides ahead and disappears. The next time Colleen looks around for her tall thin eldest child she simply doesn't recognise him among the pink herd. She puts her arms possessively around the shoulders of the twins, who squirm and wriggle and roll their eyes at each other. Nobody else's mother is fussing over them, they'll be teased about it at break and it's not fair on their first day, it's bad enough being the only new boys. A bell rings and the pink blazers form lines like beads in a kaleidoscope. Colleen's suddenly aware that she's the only female here. One of the masters shows her the way to the headmaster's study and as they walk down corridors, she smells custard and cabbage and hears a dreary hymn being sung half-heartedly. It could be St Joseph's Bangalore. It seems odd that school hasn't changed when everything else has.

After she has handed her sons over to the headmaster who, she hopes, is as affable as he looks, Colleen hurries to her appointment in the café in the Finchley Road. She met Mr Curtis at one of the agencies she has registered at and he very kindly offered to look after her. He owns a lot of property in this part of London and today he's going to drive her around 'until we find lovely home for beautiful lady', as he says in his charming Continental English.

He arrives on time in an elegant camel coat and kisses her hand. As they tuck into coffee and apple strudel Colleen explains all the complications—four children, a mountain of furniture to store, she doesn't even know how long they will need to rent this temporary flat for. Mr Curtis is older than Maurice, about fifty, with grey hair and distinguished features. He says he had a terrible time during the war, she lowers her eyes to her cake, not wanting to pry but imagining vast estates confiscated. Or perhaps he's Jewish and was in one of those horrible camps. One of the reasons she finds this part of London depressing is that it's full of tragic looking refugees. Anyone can go through a bad patch, but Colleen thinks it's bad form to go on and on about it. She dislikes politics almost as much as religion and disapproves of people who talk about their suffering. You have to pull yourself together and snap out of it. Mr Curtis has obviously snapped into a very successful business and Colleen is reassured by his fatherly manner. She doesn't want to organise the move by herself; men should do these things and she's annoyed that Maurice has left it all up to her.

Mr Curtis pays the bill and escorts her out to a wine-coloured Jaguar.

Fourteen

On the day of the move Charlotte offers to look after Viola. After the chaos of removal men, empty rooms and bewildering goodbyes to Susie and Johnnie and neighbours, Charlotte's house is a calm wooden box lined with silence. Viola can hear the grandfather clock on the landing tick-tocking like an extra grandparent sheltering her and the comforting smell of polish and lavender tickle her nose. The floors are so slippery that she skates on rugs as she walks from room to room.

Today the creamy globe of Charlotte's face is particularly gentle. She's sad that her two little protégées' families have both crashed. Emma has disappeared and doom-laden gossip surrounds the Samuells. She feels sorry for Colleen, who seems so incompetent, always late and flustered (and too fond of the bottle, the servants say). Mrs Bream, the cook, and Nanny Conway used to drink when her parents went off for months on long holidays and when they were drunk they devised horrible punishments for the three little girls in their care. Charlotte still can't see a cupboard without remembering how it felt to be locked up for hours, alone, sobbing, in the dark pantry. Yet there's no evidence Viola has ever been mistreated. All her life Charlotte has seen herself in little girls, has felt that by reaching out to them she can finally comfort that other little girl in the cupboard.

A grown-up friend comes to tea. Like all Charlotte's friends and relations, he's amused by her eccentric habit of collecting children. He has met this one before and has brought her a present: a papier mâché model he has made of a hunting scene. The three of them sit around the dining table, Viola concentrates on her boiled egg and fruit cake while the grown-up conversation washes over her. She likes this old man; she isn't sure if his name is Colonel or Gilbert or Kilpatrick so she doesn't call him anything. She thanks him for the model but is more interested in her food.

'It's disgusting! I don't want the child to even set eyes on such horrors.'

'Nonsense, Charlotte. All children like animals.'

'Dead ones? Murdered ones? You know how I feel about hunting.'

'Of course I do. But why should little Miss Samuell share your views?'

'It's obscene! I don't want it in my house.'

'I spent days making that thing. Thought you'd be pleased.'

Viola's trying not to laugh. It delights her that two old people should still be going to tea with each other and squabbling. She feels rather sorry for the old man.

'I do like it very much,' she reassures him, lying on the floor beside the model and trying to make sense of the men in red coats sitting on horses among trees made of feathers. There are dogs and another animal, a pointy-faced dog with a tail made of feathers. It isn't a toy that you could play with, but it was clever of him to make it. 'What are they doing?'

'Enjoying a sport.'

'Torturing innocent animals.'

They speak simultaneously and then glare at each other. Gilbert isn't sure, now, whether he meant to provoke Charlotte. Perhaps he did. He likes her clean, uncompromising rage and it somehow makes him feel younger when her blue eyes hurl fireworks at him. Charlotte swoops down on the model, her richly coloured silk shawl like wings as she carries it through the glass double doors to the drawing room, where she flings it on the fire. There's a horrible smell of burning wax and feathers mixed up with the sweet fragrance of burning paper as Charlotte stands, brandishing the poker like a sword, pressing the offensive images deeper into the fire.

The old man throws his napkin onto the table, goes through the double doors and closes them behind him. Viola hears them shouting as their shadows leap on the glass doors. Then the voices stop, the front door bangs and Charlotte comes back into the room, looking like a proper fairy godmother again.

Colleen is supposed to collect Viola at six but she's late.

'Are you looking forward to your new flat?'

'I don't think we're going there tonight. I think we're going into storage.'

'I think it's your furniture that's going into storage.' Charlotte smiles in a particularly nice way she has, so that you know you've said something funny but don't feel silly.

'Then I think we're going to a hotel.'

'Where?'

'Near a toyshop.'

'I shall miss you. Will you come and see me sometimes?'

'Of course I will. Are you going to die soon?'

'Not just yet. By the time I do you'll be grown up and you will have forgotten all about me.'

'No, I won't. I'll always be your friend.'

They stare at each other, sitting on the white armchairs on either side of the drawing room fire. Charlotte feels her own sadness swell until it fills the room. All the people she has lost come together into this small girl, who isn't afraid of change because she doesn't know what it is. Charlotte hates goodbyes so much that she evades them; this extended farewell twinges her nerves, intensifying the headache she has from the row with Gilbert. But it isn't Viola's fault her mother is late. She's glad when her maid, Letty, comes into the room to announce supper is ready. Charlotte insists on sharing her frugal supper of scrambled eggs on toast and stewed pears and caramel custard; the picnic atmosphere as she divides the food in two reminds her of the nursery suppers of bread and milk she used to eat with her sisters, when they weren't quarrelling or being punished. She tells Viola about them.

'What happened to your sisters?'

'They married and had children and died.'

'Is that all?'

'What would you have liked them to do?'

'Something famous.'

'I wonder what you will do.'

'I don't want to be an engine driver.' Viola has heard this is a traditional ambition for children and doesn't think much of it.

'I believe there are quite a few other professions open to girls these days.'

Colleen finally rings the bell at nine-thirty, flustered and apologetic. Charlotte sees Colleen's exhaustion and almost offers to let Viola stay with her for a few days. She's touched by the tall heavy woman's loneliness, her air of a queen who has mislaid her crown. Is that gin on her breath? She has always thought of Colleen as a young woman and is rather shocked to see her looking distinctly middle aged, with bloodshot eyes and cheeks billowing like curtains over her double chin. She looks very cold, standing there with the wintry night behind her. Perhaps she needs her children to keep her warm, Charlotte thinks as she puts on Viola's duffle coat, embraces her one last time and watches them both get into the waiting taxi. The removal van blocks the night sky.

Viola sits back in the taxi and scratches her nose where the fringe of Charlotte's silk shawl has tickled it. She falls asleep and when she wakes up feels so light that she thinks she's flying when she finds herself moving upwards with her rocking horse and two men in overalls. Then she's following the two men as they carry the rocking horse. They're in a warm, pale room and she thinks this must be her new flat. She has moved but the rest of her family has disappeared, she will have to live here alone with her rocking horse. Then she's sitting in an armchair in a smaller room and Susie's there, smiling at her, leaning over a cot where a huge baby's sleeping.

'Isn't she beautiful, Viola?'

'What is it?'

'It! Her name is Barbara. I will look after her now. My little Barbara!'

Viola watches indignantly while Susie strokes and kisses and adores the thing in the cot. She has always been the youngest, the baby, the little one; Susie has never looked at her like that. What if Mummy comes back from one of her shopping excursions with one of these new things? Viola stands beside Susie, staring through the bars at the fat pink curves that are supposed to be beautiful. This Barbara has stolen Susie and her rocking horse.

'Viola! Don't be naughty.'

Susie knows her so well that she can see the naughty thoughts before they come out. But before she can cry or bash the baby Viola falls again into a swirling pit of sleep.

She wakes up in a cot. She still has her clothes on and when she stretches her legs they kick against the bars. Perhaps she's got mixed up with that Barbara thing and she'll have to just lie here being gurgled at. Then she hears voices and recognises Mummy's angry one being nasty to Daddy. That dark shape on the other side of the room must be their bed and she's quite glad to be in the right family again.

'Where are the boys?' she demands.

'I told you she could hear,' Daddy says.

'They're at school, darling,' Mummy says in her mummy voice.

'Are we there? Is this the new flat? I like it.'

They laugh and the anger is squeezed out as they get up, bumping into each other in the small, crowded room. They open the door onto a corridor full of people and go downstairs to have breakfast in a huge restaurant. It's like a holiday but Daddy keeps sighing and Mummy keeps hissing at him like a snake when she thinks Viola can't hear.

All their furniture is stored nearby.

'Can I see Mr and Mrs Bear's shop? Where's Dandy?'

'Pipe down.' Daddy looks old and tired; he hasn't eaten any breakfast and neither has Mummy. Viola tucks into scrambled eggs with mushrooms and toast and marmalade.

'Shall I go to school now?' It seems the right thing to do after breakfast.

'No, you're not going back to that school.'

'Never?'

'No. We'll find you a new school, but not just yet.'

'Can I just stay at home all day then?'

'Yes,' Mummy says.

'Might be a good idea until we get all those other bills paid,' Daddy says. 'You don't mind, do you darling?'

'No. I don't like school, anyway.'

Maurice goes off to see his bank manager, which always makes him look ill, and Colleen and Viola wander around an enormous shop called Barkers. This feels normal, except that Colleen keeps crying and saying she has a cold. In the toy department Viola is allowed to choose whatever she likes because most of her other toys are in storage. She chooses a baby doll in a cradle. She has never liked dolls, she usually plays with her cuddly animals. This doll is peculiarly ugly: shocking pink and bald with bulging plastic cheeks as if she's sucking two gobstoppers and pouting lips with a hole where you're supposed to stick her dummy. Her body's made of hard plastic, she has spiky hands, no bottom and wears a pink frilly dress. Her brown plastic cradle is full of sharp edges with rockers like plastic knives. Viola takes her new toy out of the paper bag and tries to cuddle it, but it hurts. She wishes she'd chosen a toy poodle instead, to make up for Dandy, who is in kennels.

An old lady in a fur coat and a hat with a net that sticks out over her nose comes up. 'Is that your little baby, dear? Isn't she lovely!'

'She isn't a real baby,' Viola says contemptuously.

The old lady laughs and looks knowingly at Colleen, who

smirks back. Viola hates it when grown-ups gang up on her like this.

'What's her name?' The old lady insists.

'Barbara.'

Fifteen

When Colleen first saw the flat it didn't look too bad. It's on the top floor, like the flat in Rosemoor Street where she and Maurice lived and were blissfully happy when they were first married. There are three bedrooms, a small kitchen and a living room. Furnished, according to Mr Curtis, with antiques. The furniture certainly looks old but isn't objectionable, the rooms are bright and it's only for a few months.

When she and Maurice and Viola open the door for the first time, she isn't so sure. It smells stuffy and damp and seems overcrowded even before they unpack their suitcases. Viola is enchanted to be told she's to sleep in the corner of Maurice and Colleen's bedroom; she arranges her beloved animals and Barbara on her new bed before going downstairs to explore the garden.

Alone, Maurice and Colleen stare at each other. They are both miserably conscious of the irony that this flat is a mirror of Rosemoor Street. Cruelly, their present images mock them from that distant reflection of sensuous romance. Maurice sees a fat middle aged woman, her eyes and nose red from crying, her mouth set in discontentment. Colleen sees a shabby, flabby man whose good looks are crumbling into an expression of permanent surprise and indignation.

Colleen is determined not to cry or complain again and Maurice is determined not to upset her. So there's nothing to say. The silence is unbearable.

He continues to unpack the clothes he has carefully folded, and she attempts to get the tiny kitchen into some kind of order. In a few hours she must prepare supper for six people in here. She has brought a few cans of tomato soup and sweetcorn and tongue, some cheese and bread and a fruit cake: they'll just have a picnic tonight. She hums 'Only Make Believe', flatly. Then she stops because it really is only make believe, they don't love each other anymore. Her eyes fill with tears she's determined not to shed. From the bedroom she hears Maurice whistling 'She was a Sweet Little Dicky Bird'. Then he stops too because he can't face the line, 'sweetly she sang to me till all my money was spent'.

When the three boys ring the bell at four-thirty Maurice comes down to let them in. They stand there in their bright pink uniforms, loaded with satchels and cases and muddy football boots. His darling sons. Maurice embraces and welcomes them without quite meeting their eyes, making hearty noises he hopes will cover up the deficiencies of their new home.

'You said you'd meet us,' Alex says angrily.

'Oh dear, did I? Didn't Colleen phone to explain?'

'No. And we got lost. And Will cried.'

'No, I didn't. I was only pretending.' Will stares at the stained-glass windmill set into the front door and the broken mosaic tiles in the cold hall. The building seems to be a fake church and there's something fake about Daddy, too, that makes Will feel ashamed. Ben tugs at his arm, worried that they'll have to sleep in separate rooms. At school he's in a lower stream than

Will and hardly sees him. Alex charges past them up the stairs to inspect their new flat.

Colleen steps out of the kitchen into the tiny hall to embrace Alex but he ignores her, dumps his suitcase and satchel and darts around the flat, his incredulity and disgust so obvious that she shivers. Then Maurice and the twins come up the stairs and the flat is full. The three boys go into their bedroom where there's scarcely enough space to walk between the three beds.

'I thought you wouldn't mind sharing, after sleeping in a dormitory at school,' Colleen says nervously.

The twins are taking their mood from Alex. He's so angry that for a few minutes he can't speak. Then he says very loudly, 'It's a slum. I don't want to live here.'

'Now don't be cheeky,' Maurice says. But he looks more injured than insulted. His eldest son is eleven now, almost as tall as him, with an air of outraged innocence. The twins sense that there's been some tectonic shift between children and parents, they glare reproachfully at Colleen and Maurice who in self-defence become a couple again, working together to prop up the illusion of family mealtime. They move the dining table from the living room to the hall so that there's enough space for them all to sit down together.

Colleen opens cans and lays the table. 'We'll all feel better when we've had something to eat,' she says with her usual mystical faith in food.

Ben goes down to the garden, where Viola's crouching happily in the ruins of a bomb shelter, playing muddy games with a little boy who lives on the ground floor.

'Isn't it nice here? Ben, this is my friend. What's your name again?'

'Adzuli.'

'It's supper, Viola. You've got to come.'

'Do you like our new house?'

'No.'

'Why?'

'You're too little to understand.'

Upstairs the air is thinner and the meal that comes out of tins is congealed with silence. As if all the words got left behind in their old house or put into storage. They eat but there are none of the usual compliments about Colleen's food and the boys don't want to answer questions about their week at school.

'Who's going to sleep in that room?' Alex asks. The third bedroom is stuck between the kitchen and the living room, just big enough for a single bed and, for some reason, an empty fish tank lined with green slime. But any kind of room would be better than sleeping with the twins.

'Mrs Hunt's coming on Monday. To help me.' Colleen's voice quivers. There hasn't been nearly enough recognition that she needs help.

'I need my own room.'

'Viola ought to have that room. She's the only girl.' Will doesn't see why Alex should always have more.

'I'm going to sleep with Mummy and Daddy,' Viola says happily.

'Tell them, Maurice.'

Maurice drags himself back from daydreams of an auburn-haired actress he spent a weekend in Brighton with in 1938 to his paterfamilias present. 'Your mother and I have decided that Mrs Hunt is coming.'

In his own family his father Aubrey's decrees, issued at the breakfast table, were never contradicted. But his sons ignore him, their squabbling only becomes shriller as the boys kick each other under the table.

Grandma phones. 'Is that you, Colleen?'

'Yes, it's me.'

Edie makes her unique tutting noise, an expression of disappointment and disapproval. Colleen can imagine her pursed lips as she prepares to say something infuriatingly obvious. 'You sound exhausted. I hope they're all helping you?'

'Who?' Colleen feels a wave of self-pity.

'Why, the children and Maurice and the servants.'

'Oh, the servants.'

'How do you like your new house?'

'It's a flat.'

'Is it spacious?'

'No.'

More tutting. 'I was wondering, will I come on Christmas Eve or would the twenty-third be better?'

Colleen gasps with horror. 'I'm afraid—look, Mummy—I don't think you're going to be able to come this year.'

'But I always come.'

'I know you do, and of course we want you to, but we just haven't got room.'

'Can't the children share?'

'They are sharing.'

'By Jove! It must be a very small flat. How many rooms are there?'

'I know what, we'll come to you. We'll have Christmas lunch in that nice hotel in Epsom.'

'An hotel? But I've made you my Christmas cake. I used a whole bottle of brandy. And two puddings, so Alex can eat as much as he likes.'

In her voice Colleen hears all the bleakness of waking alone on Christmas morning in a cold house. It's her own fault, she thinks, for being such a misery all her life and not making friends. She says angrily, 'Now don't argue, Mummy. We'll come and pick you up.' A hurt silence. 'Next year we'll have a proper house again and of course you can come. How have you been?'

'I had to go to the doctor for my rheumatism.'

'Oh dear. Have you seen anybody else?'

'I had tea with Mrs Williams.'

'And how was it?'

'Very nice. And then I went next door to wish little Rodney for his birthday.'

'What are you up to tomorrow?'

'The plumber's coming.'

Colleen runs out of questions. She needs a different mother, husband and children; the happiness she's owed has evaporated.

'And how was old Edie?' Maurice asks.

'Waiting for the plumber.'

They all laugh because the emptiness of Grandma's life guarantees the fullness of their own.

Washing up in the tiny kitchen, Colleen mutters and curses. The children disappear into the bedrooms and Maurice asks nervously, 'All right, darling?'

'No, I'm not. It's like the black hole of Calcutta in here.'

'Can I do anything to help?'

'That'll be the day!'

It's true that Maurice has never washed up in his life, but her sarcastic tone jars on him. All night, it seems, her complaints are listed, dwindling to a hiss when they go to bed and Viola's asleep a few yards away. When Maurice wakes up on Saturday morning Colleen's lying beside him, staring at him with tragic dark eyes. Before she can start again, he gets up, dresses, and makes a pot of tea (his only domestic skill, learned when he was in the navy). Viola gets up too and catches him putting his coat on, attempting to escape. She takes his hand firmly and accompanies him on his walk.

They come to a roundabout where there's a sweet shop. He buys her a bag of her favourite sweets, honeycomb coated with chocolate, and a bag of humbugs for himself. Walking up to the Finchley Road sucking them, Maurice experiences a wave of nostalgia for his own Hampstead childhood. He hasn't been back to the Finchley Road since his early teens and it has changed, the buildings are much taller now and there's more traffic. He finds himself searching for traces of the memories that are suddenly so turbulent: going to Synagogue with Aubrey and Benjamin; visiting his grandmother, Rose, in Bishops Avenue; taking the train into the City with Aubrey. It strikes him that although he has always said, and believed, that he adored his mother, she doesn't appear in any of these early memories. Aubrey, who wasn't his father at all, seems to have spent more time with him. He searches for the station but there's a brash new tube station on the corner now. A few yards away he finds the old station, his station, the real station. Derelict now.

'What is it?'

'When I was about your age I used to come here with my father.'

'Where did you go?'

'To the City, where he worked. I remember standing on the platform, holding his hand like you are now. I was wearing a sailor suit and a straw boater, and he was wearing a top hat and tails and a gold watch across his tummy, even though it was summer. People wore more clothes then.'

Together they walk past the dusty ticket office, down the wooden steps to the platform where the train will never come. Aubrey used to take him to the City with him because he hoped Maurice would be interested in business and follow in his footsteps. Maurice hated the Stock Exchange, its noise and speed and aggression, the horror of a life that revolved around maths. Aubrey, who had made his fortune founding the Johannesburg Stock Exchange, was always surrounded by admiring old men and in his office he was treated like a king. Perhaps Aubrey had wanted Maurice to see the contrast between his home, where Florence regarded him as a necessary old bore, and the City where he was a hero. Maurice sighs because it's only now, twelve years after Aubrey's death, that he's beginning to understand him. Something stirs on the rusty tracks. A huge grey rat stares up at them. Another, even bigger, with entrails spilling out like gory sweets, lies near their feet.

Sixteen

Viola and Katie are digging for treasure. Katie's mother, Anne, sits near them in a deckchair, knitting a grey school cardigan for her daughter as she listens to the two little girls talking.

Katie has short brown curly hair and a pale intelligent face. She gazes, puzzled, into the hole they've been working on since the beginning of the Easter holidays. 'Are you sure it's here?'

'Yes. I heard my brothers talking. All these people called nasties came from Germany and they stole the nice people's money. It's called nasty gold.'

'Why did they come to my house?'

'Lots of people from Germany live around here. Maybe one of them came and buried it before you moved in.'

They dig for another ten minutes, using red seaside spades with wooden handles bought in Woolworths.

'What are you going to do with your nasty gold?' Katie asks.

'I'm going to go to Toys Toys Toys on the Finchley Road and buy all their Pez sweets and a toy spaniel and that witch puppet and I'm going to give my mummy and daddy some of it because this horrible man called Sydney froze all their money.'

'Do you mean they put it in the fridge?' Katie asks.

'It isn't in our fridge. I looked.'

'That's very nice of Viola to think of her parents,' Anne says pointedly. She works as a secretary in a school, carefully arranging her hours so that Katie is never alone.

Katie has forgotten her mother's listening. 'I'm going to pay my school fees and buy you a house,' she mumbles dutifully.

Their arms are aching, the fun has gone out of digging. They go through the French window into Katie's living room, where there's a piano and a dolls house Katie's father made before he left. He is never mentioned. Viola imagines him toiling over the dolls house, then suddenly deciding he has had enough and putting his coat on. The dining table's laid for tea with two bowls of fresh fruit salad, egg and cress sandwiches, a chocolate cake and mugs of milk.

'I like your house.'

'I wish I had brothers to play with like you.'

'They don't play much. They're too old.'

Colleen comes to pick Viola up and the two women regard each other with interest, if not exactly friendship, like two different breeds of dog sniffing around each other. Colleen suspects Anne of being a bluestocking and can't understand why she dresses so dowdily if she wants to find another husband. She pities women who work, as it means they haven't been attractive enough or clever enough to find a man to support them. She's slightly jealous of Viola's passion for Katie and her mother. On the other hand, it's wonderful not to have to entertain Viola and she knows she ought to invite Katie back more than she does.

'Thank you so much for having her!' Colleen gushes as Katie stares in admiration at her pointed white shoes with high heels and pink and white flowery dress. When she draws fashionable ladies they look like Colleen. When she draws mummies they look like Anne.

'It's a pleasure,' Anne says. 'They're so happy playing together. Viola loves puzzles and books. Don't you think she ought to be going to school?'

'Oh, alright, I'll find a school for her in the autumn.'

'But she could start next month. I don't mind taking her and picking her up.'

This is a masterstroke. Colleen detests the hills of Swiss Cottage and Hampstead and comes back from shopping trips to the Finchley Road exhausted. Shopping is no longer any fun, now that there's no money; she loves to compare the deficiencies of John Barnes, which is now her local department store, with the perfection of Peter Jones. When Maurice points out that the two shops are owned by the same company Colleen shoots him the reproachful look of an exile pining for home.

'Well—maybe—'

'I'm so glad! I already mentioned it to the headmistress, they do have room in the kindergarten class.'

'I'll have to ask my husband.' Colleen has just remembered the cost of school uniforms, and the grasping way schools have of insisting on being paid.

'Am I going to school?' Viola asks as they walk next door.

'You don't want to, do you? Don't you remember how you hated school.'

'I don't mind if I can go with Katie. Hello Adzuli!' she smiles at the little boy who lives on the ground floor. Colleen hurries her up the stairs. 'Can I go and play with Adzuli tomorrow?'

'No.'

'Why?'

'You're going to play with Katie. She's a very nice little girl.'

'Adzuli's nice too. I know, he can come to Katie's house and we can all play together.'

'No!' Colleen remembers Mr Curtis's assurance that only the best people lived in this house, 'businesspeople and diplomats.' He didn't mention that they were Nigerian diplomats. Alex is becoming far too friendly with their daughter, Sokari; he disappears into their flat for hours and Colleen is determined to put a stop to it.

At the top of the stairs there's the usual smell of burnt food. The door opens onto a scene of chaos: the twins have barricaded their bedroom so that Alex can't get in. He's trying to kick the door in and Maurice, who has just come back from work, is feebly telling them all to shut up. In the tiny kitchen Mrs Hunt has incinerated the sausages and has just dished up carbonised potatoes to go with them. She stands in a cloud of evil-smelling smoke, muttering and blaming the oven. Colleen blames Mrs Hunt. Over coffee and an occasional gin and tonic Mrs Hunt has confided in Colleen, who now knows far more than she wants to about her awful life. She knows Mrs Hunt has nowhere else to go and that it would be brutal to sack her.

But somebody has to go. In the house in Chelsea there was always another room you could go into; here, there's no safe distance between people. The bathroom, like the kitchen, seems to be designed for maximum discomfort, with a water heater that has to be coaxed and then ignited with a match into a menacing whoomph that doesn't even produce any hot water. Viola is filthy after digging in Katie's garden; Colleen has to force her into a tepid bath and sponge her while Mrs Hunt tries to wash the dishes in equally tepid water next door. Alex is reading *History Today* in the sitting room, while in the bedroom Will is drawing Gandalf, his favourite character in *The Hobbit*. Ben is organising his collection of medals with military precision.

Maurice sits hunched over the remains of the inedible supper, smiling politely at nobody in particular. He's telling himself that this is only a temporary arrangement, that the court case against Sydney will be over soon and they will be able to rent or buy somewhere bigger. Maurice's optimism is deeply ingrained; it's his private, his only, religion and he clings to it now. This ugly rabbit hutch of a flat, Colleen's bad temper, the noise and mess when they're all here together, the grease on the plates, the gas fires that either scorch your flesh or trap you in ferocious draughts—this isn't what he meant by family life. Whenever he thinks of a book he'd like to read or a chair he'd like to sit on, he remembers it's in storage. To avoid using the squalid bathroom, Maurice has himself shaved and uses the Turkish bath and showers at the RAC club in Pall Mall he was given life membership to on his twenty-first birthday. He goes to see Gertrude, whose scandalous memoirs, he tells himself, are certain to be a bestseller. He has told Colleen he has to work late in order to earn more and she's too distracted to be suspicious.

'Where shall I sleep tonight?' Viola asks as she comes out of the bathroom in her pink candlewick dressing gown.

Maurice kisses her goodnight. 'We'll put your bed in the boys' room.' There's a faint possibility of sex if he and Colleen have their bedroom to themselves.

'OK.'

'Good girl.'

She isn't good, she's just the only one who enjoys their reduced circumstances. This whole flat could fit into the nursery at their old house and it's this reduction she likes; the shadows and silences and loneliness and bedtime terrors have shrivelled and vanished. When her canvas camp bed is arranged under the window in the boys' room, she climbs into it happily and waits for them to come in, arguing as usual, in their striped pyjamas. Colleen calls out to them to be quiet because Viola's asleep and she smiles under the blankets because she isn't, of course, she's waiting for stories.

'Let's play Good Dog Land and Bad Dog Land,' she demands as soon as they've settled in bed.

Her brothers groan and try to return to those innocent games in the cloakroom. Even then, particularly for Alex, there was something forced and silly about it. They were pretending to be the kind of children who pretended to be dogs to please their little sister. Now, from the shattered splinters of his old identity, Alex tries to remember who he was.

'I can't remember.' His usually confident voice is dull. It hurts to go back in his head to his old house and school, to the time when he was a little prince and there was no shame.

'Yes, you can,' she says relentlessly. 'You're Boney, you're the chief dog in Bad Dog Land. You bully the other dogs and steal their bones and you boast all the time. Go on!'

'Who was I?' Will asks, not wanting to be outdone in world weariness.

'You're Towser, of course. You're a cry-baby dog and you're frightened of Boney but sometimes you rescue the little girl, that's me, and the Galloping Major helps you.'

Ben gives a military bark from the fourth bed and Alex's voice sets the scene in the dark. 'We'll have to do it as a story. Once upon a time Napoleon Boneydog lost a great battle and he went into exile on the island of Elba.'

'What's Elba like?' Viola asks.

'It's a beastly bloody ugly nasty little place,' Alex says savagely. 'And he hated it.'

'And all the good dogs were glad he'd gone so they had a party. Let's do a happy song. Ben?'

Will and Ben sing 'Nymphs and Shepherds, come away', in flat piping voices.

On the other side of the wall, where love has not been made in the double bed, Maurice says grumpily, 'I wish those children would shut up.'

'Let them play,' Colleen says. She thinks how lovely it must be to have brothers and sisters and how different her own childhood would have been if she had.

Seventeen

One day at lunch Colleen and Mrs Hunt have a couple of gins together. They've eaten a pork pie with salad as they're both trying to lose weight; the alcohol seeps through the lettuce leaves and tomatoes to infiltrate their emotions as they sit back in the hall that has become the dining room and stare at the washing up neither of them wants to do.

'How's Viola, then?'

'She's just having a little sleep.'

'Bored, probably. She ought to be at school if you ask me.'

'I didn't ask you.' Colleen wants to rebuild the barrier that once separated them: Madam and Sir and Miss Viola.

'Yeah, she needs to be with kids her own age. How about that Alex? Did he find his football socks? Don't think he likes living here. Well, it is a bit of a come down.'

This woman is discussing our family as if she's a visiting aunt. Colleen runs her tongue along her teeth to sharpen it. 'Thank you, Mrs Hunt. You can do the dishes now. And I'd like a coffee, please.'

Lady Muck. Slipping on the greasy linoleum in the tiny kitchen, Mrs Hunt fumbles in the pyramid of dirty dishes in the sink until she finds two cups and saucers. She rinses them and fills them with instant coffee. 'Fancy a biscuit?'

Something about her tone and the lumps of brown powder

floating in the tepid brown liquid make Colleen hold her breath and go red. Mummy's going to blow up, the children say when they see this expression.

But Mrs Hunt is not an explosives expert. She thinks they're getting on and is astonished when Colleen suddenly says, 'I'm afraid you're going to have to leave.'

'When?'

'As soon as possible.'

'But why?'

'This flat is really far too small for seven people. Viola needs her own room.'

Mrs Hunt stares at her and hates her fat la-di-daness. Mrs Colleen Fucking Samuell's no better than me only her husband isn't in prison. Yet. She gets up to go to her room but holds the back of her chair because she's shaking as she says, 'I'd watch that husband of yours if I was you.'

'What can you mean?'

'Working late, my foot. He's got a bit on the side, I been watching him. You can always tell.'

When Viola wakes up an earthquake is happening in the hall. She opens the bedroom door and sees Mummy screaming at Mrs Hunt, who rushes past with a suitcase and disappears downstairs.

Colleen's so upset that she has to lie down on the sofa in the living room. Viola sits on the floor beside her. 'Was Mrs Hunt naughty?'

'Darling, I need to rest. Could you play in the other room?'

Viola's favourite toy is a white plastic toy piano. She's convinced that if she can just get the knack it will make beautiful rolling sounds like the one at Katie's house; but all she can thump out of it is a melancholy plink plonk. She punishes it by pressing even harder and the piano loses a leg, sinking lopsidedly into the carpet.

Even the sofa's uncomfortable, too short for Colleen's long legs. He wouldn't do that to her. The old bitch was just trying to hurt her. It hurts so much that she feels as if she's been strangled and flung down, all the breath squeezed out of her. Thirteen years. Of course he still loves her, all her friends are envious. There aren't any friends since they moved to Mr Curtis's hellhole; she and Maurice have tacitly agreed not to let anyone see it, not even Edie. Specially not Edie. But somewhere there's this group of benign people: Sally, Billy, Jim, Rex, Mary too, they are the audience of her life. They all say, why she can hear their voices: Maurice adores Colleen. Who could it be, anyway? Some tarty little secretary at the oil company where he works? Or that raddled old gold digger?

'Have you seen Gertrude lately?' It's supposed to sound casual but because she's been rehearsing the words for hours they come out in a venomous hiss. Luckily Maurice can't see her face as they lie in bed that night in the dark.

'Gertrude?' He's reassuringly vague, as if he can't quite remember who she is.

'I thought you decided to go ahead with that book after all.'
'Oh, that. Well, I might.'
'I don't want you to see that woman.'
'Whyever not?'
'I don't like her, Maurice. I don't trust her. I don't want you going to that flat of hers.'

'You mean—' he laughs incredulously. 'Why, darling, she's years older than you. Older than me, in fact.'

'Maurice, I want you to promise me.'

'But if we go ahead with this book, I'll have to see quite a bit of her and she can't very well come here, can she?'

'Then don't do any more work on it until we move.'

They hold each other in the dark. Maurice changes the subject, stroking her hair so tenderly that she doesn't notice. 'What happened to poor old Hunt?'

'I had to get rid of her. She was insolent.'

'What did she say?'

'Oh, she's an old bitch. And she can't even cook.'

'You were the one who insisted on bringing her. You said you'd never lived without a servant.'

'Well, there's a first time for everything.'

Neither of them can quite believe they're still here, after seven months. It's as if a power cut that should have lasted a few minutes has gone on and on; they're cut off from light, from their old friends, assumptions and identities. Even the children seem different: bigger, noisier, monsters that hoover up vast quantities of food and grow out of clothes with perverse speed.

We only have each other, Colleen thinks, and then tries it aloud, a timid exercise in optimism.

'Yes, that's right, darling. We still have each other,' Maurice booms in the dark, his voice just as robust as ever.

Eighteen

On the last day of the summer term the three boys cross the Finchley Road, carrying an assortment of satchels, books, rolled up paintings, cricket bats and tennis racquets. As they begin the descent Alex feels a wave of disgust and anger. In stories, when the prince is forced to live in a pigsty, obliging magical mentors help him get back to the palace. Even the pigs notice. Alex doesn't read books like that anymore, he prefers history books that debunk generally held beliefs. With a schoolfriend, Tom, he has started a newspaper, Samuell's Weekly, which reports the follies and stupidities of adult life. Tom types it on his father's typewriter and then Alex produces it on a second-hand duplicating machine in what used to be Mrs Hunt's room. Maurice is delighted by his enterprise and doesn't mind, or perhaps doesn't notice, the rebellious and contemptuous tone.

'Down to the mines of Mordor,' says Will, who knows their new flat is disgraceful.

'Beastly smelly dump,' Ben agrees, although he isn't really angry but pleased at the thought of having Will to himself all summer. At school Will has made new friends and the twins hardly see each other.

Colleen keeps telling herself it's lovely to have all her children at home. But it isn't. She wakes each morning with a heavy sense of failure that she knows will turn to bad temper before the day is out. She can't blame the children for being on holiday, so she blames Maurice, who often has to work late. Nervously, she watches the children demolish the flat. Each time a large Samuell bottom sits on one of the fragile cane chairs it cracks and stains have appeared on all the carpets. Most of the beds and chairs are balancing on books now, or not balancing at all so that you have to sit at an awkward angle. When Mr Curtis comes to collect the rent on the first of August he sighs and shakes his head as he looks around. His charm has deteriorated with the furniture.

'Too many children, Mrs Samuell.'

'Well, what do you expect me to do about it? Drown them? Here's the rent.'

He counts the money. 'When did you say you were leaving?'

'I told you, I don't know.'

'If you are staying more than one year we will have to make new contract. New year, new rent. And so much damage! I did not think you would be such a family. When you leave, I will have to make my flat like new. Very expensive.'

'That geyser in the bathroom still isn't working. I'm sure it's going to explode one day.'

'Ah yes.'

He says this every month. No repairs are ever done and the damage they do to the flat just by existing ticks on like a taxi meter. Colleen's alone with him because the children have been herded down to the garden. Colleen longs to push him downstairs and wishes she could sack him but keeps her temper until he leaves. Then she looks in despair at the blitz of breakfast on the table in the hall, the dishes rotting in the sink, the tangle of wet dirty towels in the bathroom. A year. She remembers the last time she hated her life like this: Epsom. That cold dreary house where Daddy was dying, and Mummy was ill yet again and said it was Colleen's duty to stay at home to look after them both. Then she escaped, to a typing job at the American embassy in Grosvenor Square, in proper London, and met Maurice and—Colleen can't bear to finish the thought that this, finally, is where her escape has led to. She sees this flat through Edie's eyes; then shuts her own to keep out the singsong voice of her imagined mother stating the obvious: It's very dirty, Colleen. Will I help you with the dishes and the hoover? Whatever made you take such a poky flat? I thought Maurice was supposed to be rich.

Edie's tutting rises to a crescendo in Colleen's head as she takes two Disprin, kicks off her shoes and lies down. From her bed she can see Viola and Katie in the garden next door, chatting and laughing and digging away. No nasty gold has materialised and Samuell gold is just as elusive, frozen by Sydney and locked in mysterious lawsuits. There's no money to move or have a holiday, they might have to spend a second Christmas here. Every weekend Maurice hires a car so that they can have family outings. Last Saturday they went to Epsom to take Edie out to lunch and this weekend they're going to Bognor Regis where Jim Bates, whose photographic company is flourishing, has a yacht.

The twins come thumping up the stairs again. Alex has been invited to Tom's house, thank God, and Viola will be happy to stay at Katie's all afternoon. Colleen lies on her bed as long as she can, not sleeping, reciting to herself the litany of reasons why she has to carry on: the children need her;

Maurice loves her really; she has to show Edie; trusts will be bust and paradise, which is situated near Sloane Square, regained. She doesn't have Maurice's blithe optimism, she has to crank herself up every morning to the point where she can face them all as Mummy.

When she comes out, dressed and freshly perfumed (her *Femme* is running out and she doesn't know when she'll be able to afford any more), Ben and Will are in the living room. Ben is curled up in one of the battered wicker armchairs reading *The Eagle* and Will sits opposite, drawing him. The twins' intimacy is a secret chamber locked against the rest of the family. Of course, it's good that they play together happily and don't get bored like Viola and Alex but still—Colleen is beginning to resent their collusion. It's too intense, all that whispering and giggling gets on her nerves. Ben is a dear little boy but she doesn't like the way Will looks at her these days, she's worried that he might be setting Ben against her. She hovers behind Will, watching the soft black pencil overpower the white paper.

'It's too much of a caricature. You know what your art teacher said in your report, your drawings are too grotesque. I wonder why.'

Will closes his sketchbook and turns to glare at her. His eyes make her feel ugly and unloved. She finds herself hoping he never draws her as she says brightly, 'Well, I'd better get us some lunch.'

Will goes on watching Ben read although the sketchbook remains closed on his knee. She has spoiled it again. Ben is deeply involved in Dan Dare's adventures, he's thinking he will probably go to the moon, after he has explored India and Persia and won lots of medals like his grandfather. Ben inhabits his body quite unselfconsciously and has no idea how others see him. Will sees him with love and envy, as the face and body he ought to be inside. Ben's dark, sullen face and long, graceful body make Will feel even more blubbery and clumsy. If he'd come out of Mummy's tummy half an hour earlier—Will hates to think of coming out of her, although Alex and the boys at school insist it's true. He imagines a vast female butcher covered in blood and slime. On the wooden board in front of her is a Ben chop, lean and neat, surrounded by the fatty yellowy heap that has been trimmed away to make Will. Brutally the giantess wields her chopper.

On Saturday morning they get the bus to Victoria where they are hiring the car that will take them to Bognor. Colleen has looked forward to this day when they will all be together, a family at the seaside. She's wearing a blue and white cotton dress and has dressed Viola in a sailor dress in honour of Jim's yacht although she can't help feeling it's rather unfair that little Jim, as she thinks of him, should be doing so well when they are not. The Samuells, with their weekend bags full of towels, bathing things, Viola's bucket and spade and shrimping net, pyjamas, books, and the enormous picnic Colleen has prepared seem to take over the bus. They'd hoped to leave early but by the time they get to Victoria and collect the car it's nearly lunchtime.

Instead of the Humber he's used to driving Maurice is given a new Rover that looks horribly unfamiliar. The children admire the leather upholstery and gleaming dashboard while he tries to work out where the gears are. Maurice was taught to drive by the family coachman who transformed himself into a chauffeur in the early twenties; his driving is idiosyncratic. He goes so slowly that he's frequently stopped by policemen and asked to drive faster and relies on elaborate hand signals when he wants to stop or turn right or left. When other drivers overtake him, which most do, he mutters 'Roadhog!' and Colleen joins him in a lament over the decline of good manners.

They pile into the car, the three boys in the back while Viola sits on Colleen's knee beside Maurice, who is still trying to get used to these strange new gears as they shudder and lurch through the Victoria traffic. Maurice is exhausted from his working week and still doesn't know what to do about Gertrude. He thinks longingly of his study in their old house, where he could go after breakfast on Saturday and peacefully while away the time until lunch. In this new life that has assaulted him he's never alone, there's no time to do anything except earn an inadequate salary and submit to his family's demands at weekends. Behind him Will and Alex are arguing again.

Colleen's remembering her last voyage on a friend's yacht, when she slipped on a glass roof and cut her leg and there was a storm and she thought they would all be drowned. She can't swim and detests boats, except the comfortingly vast P&O ones which used to take her to India and back. When she's rich again, when she wins the football pools or their family fortunes are restored, she might go on a cruise, but she certainly won't have anything to do with the sailing of the ship. It annoys her that other people do such foolish things with their money. She can remember Jim when he hadn't two brass farthings to rub together and had to be taught how to eat lobster; his success seems rather tactless, given their situation, although she likes him and is pleased he has finally found a girlfriend, Yvonne. Hardly a girl, they're both about forty and far too old to have children, if they do marry. Colleen's pride in her own children is immense, they're all wonderful and she wants them to be admired wherever they go. She's sure all their childless friends envy her. Jim's yacht will be horribly uncomfortable but she's looking forward to this weekend at sea as a showcase for her family.

It's the hottest day of the year. Even with all the windows open, their bare legs stick to the seats and there's a smell of boiled sweets, farts and scorching rubber.

'This is a new car, isn't it?' Colleen asks nervously at Roehampton.

'It smells funny,' Ben says.

'It's Alex, he always smells,' Will says.

'How puerile,' Alex says.

'He's not poorile,' Ben says defensively.

'You don't even know what it means.' Alex laughs at the absurdity of his younger brothers and the three boys start to fight on the back seat, kicking and punching each other. As the car lurches, they're thrown forwards and bang their heads.

'Sit properly, you stupid boys.'

'Maurice! They might be hurt! Are you all right, my darlings?'

'I feel sick,' Viola says.

'I've got a headache. And I think I'm going to be sick too,' Will says.

'I need the loo,' Ben adds.

'You'll have to stop, Maurice.'

It annoys him that they are darlings and he is only Maurice. 'I can't stop here. I'll cause an accident.'

They're on the Kingston Bypass, stuck in an enormous traffic jam. On their left, in a front garden, plaster gnomes fish and ogle and smoke pipes in an orgy of kitsch. They have time to count each pointed ear. For fifteen minutes they don't move; the heat, squabbling, and threats of imminent vomiting and bursting bladders give Maurice a headache. He wonders if all these other cars are full of families who don't like each other, going to places they don't want to get to.

They stop for the picnic and pee in the bushes. On a tartan rug they devour the feast Colleen has brought: sausage rolls, curry puffs, ham sandwiches, Scotch eggs, chocolate cake, ginger beer and orange squash. While they eat there's harmony; Colleen enjoys their healthy appetites and praise of her food. This is what she wants, all she wants; this feeling of being needed and appreciated. Their loud voices fill the terrible silence that shrouded all her childhood meals. Here on this tartan raft she sails at last with her happy family.

But the real boat is still thirty miles away. The car they climb back into is baked, the air as heavy as flannel. They drive off back into the traffic jam and one by one the children fall asleep. Maurice and Colleen turn to each other.

'What time did you say we'd be there?'

'About two.'

'It's nearly three.'

'Jim won't mind. He knows we're always late.'

At the bottom of a steep hill the drowsy silence is broken by grinding gears and the engine sounds as if it's about to have a heart attack. 'I'm sure there's something the matter with this car.'

'Now then, Colleen, don't be a backseat driver.'

'I'm in the front seat.'

'Even worse.'

'There's a dreadful smell of burning.'

'Probably that chap in front. Can't stand men who drive flashy sports cars like that—'

'Maurice! Stop! There's smoke pouring out of the engine!'

Her screams wake the children, who are thrilled. Maurice drives onto the grass verge and they abandon the car, while passing motorists honk at them and jeer and wave. Alex feels it's typical that they can't even get to the seaside. Reluctantly, he accompanies Maurice as he trudges up the hill in search of a phone. Ben climbs a tree and hauls Will, who isn't agile, up beside him while Colleen and Viola sit on the tartan rug again, making daisy chains.

'Is this our holiday?' Viola asks. 'Where's the sea?'

'I don't know where we are. Daddy will come back soon.'

Cars are masculine, nothing to do with Colleen, who shows her daughter how to pierce the juicy green stalk with her nail and pull the stalk of the next flower through the hole she's made. Viola, who hasn't had much to do with nature, is disappointed when the crisp white smiley flowers droop and go yellowy brown. Still, the chain is a marvel, it keeps her busy for hours which is just as well as the breakdown van doesn't come until ten.

Maurice walks to a pub to buy stale sandwiches, bags of crisps and bottles of ginger beer. They camp out on the roadside. As it grows cooler they are draped in towels as well as the withered daisy chains Viola has made for them all. In the dark the headlights swoop past, manic eyes watching them. Laughing at us, Alex thinks as it grows too dark to read and he puts down the book on the Russian Revolution he is reading.

On the way home, if they ever get home, he will fire questions about Russian history at Daddy and Will. Daddy will say he hasn't got time for all that now and his brother will say he isn't interested anyway. Will has gone his own way, into art and fantasy, but Alex still needs to keep reminding him he's the cleverest as well as the oldest. Will and Ben have been sitting against a tree reading *The Hobbit*, which Will knows almost by heart. Ben reads slowly and Will sighs with impatience as he waits to turn each page. When the words describing the epic journey grow pale and blurred and then invisible as it grows dark, the boys turn back to the unheroic mess of their own journey.

Colleen sits on the tartan rug, Viola asleep on her lap in a nest of towels and dead flowers. She has let go of the image of their chic nautical weekend, it has floated away and will have to be postponed.

Maurice sits beside her on the rug. 'I can't understand it,' he keeps saying. 'A brand new car.'

'It's disgraceful, we might all have been killed. Never mind, darling. I'll phone them on Monday and make sure we bloody well get our money back.'

The breakdown van arrives at last. The Rover is loaded onto the back and the driver gives the Samuells a lift to the nearest station.

Nineteen

The manager of the car hire firm says Maurice drove all the way in first gear and, he adds, it's surprising the car didn't explode. Colleen adds the car hire firm to Sydney, the bank manager, Mr Curtis and Mrs Hunt on her list of villains.

Colleen finds the school summer holidays a strain. Shopping, cooking and washing all on her own for the first time in her life, she feels like an unpaid servant. In a few months she'll be forty and the bedroom mirror isn't flattering. She tells herself it belongs to Mr Curtis and is probably distorting her reflection. All her favourite clothes seem to have shrunk. She can't possibly have put on weight, what with the stairs and that terrible walk up to the Finchley Road and back she has never taken so much exercise. Colleen avoids that puffy, bulging woman in the mirror as she avoids her friends, embarrassed to accept hospitality she can't return. When Maurice is at home he expects to be waited on hand and foot.

'The butler's off tonight,' Colleen says pointedly as she bangs the burnt casserole down on the table.

'It smells horrible,' Ben comments.

'Tom's mother is a really good cook,' Alex remarks.

'Why is it so dark in here?' Will asks.

'The light bulb's bust.' Colleen glares at Maurice, who ought to have fixed it.

They all look up at the empty socket. None of them has the faintest idea what to do about it. In the past, little men appeared with ladders to replace bulbs. Electricity is a mysterious force that might kill them. Colleen thinks that now there are no little men around, her big man should learn to do these things and her voice is dangerous as she turns on him. 'I hate this bloody flat. Nothing works, nothing's comfortable. Just get me out of here, Maurice.'

He looks at her in dismay. The children have stopped eating and are staring at her too, her rage and disappointment fill the tiny flat. Usually, these outbursts happen when they're in bed, in whispers. Viola is sleeping in their bedroom again to act as a buffer, but Maurice doesn't know how to cope with this public display.

'We'll find somewhere soon, darling, don't worry.'

'We? You never lift a finger.'

Maurice wonders if she's been drinking. He sinks into passive gloom. If he doesn't say anything her angry words will break on his head like waves dashing against a cliff. Aubrey and Mother and Benjamin used to argue endlessly at mealtimes while Maurice sat and smiled, wanting to be friends with them all. Silence is tact, as he learned again when he was sent away to school and was the only boy in his class to avoid the wrath of the headmaster's bad-tempered wife, Flip, who got her nickname because of her habit of painfully flicking at boys' ears as she walked down the rows of desks.

Just after her sixth birthday Viola goes back to school, dressed in her strange new scratchy clothes: grey knickers, a grey pleated skirt, grey V-necked jumper, green blouse and a tie that neither she nor Colleen know what to do with. It's in a knot under her chin when Katie's mother rings the bell and Viola runs downstairs. She doesn't mind the long walk up to Haverstock Hill, chatting to Katie.

But when she has to let go of Katie's mother's hand and stands alone in the cloakroom that smells of pee, vomit and sweaty shoes, Viola panics and tries to flee. The teachers, the many Misses, are gaolers who march her back to her own generation, to the seething grey girls.

There are too many children in the enormous room, too much whispering and shuffling on hard splintery chairs. Katie has disappeared among the other girls, who know her, and Viola tries to follow the activities that swirl around her in a fog of newness. A bell rings and they all stampede downstairs into a garden. She stays by the teacher's side.

'Don't you want to play?' Miss Something asks.

'No.'

'But this is break. You must play with the others.'

'I don't want to. Can't I go upstairs and sit in that room?'

'All on your own in an empty classroom? Certainly not.' She gives the lazy child a shove and Viola reluctantly sidles into the wet bushes and watches them. They stare back but don't talk. Talking is the only kind of friendship she knows, all this running and skipping and yelling confuses her.

'She's shy,' she hears one Miss say to another.

'Needs to lose some weight.'

In her family Viola feels small but here she feels like a clumsy giant surrounded by Thumbelinas.

That night, when the geyser has finally heated enough to provide a tepid bath, she asks Colleen if she's fat.

'It's just puppy fat.'

'But dogs aren't fat.'

'What did those children say to you?' Colleen remembers the bitchiness of little girls and longs to protect her daughter from it. As she frequently says, she and Will and Viola aren't fat, they are just in proportion.

'They said I was fat. And Indian. But I'm not Indian, am I Mummy?'

'Of course not.'

'Can I stay at home tomorrow? I hate school.'

'I'm afraid you'll have to go. Unless you're ill, of course.'

Viola manages to be ill quite a lot that term but most mornings, with complaints and sometimes tears, she puts on her grey prison uniform and joins the expedition up to Haverstock Hill. Her hatred of school dwindles from tragedy to a family joke.

Alex wins History prizes, Will wins Art prizes and Ben is put in an even lower stream where he floats away from Will. He's popular but he doesn't want other friends, he wants his twin. The qualities that won the talking prize don't endear the Samuell children to teachers and they're generally regarded as overconfident, precocious, clumsy and undisciplined. Maurice is proud that they're all good at English and History and equally proud that they all, like him, have difficulty with Maths. He would like them to be more athletic and less argumentative, but he reminds himself that politicians are paid to argue, and artists are usually hopeless at games and, being sensitive chaps, cry all the time. Ben's career is not yet mapped out and girls, of course, don't need careers.

On the bus coming home from Gertrude's one December night Maurice has an epiphanic moment and realises that all will be well: he can have his family cake and eat… remembering what he was doing half an hour ago he abandons this metaphor and looks furtively around the bus. That man over there, with a red face beneath his bowler hat, clasping his rolled-up umbrella and smirking to himself, he hasn't been working late either. And those two giggling office girls in the front seat, what else can they be talking about but their married lovers? Half the fellows at work go out for a Babycham with the secretaries before they go home and who knows what happens next? Instead of the background guilt that has disturbed him for months Maurice feels masculine and sophisticated.

He sees his own childhood differently now. Florence was fifteen years younger than Aubrey, who had as much sex appeal as a tin of spam. There was that obvious crisis in their marriage, when his handsome cousin Monty came to stay and Aubrey came home to find Florence and Monty in bed. Maurice and Benjamin, who weren't supposed to know, were sent on a skiing holiday while things were talked over. Maurice can see now that there were months, if not years, when Florence was in London and Aubrey stayed in the country brooding, muttering about wicked women. As a grass widower he was looked after by a succession of women known in the family as Aubrey's porpoises, presumably because they were shapeless and friendly. Maurice never knew whether any of these women had designs on Aubrey or became more than friendly. As for Florence's wickedness—she left her first husband, Maurice's biological father, and two little daughters in South Africa to go off with Aubrey. Jack was handsome but poor, he managed a store in Kimberley. Maurice met him only once, when he was in his twenties and Jack was an old man. They went out for a silent dinner together in the restaurant of the dull hotel in the

City where Jack was staying. Maurice stared at the disconcertingly familiar features, his own face aged and broken.

Maurice is enough Florence's son to be very thankful that she was wicked. He knows he'll never do anything like that; he adores his children and still loves Colleen. Really. Although she's losing her looks and developing a very sharp tongue. Gertrude isn't the sort of woman you marry but she's entertaining and appreciative. Maurice looks at his reflection in the bus window with some satisfaction. By the time he gets off at Finchley Road he's a happy man again.

Colleen is infuriated by his good humour as he comes upstairs whistling 'The Cornish Floral Dance'. She wants to snatch away the day that has left him in a good mood and give him instead her own day: another bounced cheque, preparations for a second Christmas in this hateful flat, Viola's rudeness.

'What did she say?'

'I asked her if she wanted to go to Selfridges to see Father Christmas in his grotto with Uncle Holly.' Her voice is strangled with pain and with fear that he will laugh.

'Well?'

'And she said, Uncle Hollic! Like you, Mummy.'

Maurice struggles with his facial muscles. 'She probably doesn't even know what it means. She picks up words from the boys.'

'And what have they been saying about me?'

Her loneliness touches him. He promises to back her up and the next day, Saturday, he summons Viola to the bedroom after breakfast and tells her he's going to punish her because she has been cheeky.

'No, I wasn't.'

'Mummy says you were rude to her.'

She goes on arguing but Maurice, wanting to get the scene over with, tells her to pull down her pants and lie across his knees as he sits on the edge of the bed. Reluctantly, he picks up one of his leather slippers. Boris, he remembers, used to enjoy this kind of thing, paid women to beat him and be beaten, but he detests it. 'You've been very rude to your mother and I'm going to have to spank you,' he declaims in a loud voice for public effect. He taps his daughter's fat buttocks with the edge of the slipper.

Viola roars and screams with indignation. Maurice thinks he has really hurt her and his hand refuses to lift the slipper again. He's a gentleman, a gentle man, hurting little girls degrades him. Maurice pauses for so long that Viola wriggles off his lap, pulls up her pants and glares at him reproachfully. 'It's not fair. You're not my daddy anymore.'

Twenty

The long fur that tickles her nose smells of perfume and the animal it once covered. Now it crouches on Mummy's shoulders and Viola loves to lean against her on the bus, pretending to sleep in the itchy forest of security. Colleen puts her arm around her daughter and feels the intense joy of protecting her young, as if the fur covers all of her. She wishes all her children could have stayed like this forever, pups or kittens, dependent; Colleen's maternal heart yearns to shelter her children from all danger—the Mutiny, Council schools, unsuitable friends.

Outside the shop Colleen calls DH Heavens they cross Oxford Street and go down South Moulton Street to Sally's dress shop. Colleen pauses outside and stares at the window where a blonde dummy as slender as she once was models an apple green straw hat and spring costume, waving her arms and pirouetting as if she's about to fly. Sally's clothes, imported from France, have been written about in *Vogue* and *The Queen*. Behind this window her friend earns enough to pay for Martin's school fees. Colleen seethes with admiration and envy. Women shouldn't have to work; their husbands should support them— yet how wonderful to earn money of your own. In the white and gold interior Sally is chic in black, her defiantly blonde hair in a chignon.

'You look beautiful,' Viola says as this vision, a peach surrounded by a golden halo, stoops to kiss her.

'Darling! What a lovely shop. You look terribly glamorous.' Colleen thinks she looks tired underneath all that makeup. She probably has to get up at crack of dawn. Inside her carpeted, mirrored kingdom Sally gives orders to her shop assistant and crisply answers the phone.

The three of them go to have tea in Fortnum's where Colleen and Viola tuck into meringues with whipped cream while Sally has coffee and a cigarette. Both women smile and chatter as they try to stir the embers of their old friendship. Billy joins them, red nosed and bloated. A sour gale of alcohol on his breath as he kisses Colleen confirms her worst hopes and she watches as Sally passes him a five-pound note under the table. He's the only man here; men are supposed to work in the afternoon while their wives shop. Maurice is finally working. Billy's a bounder, a cad, a lounge lizard. Actor my foot! Colleen beams with relief. Sally's only being brave because she has no alternative, no man to speak of. Maurice is still Colleen's knight in shining armour even if his armour's a bit rusty. He's going to do the book with Gertrude after all and it's bound to be a great success.

But when January comes, they're still in the flat and Christmas cheques are bouncing like tennis balls as the children go back to school.

Colleen watches from the living room window on the first day of term as the children gather on the pavement below. The three boys in their pink caps and blazers turn right and walk in a triangular formation, Alex striding ahead while the twins walk behind him, whispering and giggling. Viola in her grey hat and overcoat joins Katie and her mother as they walk off. Colleen sees the four of them as children among other children, not as demanding monsters whose needs have sucked her blood for the school holidays. None of them looks up at Colleen or waves. She feels abandoned but also relieved to have the flat to herself, to be able to tidy and think about how they're going to move. She knows that it's up to her, Maurice will never sort it out. Suddenly she wishes he was here, now, wishes he could come in as the children go out and they could be lovers again. They could lie in bed together all day and make love and talk and then perhaps it wouldn't matter that the bed was in this hated flat.

For Alex school is more satisfactory than home. He shines at History and English and he and Tom lead a gang that terrorises the weaker boys. He's in charge of the library which means he can devour as many books as he likes. When he sits there, surrounded by books, he feels powerful, confirmed in his future greatness. Next year he will float above these petty rules, the insults of the Games and Maths masters, the muddle and squabbling at home, and go to his real school, where his brilliance and originality will be recognised; he will make friends with boys who are his equals. His family will be killed in a car accident, only too likely with Daddy's driving, and he will inherit the money that is rightfully his.

Will has become a star at art and the centre of a group of friends. With Stevie, Tom's younger brother, he forms a close alliance based on annoying their presumptuous older brothers. Will is subtle in his emotional dealings and is searching for an ideal friendship, a companion who will understand and admire him and laugh at all his jokes. Ben is the only perfect mirror he has found but he's in a lower stream and in the savage competition of school life this belittles him. Will would like a larger, shinier mirror. In the art room he sits making a picture of Gandalf with blue and grey and green plasticine. Rolling it between his fingers, Will inhales the fishy, slightly disgusting smell and makes the magician's eyebrows more bushy, his cheekbones more noble. Gandalf hasn't got any children, he's wise and powerful and Will wishes he would appear now in a puff of smoke and take him off on a very long journey. The other boys will watch admiringly as they disappear.

Ben watches him from the doorway of the art room and Will knows without looking up that there's love and devotion in his eyes. Ben's loyalty is like a carpet that always unrolls beneath his feet. Pretending to be so absorbed in his art that he can't see or hear anything, Will finally does look up and grins at his brother, whose darkly handsome face is illuminated by delight. For Ben school is always confusing, an arbitrary string of tests he fails without understanding why. He doesn't complain but has become surly, his dark brown eyes veiled by resentment. It's only Will, and occasionally the rest of his family, who see his sweetness now. He dreads Common Entrance, the final exam he will have to take in the top class, so much that he feels sick whenever he thinks of it. He doesn't think of it, his mind skips past it to the palatial school where Will and he will have adventures together.

Viola still doesn't understand what school is for or why she has to go there every day. She looks around the huge room with French windows leading to the playground, wishing she could walk through them and run home down the hill. The teacher tells her to sing with the other children. They're singing a silly song about a man who has whiskers on his chinnigan. She tries to sing. The teacher tells her to keep quiet because she's tone deaf. Viola sighs, she always seems to be doing things in the wrong way or at the wrong time. Although she was given a watch on a blue leather strap for her sixth birthday the numbers on its moony face don't make a lot of sense. She knows the friendly shape of home time at four o'clock, but the rest of the school day seems to consist of being pushed and dragged, of sitting down when she wants to walk around and being told to go out and play when she wants to sit in the classroom.

She feels like a glove puppet with an enormous hand inside her. Upstairs in the classroom, where it's freezing unless you sit right next to the huge black metal stove, they're embroidering tray cloths as presents. Viola doesn't know why trays need cloths, it's like the whiskers on Michael Finnigan's chinnigan, nobody explains. Her tray cloth is pale blue with mauve flowers, it's grubby and sweaty and she's quite sure nobody would want it as a present. Sewing is also Reading; they have to queue up at the teacher's desk to be heard. They have special nasty books at school, with poo-coloured soft covers that smell of old metal, boring pictures and even more boring words. Viola listens to Jane, in front of her, going on about the fox and the log.

When it's her turn Viola holds the book up to her nose and tries to explain to the teacher that she knows much better stories than this about foxes: Charlotte's foxes, yelping with terror as they're hunted by dogs and men in red coats; the fox that ate her father's pet rabbits when he was a little boy—

Miss Carter, who has to hear six more little girls read aloud before Break, glares at this fat little show-off. 'Just read what's in front of you, please, Viola.'

But she can't. She has been corrected so many times that she's afraid of that stupid fox jumping over its stupid log and the words won't come out.

Then there are the white squiggles on the blackboard. You're supposed to copy them into your exercise book in pencil and then the teacher comes round and gives you a red tick, a slash of adult approval on your childish pencil marks. But Viola never makes the right marks and there are holes and smudges on all her pages. Her exercise book looks as if it has fought and lost a war whereas Julie and Katie, who sit on either side of her at the long table, have beautiful clean pages full of neat pencil marks, red ticks and even triumphant gold stars.

All the Samuell children have a complicated relationship with order. What is obvious to other children is not obvious to them and in their satchels chaos reigns. All four of them lose their homework, fall over the pavement, fail to understand the rules of games and social conventions. School uniforms that look immaculate on other children always look messy and bedraggled on them. Ties are crooked, shoes unlaced, their hair is uncombed. They talk too much, eat too much, demand too much attention, seeming to be both precocious and retarded; they all live a rich inner life nourished by books and stories and a clownish outer life. Which is what the world sees.

Colleen is indignant when teachers criticise her wonderful children. Again and again the same words crop up in their school reports: untidy, lazy, undisciplined, inaccurate, arrogant, uncoordinated, careless, uneven. Maurice, with seasoned optimism, constructs a family mythology which accounts for his children's apparent weaknesses and also for his own failures. Samuells, he explains, are good at English and History and bad at Maths and Science. Since this is in their blood there's nothing that can be done about it. Alex's illustrious political career and Will's future as a great artist will blossom regardless of the niggles of teachers, who wouldn't be teaching if they had any talent. Ben's future is still in doubt but at least he's handsome and can play football and cricket and Viola, of course, is only a girl, so her education isn't important.

Alex is the first to crack under the strain of the dissonant messages from home and school. For days he lies in bed in the room the four children still share, looking pale and clutching his stomach. Colleen calls the doctor, an unreliable North London doctor, not nearly as charming as Doctor Lowndes who can't be expected to schlepp all the way over here from Chelsea. The doctor says Alex will have to have his appendix out, which will cost a fortune but will of course have to be done privately because, as everybody knows, National Health operations kill you.

Viola is fascinated by the invalid. Mummy has gone out to the shops and has told her to look after Alex. She sits on the end of the bed and gazes at him, amazed that someone so huge and loud and confident has been struck down by illness.

'Are you going to die?'

'We're all going to die.'

'When?' she asks, alarmed.

'If you mean, am I going to die now, I think it's extremely unlikely.' He bounces out of bed and goes to the bathroom in his striped pyjamas.

'But Mummy said you're not supposed to walk. Doesn't it hurt?'

She hears the toilet flush and then Alex's laugh, confident

and knowing. He comes out of the bathroom and goes into the tiny kitchen where he slaps chocolate spread and peanut butter onto eight slices of bread. Viola has never seen food disappear so quickly. She thinks it's unfair that she's fat and he's skinny.

'Are you feeling better, Alex?' She takes Mummy's orders very seriously. If he dies before she gets back from the shops it will be her fault.

'I wasn't ill, silly.' He burps, strides back to bed and lies down again.

She stares at him in awe. 'Were you just pretending?'

'Of course. I don't want to go to school.'

'Will you go to hospital like Madeline and get lots of presents?' Madeline is the heroine of a rhyming story Alex has read her. She is sent to boarding school and then pretends to have appendicitis to get attention from her papa. In hospital such a fuss is made of her that all the other little girls she shares the dormitory with pretend to have a tummy ache too. *In the middle of the night Miss Clavel turned on the light and said, 'Something is not quite right.'*

'You mustn't tell anyone.'

The combination of secrecy and acting out a story thrills Viola and also opens up vistas of possible deception. She has never pretended to be ill for more than a day. She stares at maestro Alex, deeply impressed. *And all the little girls cried, 'Boohoo, we want to have our appendix out too.'*

Alex stares back at his little sister and wonders if she could be his ally against the twins, his confidante. He was the age she is now when she was born. Her eyes are popping with helpfulness but she's too young, she can't possibly understand and will probably go blabbing to Mummy. Already he wishes he hadn't told her. He won't tell her about the other things, won't admit to anyone they happened. Mummy and Daddy will believe him, not the headmaster.

Alex remembers the thrill of pleasure as he and Tom tormented Bumface in the cloakroom. It got a bit out of hand, but it was only a game, really, and it was Bumface's fault for being so pathetic and weedy and repulsive. They didn't really hurt him, not much, Mrs Bumface was being hysterical when she said she was taking him away from the school. It was just bad luck that someone sneaked. Bumface is delicate and sensitive, apparently, revolting little runt, so Alex is going to show them all he's delicate too and then they'll feel sorry for him and by the time he goes back to school it will all have blown over. Soon he'll escape to his new school, which will be bigger and better in every way, escape from this horrible little flat where he feels like a changeling.

When Colleen comes back from the shops her eyes fill with tears as she sees her dear little daughter nursing her big brother. He looks dreadfully pale and thin. Colleen tries not to think about her cousin Mavis who died of a burst appendix. The doctor says it isn't an emergency, but the ambulance is coming in the morning to take him to hospital just in case.

Alex is in hospital for a week and on Saturday they all visit him with grapes and flowers and books. He shows them his magnificent scar and the deliciously revolting organ that has been cut out of him, a piece of withered rubber crouching in a jar like a pickle not even Alex would want to eat. Will is torn between envy of the attention Alex always attracts and fantasies that his brother will die. Ben wonders if he could arrange to have appendicitis the day before his Common

Entrance exam. Maurice, who has herded them all into an expensive taxi to go to the hospital, sits on the only chair biting his nails as he tries to calculate how much all this is going to cost. Viola sits on his knee, feeling proud and rather possessive because she hasn't told anybody that Alex is faking. Alex thinks how shabby they all look and how embarrassing Colleen is as she fusses around his bed.

When they get home Edie phones. Colleen flinches at the sound of her voice, as she always does. It's her private superstition that her mother can smell bad news thirty miles away and comes circling in like a vulture.

'And how is Alex's stomach-ache?'

'We've just been to visit him, as a matter of fact,' Colleen says in the tight voice the children associate with their grandmother.

'He's in hospital?'

'It's nothing serious, Mummy, just appendicitis—'

'Not serious? Don't you remember Mavis?'

'That was donkey's years ago, and they didn't have proper hospitals in India. He'll be fine, he had the operation on Thursday.'

'Why didn't you tell me?'

'I didn't want to worry you.'

'I won't be able to sleep now.'

Her querulous voice stirs violent memories in her daughter. It's croakier now but the same voice, fretting and nagging, that has forced Colleen to insist that all is perfect in her life, to look on the bright side until it blinds her. She knows that if she was being bludgeoned to death and her mother phoned, she would gasp that she was enjoying herself.

'Now I'm afraid I must go. Maurice and the children are waiting for their supper. Everybody sends their love.'

Where is it then? In the cold hall of Quetta Edie puts the receiver down and stares at the photograph of Carr as a young soldier. Its frame, like the tables and chairs and screens in the living room, is made of dark wood carved with flowers and leaves. Each piece of furniture was made so that it could be folded and moved easily to the next army bungalow. Now the tables, chairs and screens are wobbly, as if waiting to collapse for a move that will never happen. As she prepares her frugal supper of ham salad, Edie thinks of that other household, the noise and mess and mountains of food she's excluded from. It's beastly of Colleen not to have invited her to the new flat, not once in eighteen months. Edie suspects there's been some kind of financial crash, she wants to turn up on their doorstep with the five hundred pounds she has saved and offer it to them but knows that if she does Colleen will be furious with her (although she will probably take the money anyway).

Colleen bangs the phone down. The thought of that dreary little house in Epsom suffocates her and makes her clench her hands with rage; the bedroom where Daddy died in pain and bitterness; the chest of drawers where Edie keeps all the expensive handbags and gloves Colleen has given her over the years (too good to use, dear) together with the paper they were wrapped in, neatly folded, as if it was too good to throw away; the living room where Edie announced, on the day of Carr's funeral, that it was a daughter's duty to look after her mother. Colleen packed a suitcase and fled to Maurice.

Fourteen years later, Colleen turns to him with a radiant smile of gratitude because he's still here and she did get him and children and London instead of being entombed.

'And how is dear old Edie?' Maurice can't mention his mother-in-law without a twinge of malice. He has never forgiven her for opposing their marriage because he was Jewish, and he detests her cautious, timid, banal personality. Usually, Colleen is in a bad temper after speaking to her; he's surprised when she comes over to kiss him on the forehead and then on the lips. The children look away in embarrassment while their parents are being soppy.

That night Viola sleeps in the boys' room again.

'Let's play Good Dog Land,' she says as soon as the lights are out.

The boys groan because it's so babyish and boring and they want to tell ghost stories.

Ben begins. 'One night, at midnight, a man came to a lonely cottage in the middle of a dark wood. He knocked on the door, but nobody answered. So he pushed open the door and went into a cold dark room. He put his hand on the light switch—your turn, Will.'

'He put his hand on the light switch but there was another hand there. A slimy, green—'

'How could he see it was green if it was dark?' Alex objected.

'It glowed in the dark. So there! And he touched it, and the fingers gripped his and wouldn't let go and he tried to escape but the hand clutched his and then he felt another hand at his throat—your go, Alex.'

'I'm going to sleep.' He hates sharing a room with all these children. He wishes he was back in hospital, where there were pretty nurses and presents. His scar hurts—how strange that real pain should have come out of an imaginary illness. Tomorrow, he has to go back to school and he's dreading it, afraid that he will be caned for tormenting Bumface.

'Viola then.'

'I can't!'

'She's frightened,' Ben explains.

'No, I'm not.'

She's terrified. She wants the man to get out of the door and run away. Get a bus, don't run through that horrible wood. If you wriggle and bite perhaps you can escape from the hands but what if they follow you forever? She will never put her hand on a light switch again. She pretends to be asleep.

A few days later Viola is walking home from school with Katie and a group of schoolfriends. They're all going to tea at Katie's house. Viola wants to go too but isn't sure if she's been invited. She looks up at her window and sighs as they pass her house. 'Oh dear, I hope my animals will be all right.'

They all look at her and she feeds on their attention, hears the words pour out of her, wonders where they come from. 'Gulliver doesn't like it when I go to school and leave him at home. He's a teddy, he's yellow, he's bigger than the other animals and he's really naughty. One day he tried to follow me to school and my mummy had to come and fetch him. Then there's Dandy, my black poodle, he tries on all my clothes when I go out and then he goes into the kitchen and eats up all the food. Ginger's my nightdress case, he's really old, so old all his fur has gone white. He's got a zip in his tummy where you put the nightdress. He had to go to hospital to have an operation to put the zip in and he used to live in India with my mummy when she was little. He just wants to sleep all day, but Gulliver and Dandy want to play and they really annoy him. Look, can you see them at the window?'

They all look up and for a split second they do see them, the bear and the two dogs. They laugh and Viola feels a sharp pang of triumph because they listened; her head isn't empty after all but full of stories waiting to come out. All those toys that are in storage have come back to life now that she has put them in a story. She goes to tea at Katie's and joins in the games instead of standing awkwardly watching as she usually does when she's in a group of children.

Twenty-One

While her children are at school Colleen hunts for somewhere to live. The new solicitor, David, is an angel compared to Sydney but not quite enough of an angel to let them have all the money that's rightfully theirs. Whenever she sees an advertisement for a house that sounds wonderful, the price is less than the money she knows is locked up in those blasted trusts but more than the money they're allowed to spend.

Looking at houses becomes Colleen's hobby. She knows all the little tricks estate agents use to lure you to their dumps; the exquisite rooms that are poky; the nobly proportioned reception rooms the wind whistles through; the conveniently positioned houses with a railway line at the bottom of the garden; the secluded ones up a dark alley; the house in need of modernisation that has Victorian plumbing and the airy modern one that's pseudo Tudor, like Edie's house in Epsom. Colleen knows now that Mr Curtis has swindled her, they're paying far too much for this horrible little flat. Although she dreads the bill for breakages they will get when they leave, she's desperate to move. She works at house hunting as she has never worked at anything before and registers with six estate agents. They're all charming as they drive her around but she doesn't trust any of them.

There's always a problem. Often, it's something depressingly obvious, like galloping damp or a smell of drains. Other houses feel miserable or neglected, or as if a murder's been committed. When the politely condescending man beside you opens that front door there's always a spirit that rushes out at you before you can register the size and shape of the rooms, and Colleen knows that the next place they live in must be perfect. If there are ghosts, they must be happy ones, they can't afford any more periods of exile. It's time for her family to come home, to be cheerfully united under the right roof. The twins can share but Alex and Viola need their own bedrooms, Maurice needs somewhere to write, she needs a kitchen and bathroom that work properly and a drawing room and dining room where she can entertain. All their friends will come back, their life will return to normal. Which is happiness.

But every time Colleen thinks she has found her house, *the* house she knows is waiting for her somewhere in London, there's a problem. It's too small or too expensive or needs thousands spending on it or it's miles from a tube station. It's a bit like hunting for a husband—Robin was sweet but a Yorkshire farmer, that American GI was charming but a total bastard; dozens of others were too poor or ugly or unambitious or boring or bad tempered. Butter wouldn't melt in your mouth when I met you, Colleen, Maurice says—he always says these things at least a thousand times. But in fact, butter melted copiously, great slabs of it, water under the bridge, trips to the moon on gossamer wings. Not that she was promiscuous, but how were you supposed to find Mr Right without sampling a few Mr Wrongs first? If she didn't find a husband a lifetime of looking after Mummy loomed. Colleen only had a few years to cash in her assets and she knew exactly what they were: she looked like Jessie Matthews, the nation's pin-up, and she had plenty of willpower and quick wits even if she wasn't what you'd call an intellectual. After thirty she'd be a spinster, an old maid, yesterday's newspaper, returned empty, on the shelf, not even a maiden aunt as she had no brothers or sisters. Maurice really was her saviour: the kind, handsome, rich, charming, cultured (in that order?) antidote to the poison of life alone with Mummy.

Now the object of her romantic fantasies isn't a man but a house. If love conquered all in her twenties, she needs money to sustain love in her forties. Not for herself but for the children, she reminds herself, and as it turns out some of the things she said to Maurice in the early days, like darling I'd love you even if we had to live in a hovel, weren't quite true. She knows now that family life in the farmyard (that farm she so desperately didn't want to live on with Robin) is nasty, brutish and long. The eighteen months they've been in Mr Curtis's flat have aged her, distanced her from Maurice, damaged the children; Alex's bullying, the twins' rudeness, Viola's hysterical tantrums about going to school—Colleen is sure these wouldn't have happened if they'd stayed in their old house. They can't get back there but in her head there's a new house (a flat will do if it's big enough) where their squabbling, chaotic, inedible mealtimes will be reincarnated as cheerful Sunday lunches. Talking will be prized again instead of dreaded, food will cook at the right temperature in a proper kitchen and family affection will bloom.

'Well, I think I deserve a medal.'

Maurice, exhausted after a week juggling work and Gertrude and family life, looks at her wearily. 'A medal, darling?' A Victoria Cross for sacrifice to the retail trade.

'I could have just sat here on my arse—'

'Now then, Colleen, Rose and Crown!'

The children giggle and try to eat the stringy, leathery liver and bacon.

'But I schlepped all over North London, I didn't give up, didn't take to my bed like Mummy, I searched until I found it. Now eat up your liver, Viola.'

'I'm leaving it for Mr Manners.'

'He doesn't want it.'

'Neither do I.'

'Don't be cheeky. Ben, why have you left your spinach?'

'It's slimy and green and revolting.'

'Now eat it up.'

While Colleen's in the kitchen opening cans of peaches and condensed milk for pudding Viola and Ben pile their unwanted food onto Alex's plate.

'Dustbin!' all the children yell as they watch the liver and spinach disappear down their unfairly slim brother. Alex loves food, all and any food. As babies the twins were fussy eaters, but he never has been, he needs to fuel the power he feels within him, needs to be stronger and cleverer than the others and so he must eat. In their games he was Boney, the dog who stole the other dogs' bones, and although he has outgrown those games he still needs the extra bones. Colleen is pleased he will always eat her food.

'Alex, darling, you're a good trencherman,' Colleen says approvingly from the kitchen. She hates throwing food away, it means she has failed as a mother. Edie's meals were always grudgingly planned to the last mouthful; in India she would sack the cook if she thought he was wasting food and Colleen was a skinny child. She wants to give her children foodlove, lots of it, it hurts her when they won't eat. 'Are there any thirds?'

Alex asks, looking around the table.

Glutton. Show off. Maurice has eaten his overcooked liver and watery spinach to please Colleen but he's a fastidious eater, Alex's greed offends him. As he approaches puberty his eldest son looks disturbingly like Maurice at the same age. Twelve. When his mother was having that affair with her cousin and he wasn't supposed to know but did, of course, and so did poor old, dear old Aubrey. The year he was sent to stay with Auntie Connie and Uncle Jacob and overheard them say he was adopted. He doesn't like being reminded of all that. To his astonishment tears come to his eyes more than thirty years later as he relives that moment when he realised he didn't really belong in his family, didn't really belong to Aubrey and bratty Benjamin did. Florence never talked to him about it, she just packed him off back to boarding school and went on telling him that the pretty little girls in the photograph on her dressing table were her nieces in South Africa, although Maurice knew they must be his sisters. Nobody comforted him or explained. Although he and Aubrey went on loving each other, Maurice spent most of his adolescence feeling abandoned by his family. By the time he finally did meet Jack Solomon, his biological father, Maurice was an adult and Jack was old and it was too late to ask questions.

Every time Maurice looks at Alex he sees, not a little boy, but a counterfeit version of himself at that unhappy age. Colleen comes back after clearing the table and sits down with a sigh of martyrdom, to remind him that she's worn out by all this domestic drudgery.

'You've found a flat?' Maurice finds it harder and harder to drag himself back to this one every evening. Most evenings. He feels like an actor in the wrong play: shabby husband of bad-tempered woman, impatient father of four rowdy children. At Gertrude's he feels at home, perhaps because he's free to leave; in her drawing room he relaxes and expands. She is, as he archly reminds her, a very wicked woman. Her wickedness is flattering, amusing, comforting. He misses her terribly as he stares politely at his wife.

Now that she has their attention Colleen beams with triumph. 'It's in St John's Wood. Just a few doors down from the synagogue but we don't have to have anything to do with them.' (Colleen loathes all religion. She's not anti-Semitic but anti-God.) 'There are five bedrooms, so if the twins share there'll be room for a maid. Au pair they call them now. Sally says you can get them for practically nothing. There's a decent sized drawing room with a balcony and a dining room that can double as your study, Maurice, and two bathrooms. It's on the first floor, nice big rooms, high ceilings, we can get all our own things out of storage. There's a kitchen big enough to eat breakfast in, radiators in most of the rooms—oh and it's near the tube station. And we can afford it!'

'Well done, darling.' Now Maurice can see the old Colleen in her again, or rather the young one. She glows with success and her flesh looks firm as her dark eyes shine with optimism.

The next evening Maurice sits in his armchair, upholstered in oyster-coloured silk, in Gertrude's opulent, softly lit drawing room. She has just handed him the crystal tumbler full of whisky and soda, clinking with ice. He tells himself he isn't going to let it happen again. The trouble is women want things so much, they're so emotional and he can't bear to hurt their feelings. He gets out his notebook and frowns to make it clear he is being serious about working this evening.

'Now let's get this absolutely straight. You were in Beirut until you were seven and then you were sent off to a convent in Brussels. Why Brussels?'

'It was cheap.'

'But I thought your father was an Austrian aristocrat with vast estates?'

'He was, but he gambled, and he and Mama had parted company by then.'

'So, were you with your mother in Brussels?'

'I don't think so. I never saw much of her.'

'Now when was this, exactly?'

'Donkey's years ago.'

'Yes, but when, Gertrude? Before the First World War?'

'Oh yes, I should think so.'

'Before the turn of the century?'

'Darling, how can you? What a beastly thing to say.'

Suddenly he has all her attention. She's wearing a tightly fitted cream suit, with that look of being very carefully packed into her clothes that she always has. Not exactly fat or thin, but firm and waiting to be unwrapped like a seductive parcel. Her wavy hair has gone a curious shade of blue and her face is a cosmetic masterpiece. She carries a gold inlaid powder compact she takes out several times an hour to check that no cracks have appeared. Her strong features and jawline are still intact, her grey eyes have the power of her confidence in a beauty she has mislaid but hasn't lost. She reminds Maurice of his mother, not that he was in love with his mother of course, Boris was talking through his hat about that. But women of that generation do make women nowadays look like a bunch of hoydens. He's about to tell her so when he sees that she's upset.

She sits on the sofa they both know they will end up on and refuses to look at him as she stares into her whisky and says sadly, 'You think I'm old and ugly.'

'No!'

'I'm not that much older than Colleen.'

'I didn't say you were. I'm not insulting you for God's sake, I'm just trying to find out what happened, and when.'

'You're so pedantic.'

'This book has to begin somewhere.'

'I don't see why. I hate being bogged down by dates and things.'

'So, what do you suggest? Once upon a time?'

'I'd love that. I've always wanted to be a princess in a fairy tale.'

'Well, it's your book.'

'Quite. And I am paying you enough, aren't I darling?'

Over the last year her cheques have added up to almost as much as his salary. He always expects them to bounce but they seem to be, like the flat overlooking Regents Park and the jewellery and the carapace of her clothes, quite solid. Being paid by a woman is not as shaming as it ought to be, in fact Maurice finds it rather exciting, a nice change from Colleen who is always demanding money he hasn't got. He just wishes he was a bit less confused about what she is buying.

The phone rings. They both know who it is. Maurice feels panic rising as he picks up a copy of the Evening Standard and pretends to read it. Getrude, glancing at him as she picks up the receiver, thinks how furtive he looks. Not a man to trust. Can't trust any of them, married or not.

'Colleen! My dear, how lovely to hear your voice. Yes, he

is, as a matter of fact. Working away. You must come and join us one of these days although it's frightfully boring, just my silly old life. Here he is.'

She passes the receiver to Maurice, who bellows in astonished tones, 'Darling! Is that really you?'

'Of course it's me. Maurice, I want you to come home.'

'Won't be long, darling. I'll be home by ten-thirty. Just sorting out the first chapter.'

'The first chapter? You've been working on it for years. At this rate the bloody woman will be dead before you finish it, and a good thing too.'

'Now darling, don't be unreasonable. I've had something to eat, don't bother about that. I'll be home as soon as I can.'

When he raises his eyes from the black telephone, he thinks there has been a power cut. In the dark there's a shimmer of apricot satin on the sofa.

Twenty-Two

Colleen feels her confidence seep back as their possessions come out of storage like prisoners stumbling out of dungeons. Her old self jumps out of boxes at her; each pile of books and piece of china restores her a little to her matriarchal throne. Maurice is pleased by the size of the new flat; it puts thick Edwardian walls between people and gives him enough space to be a writer (between meals). He and Colleen have their own bathroom again and their own bed, his mother's pink satin bed, has returned from the limbo of storage. Altogether he feels more dignified and no longer dreads the walk home from the tube station. Mr Curtis has presented them with a huge bill for damage and breakages in their old flat, Dandy the black poodle has returned from the kennels where he expensively lodged and his confinement, like theirs, has altered him. He yelps all the time and is hysterically devoted to Colleen. When she goes out one day he destroys her clothes, like a jealous lover, and she has to leave her bedroom door locked. He sleeps outside it, guarding her, growling at anyone who dares to walk the corridor at night.

For the children the move has been confusing. From the mess and chaos, you emerge as something new, but what happens to your old flat and the person who lived there? There must be traces on the walls, echoes of your voices arguing and telling stories. Perhaps that's what Mr Curtis is charging them for. These newly decorated walls are aggressively shiny, the smell of paint gives them headaches. Alex has his own room again, next to the kitchen at the end of the L-shaped corridor. He spends all his spare time there, reading and doing his homework, barricading his door against the twins if they ever dare to try to enter. He has his books again, his grandfather's bed and curtains with the hunting pattern, and he can invite his friends home. He doesn't like the view of dirty red brick walls and pipes; it isn't the place where he ought to live but he doesn't have to feel ashamed anymore.

The twins have a bedroom almost as big as the one in their old house. They have all their books back, their fort is full of Roman gladiators and crusader knights again and Ben has his collection of medals and military buttons. They settle back into calm companionship, reading and talking. Will draws while Ben sits and watches him admiringly or struggles with his homework. Occasionally they organise skirmishing raids on Alex's room, charging down the corridor with whoops and screams of mock terror. His room is called the torture chamber.

Viola is the only one who misses the enforced intimacy of their old flat. Her room, next to Alex's, is huge and cold, with a fireplace that is hardly ever lit. There's a bookcase full of books she still can't read, although she's nearly seven. She has to go to bed all alone again. The nightmare couldn't get through to her when there were other people in the room but now it swoops, dragging her back to the burning port where the river of blood flows into the fiery sea. The city's growing up with her, becoming monstrously familiar. She recognises the cobblestones, the tall buildings consumed with flames, the silence of death. It has become a part of her, but she still can't find her way down to the water. The girl who may or may not be Viola runs down the steep cobbled street; breath scorches her lungs, her legs are weak, but she has to keep running even though she knows she can't escape the terror and loneliness. She wakes up and needs Mummy.

Dandy growls outside the bedroom door, Maurice growls in his bed. He hopes Viola isn't going to be neurotic. Colleen gets up and takes the sobbing child into the drawing room where they lie together on the green Parker Knoll sofa under a tartan blanket. Safe in Colleen's arms, Viola knows she won't be sent back to the burning port. They whisper like lovers, she has her mother all to herself.

'Have you got earache?'

'Yes. It really hurts.'

Something hurts. Perhaps the tears have flooded down into her ears. Anyway, pain is an acceptable reason to cry.

Colleen disappears and returns with warm olive oil she drips into the curved fleshy whorls. Complicated things, ears and children. She remembers nights of childhood illness when her ayah held her, and Edie didn't. Colleen knows she won't get much sleep on the sofa, but she doesn't mind, she loves it when her children are ill; Will's catarrh, when he could hardly breathe and clung to her; these nights with Viola when she feels totally needed. This visceral closeness is what she really wants.

At four, when Viola is finally sleeping, Colleen tiptoes back to the right bed. Dandy glares reproachfully at her as she steps over him, and Maurice has sprawled over to her side of the bed so that she has to lever his stripy pyjamaed leg out of the way before she can get in. That unconscious leg offends her. It's as if he (the owner of the leg) were kicking her out of the way.

He snores, too, not shallow childlike snores but deep waves of capricious quivering noise. She resents his sleeping so peacefully when she can't. It's selfish, yes, Maurice does exactly as he likes. Goes off to work in the morning without kissing her properly and phones, as he did last night, to say he wouldn't be back for supper after all because he had to discuss something with Gertrude. Well, I want to discuss something with you. She punches him viciously in the ribs, but he only smiles and rolls over, away from her. Colleen follows him, clasps him from behind and presses her lips to the back of his head where she suspects he is having disloyal dreams.

In the morning Maurice leaves her sleeping. He has a bath, shaves and dresses, putting on a sense of superiority to his torpid family with his aftershave, shirt, tie, waistcoat and pinstriped suit. They're all asleep, even though he has heard the children's alarm clocks go off. He bustles into the twins' room to tell them, with naval heartiness, to rise and shine and then knocks on Alex's door.

'Time for school!' He doesn't want to see him asleep, doesn't like being reminded of his own twelfth year. Colleen has left packets of cereal, a sliced loaf, jam, peanut butter and marmalade on the kitchen table. Maurice makes himself a bowl of Weetabix and milk. He isn't sure how you make coffee, but his secretary will make him some when he gets to the office. Then he raps sharply on the boys' doors again before he leaves. He looks into the drawing room where Viola is still asleep on the couch and decides she can miss another day of school. As he shuts the front door, he whistles 'Oh What a Beautiful Morning'. Well, it is. Spring has come to St John's Wood, the cherry blossom and daffodils coincide with a springtide in his own life. The corn is as high as an elephant's eye, well why not? Everyone's so damned cynical these days. Maurice defiantly enjoys his home comforts, the family life that's so much easier in the bigger flat.

Who is he defying? Well Boris, who also lives in St John's Wood, would certainly sneer at his present life. Maurice has been meaning to phone him but really there's no need because he can hear his voice, the upper-class drawl with exotic Russian vowels and rolled 'r's that made him such a success, once, in literary circles. *You see, Maurice, to be a writer you must rise above the little people, the Pooters. It is so easy for you, you have money and good looks, you don't have to do hack work to survive like me. Marry a woman who is rich and clever, if you must marry, and don't have children unless you have enough servants to take them off your hands. Perhaps, if you work very hard, you will produce a good novel one day.*

That was the most generous praise Boris ever offered, from his ascendancy of ten years and four novels the critics had drooled over. The unspoken assumption was that Boris was great whereas Maurice, with luck and slog, might be good. At the time, in the thirties, Maurice had smiled and stammered. The heir of Tolstoy had anointed him. Well, where is he now? Drinking himself to death in squalor, his magnum opus still unfinished after twenty years, no wife or children but a devoted secretary who, according to gossip, shares his bizarre tastes. Flogging each other to death.

The other voice that comments as he buys his ticket and descends the escalator to the crowded train is Gertrude's. Boris and Gertrude would probably be attracted to each other, he thinks with abstract jealousy as the train lurches towards Baker Street. Must be about the same age. *Maurice darling why do you stay with that boring woman? We could have such fun together. Children? Oh, the boys will be going off to school soon. I'll take care of the little girl and I'll take care of the solicitors, too. You should have seen the way I dealt with old Armie's solicitors, they didn't know what day it was. We'll soon get those trusts bust. All you need to do is write, darling, leave the practical stuff to me.*

How seductive that is, whispered in her husky voice as they lie between silk sheets in her enormous bed. She makes him feel masculine, potent, blissfully looked after. In her dimly lit rooms Gertrude is a goddess personifying a cult of sophistication, wealth and artifice Maurice has worshipped since birth. She only has to show him some of those photographs—the palatial roof garden of the Roxenbrist mansion in Geneva; the publicity shot of Gertrude in tights showing her fabulous legs and flirting with the camera— no wonder her memoirs are taking so long to write.

But I was about five when that photograph was taken. She keeps saying she was just a child then, but she looks at least eighteen. In a few years she'll be really old; it's like restoring an ancient building, you can prop it up but sooner or later it just crumbles. Living in the rubble or rather with the rubble. If only she was a bit younger, or Colleen had a bit more savoir faire or there weren't so many children or there was more money, or I didn't have to do this fucking boring job. As he rises from the underworld into the bright April morning of Charing Cross (Gertrude looks ghastly in daylight, like something out of a Hammer horror film) Maurice knows he loves Colleen. Really. Most of the time. It isn't his fault that Gertrude has thrown herself at him.

Twenty-Three

Viola takes a pencil from the red leather pencil case she got for her birthday and strains to copy between the lines in her exercise book. The letters wobble and fall over backwards.

'Use your right hand, Viola.' Miss Chamberlain advances to practise the theory she learned at Teacher Training College. Left-handedness is quite literally sinister but it's a misfortune that can be cured. She hasn't yet resorted to tying Viola's left hand to the chair while she writes although they've discussed this possibility in the staff room and agreed it would be good for her. Viola sneaks out her left hand again while Miss Chamberlain turns away and completes the 'y' and the 'g' easily before the teacher turns back to her, like Grandmother's Footsteps. What's a tyg anyway?

Know-it-all Jane, who has finished copying the whole calligraphy card in beautifully neat letters with no rubbing out, reads aloud: Tyger tyger burning bright in the forests of the night. Even through Jane's flat voice the eyes and fire and nightmare forest glow thrillingly. The letters that lie squirming and mutilated on Viola's page leap in the air, brilliant and mysterious flames. There is magic in the squiggles on the board, heart stopping excitement in the dirty smudges she has made in her exercise book.

In her room the books that her brothers have read and passed on stand in rows with their backs to her, keeping their secrets. She sits cross legged on the floor under the window and slides out a big red book with a picture of a crowned elephant. Viola knows it's Babar, Mummy and the boys read it to her dozens of times when she was younger, but when she opens it and holds it up to her eyes the words run away and hide. So she makes up her own story for the pictures, makes sense of the grey blur. She wants someone to come into the room and see that she's reading, more or less.

On Saturday morning she's allowed to get dressed in her parents' bedroom, in front of the gas fire that scorches your knees as it flickers orange and blue in its white waffle. She loves being in here and often pretends to be ill so that she can sneak into the safety of their bed in the morning. Mummy and Daddy bustle around her getting dressed, huge and comforting like Babar and his wife Celeste.

Lying on her tummy in front of the gas fire Viola struggles to read *The House of Arden*. She likes books like this that have lost their covers because the pictures on the covers tell you what to think. There's a little picture of four children on a flying carpet, dug into the hard blue cover. There are two girls and two boys, she wants to know where they got their magic carpet and whether they play together all the time or only when their Mummy tells them to. But inside she can't find the four children, only two, a girl called Elfrida and a boy called Edred. There's a picture of them in funny clothes, tights and baggy knickers, bowing to a beautiful lady in a wonderful dress like a tent with a triangle on top.

'Did people really look like that? In olden days?'

'Elizabethan. Time of Shakespeare. About four hundred years ago.' Daddy, who knows everything, tosses this over his shoulder as he ties his tie.

Viola needs to finish this book; she tries to burrow into the story like a maggot into a cheese. At moments she can do it, she enters the lives of the brother and sister who live with their aunt and ought to be rich but can't be until they find the treasure buried in the castle their family used to live in. A bit like me, she thinks, I just need to find a magical mouldiwarp to help me. When a word she doesn't know pushes her away, she tunnels around it, skipping a sentence or a paragraph before she can return to the warm embrace of the story. She stops needing reassurance that these things have really happened because they *are* happening to her, now, and she's happily swept away by them, away from the boring grown up voices droning on above her head.

'I don't see why you have to go there. Gertrude can come here, you could work in the dining room.'

'I can't possibly concentrate with all these children around. It's just a matter of concentration, darling. It's only at the weekend that I can really put my whole mind to it.'

'Can't see why you need to. All she did was lie on her back and open her legs.'

'Now, darling, don't be—'

'Don't be what? Possessive? Of course I am. I never see you anymore and I don't trust that woman.'

'We've been into all this before. It's purely a business arrangement, I need to finish the book this year so that we can sell it. I'm sure there'll be a lot of interest. Armand was one of the richest men in the world and Gertrude has had a very interesting life.'

'Beastly old tart.'

'How can I invite her here when you can't even be polite to her?'

'I warn you, Maurice, I won't put up with this.'

At lunchtime Daddy isn't there and the word has spread among the children: Mummy's on the warpath. She looks red and unhappy as she bangs down their plates of sweetcorn and bacon and fried bread. The children are subdued, even Alex, afraid of triggering an eruption. After lunch Alex and Will leave together to visit their friends Tom and Stevie. Will avoids Ben's reproachful gaze and submits to his mother's crimson kisses. As they gallop downstairs, they both wipe her lipstick off their faces, gasping for breath in the neutral air of the street. When they're alone together, as they hardly ever are, the ferocious competition between the two brothers fizzles out into an armed silence. Soon, when they get to Tom and Stevie's house, they will have to pick up their swords again. On the bus Will is happy because he's going to Stevie's and other people's families are always easier.

Ben hasn't eaten his lunch. He wanted to tie Will's shoelaces to the table so that he couldn't leave; run down the corridor and lock the front door; now he longs to fly ahead to Stevie's house and hang, draw and quarter him before Will arrives.

'What's the matter, Ben?' Colleen asks.

'Nothing.' He glares down at his plate. Crying in front of Mummy and Viola would be pathetic but he can feel the tears burning. He scowls and charges off to lock himself in his room, their room.

Three of them out of the way. Colleen dreads Viola's clinginess but to her mother's surprise she picks up her book and disappears into her room. Alone, Colleen stacks the dishwasher and mutters to herself.

'Bitch. Working my foot. He's such a fool, he'd believe anybody. Bastard. How dare he do this to me. Raddled old bag.' Colleen sees and hears the scene she longs to make: Maurice apologetic, Gertrude terrified as Colleen the avenging angel waves her flaming—no need to get religious about all this. 'It's just wrong, that's all. Stealing. He's mine. He adores me really and he'd never leave me. Well, I'll bloody well leave him, find someone else. Fat chance with four children.'

She strides down the corridor and Dandy, asleep outside her door, yelps with fear. He sees through her familiar, beloved pink floral dress to her fiery heart and crawls out of her way before she kicks him. Seeing their unmade double bed only makes Colleen feel worse. She takes off her shoes, throws them at Maurice's smiling photograph on her dressing table and lies down, exhausted. If only she could sleep. How long? He's been going there for years. Mrs Hunt's warning. She can smell his hair oil on the pillow beside her and the sex they had last night on the sheets. She gets up to lock the door before flinging herself down again to cry.

Children shouldn't see these things. A memory rolls towards her; another bed with another woman lying on it. Mummy and Daddy shout, Daddy goes out, Mummy goes to bed. For twenty years. I'm not going to be like her, I'm not going to take to my bed and say nothing. The third bed, in Gertrude's flat where Colleen has never been, tortures her all afternoon.

Alex and Will come bouncing back at six, ringing the bell exuberantly. Colleen opens the door in her cream coat and gloves, a shiny straw hat perched on her brown permed hair. She doesn't even ask if they've enjoyed themselves.

'Just popping out. Won't be long.'

Colleen walks to the end of the road, hails a taxi and gives the address that screams in her brain. When we lived in Quetta there was always a cosh under their bed and a loaded rifle beside it. You never know, Daddy used to say, when a band of dacoits might break into the bungalow. If there'd been a cosh or a loaded rifle she might have taken them with her. She counts out her fare and turns to the elegant Nash terrace.

The bell rings, a mad unbroken peal.

'Who the hell is that?' Gertude asks lazily.

Maurice knows. Through three walls he can see Colleen's thumb with its scarlet varnished nail pressing down relentlessly. It was her idea, nothing much happened, of course I didn't really, darling, she means nothing to me, he rehearses as he pulls his clothes on. Watching him dress for what she knows is the last time, Gertrude lights a cigarette and exhales the abject cowardice of husbands. All of them, everywhere. Sometimes you're married to them, sometimes you aren't. Once she thought she might like to be married to this one but now she can see what a pitiful creature he is. Not her creature.

The bell screams again. 'Your owner's come to fetch you.'

Maurice is quivering with terror that he will be caught, divorced, his guts will be garters. There isn't enough of them to make one decent sized ring, Gertrude thinks as he says, his voice as charming as ever: 'Must go, Gertrude dear. Thank you so much.'

He scurries out and the bell stops. Will his wife come marching through to confront her in bed? Gertude inhales and taps her ash on the onyx ashtray. She can handle wives. But nobody comes. Thank you so much for what? Two years of sex, talking, useful little cheques. She picks up the phone to have a good laugh with Rex, who knows the Samuells, who introduced her to them in fact.

For Colleen this is tragedy, not bedroom farce. She stands on the doorstep with tears streaming down her face. Maurice puts his arms around her, feeling her pain and love and passionate jealousy. 'She means nothing to me,' he whispers into Colleen's wet ear. Her tears are everywhere, a fountain, Niobe; passers-by are staring.

By the time the taxi delivers them Colleen is Mummy again. Refusing to look at Maurice, she prepares supper for them all. Her fingers wash the mushrooms and roll the veal escalopes in the slimy breadcrumbs.

'What's for supper?'

'I'm starving!'

'When are we going to eat, Mummy?'

Maurice comes down the corridor with a gin and tonic for her and offers to lay the table. She glares at him. At supper the children chatter and bicker, but an ominous silence hangs over the end of the long mahogany table. Then Maurice tries to snap out of it, to return to the normal tedium of domestic life he suddenly, desperately, needs. After the pudding of brick-like lurid pink strawberry mousse he announces he's going to sing. The children like his songs but this isn't for them. He stares straight at Colleen, stands up and sings, in a lovely baritone, 'If You Were the Only Girl in the World'. When he finishes the children clap and cheer, although they think it's a soppy song. But Colleen just looks down at her plate and Maurice has no idea what's inside her head.

Thinks he can smarm me now well he's got another think coming God knows how many other girls there have been—the children don't care just think of me as their cook and chief bottle washer unpaid bloody servant—well I won't put up with it—the only one who really loves me is Dandy.

When Colleen goes into the bedroom Maurice thinks she's having an early night and supervises a chaotic tidying of the dining room.

'Mummy's resting!' the children roar as they galumph down the corridor to the kitchen, dumping dirty plates and glasses in the sink on top of the heap of greasy pans. They're milling around when Colleen comes out of her bedroom, wearing her coat and carrying a small suitcase. She picks up Dandy and waves him like a shield at her astonished family who are, for once, lost for words.

'I'm leaving,' Colleen announces, pushing through them like a juggernaut.

Alex wonders if they're going to divorce, like Chris's parents; the twins look at each other, not sure whether to giggle or cry; Viola bursts into tears because Mummy's disappearing into the night forever and is taking Dandy instead of her.

'And where will you go, darling? Back home to your mother?' Maurice blocks her way as Dandy jumps out of her arms. Colleen, who had counted on at least getting to the front door, feels her terrible vulnerability. If I could drive if I had money if I had a lover too if I didn't love them… Maurice puts his arms around her and kisses her on the mouth, a reckless not-in-front-of-the-children kiss in front of the children who watch, fascinated and embarrassed, as their parents slink into their bedroom.

Twenty-Four

Maurice is typing at his desk behind the dining table, near the balcony that overlooks the leafy street. It's a pleasant view but he wishes he didn't look at it so often as he tries to make a coherent narrative out of Gertrude's lies, fantasies and self-justifications. He still doesn't know where or when she was really born. He has stopped adding to the list of questions he needs to ask her because he isn't allowed to visit her unless chaperoned by Colleen. She can come here, Colleen retorted when Maurice said that was unreasonable. Last month she did come to supper and Colleen refused to leave the room, answering Gertrude in monosyllables and abruptly pushing food at her. Did you have to be quite so rude? Maurice asked later. Just you wait, 'enry 'iggins, Colleen quoted ominously from her favourite song in *My Fair Lady*.

Alone at his desk in the dining room Maurice surveys the piles of box files and document folders that contain his life; old scripts, ideas for novels and TV series, threatening letters from banks and solicitors. He catches sight of a battered pink cardboard folder with "Colleen, Wartime" written on it, slides it out from the surrounding folders and reads her letters for the first time since they arrived in pale blue envelopes, to be torn open by Maurice's fingers, hot with desire and excitement. Her letters have been through the indignity of storage and have aged, like the hands that wrote them. The ink that was once as fresh as the geraniums blooming in the communal gardens outside the window looks faded now, the paper's brittle and the envelopes that once made his heart beat so ferociously have a dated look. Even the stamps and postmarks have slipped into history.

Maurice settles down to savour his past. More of her letters have survived than his; the story about their meeting and love affair that Maurice has been telling himself for twenty years isn't the same as the drama played out on this old paper stage; the voice that demands and manipulates out of the letters is not that of the shy ingénue he thought he'd married.

They met because they'd both volunteered for the ARP post at Grosvenor Square. In that first year of the war, working as an air raid warden was a bit of a lark, as much an opportunity for flirtation as heroics. Maurice can still see Colleen that first evening when she walked into the shabby office and smiled at him: a tall, skinny girl of twenty-five with huge, soft dark eyes and brown hair fashionably frizzed. What was she wearing? It's her face he remembers, and her long legs. He has always been a legs man. Actresses and rich young women crossed his eligible path all the time so there was no reason why he should have been smitten by one more pretty girl, yet he was. He remembers saying to his friend Joseph, 'That's the kind of girl I'd like to marry.' Did he really say that or just wanted to sleep with her and sanitised the anecdote for later consumption? Maurice isn't sure.

Anyway, penniless Miss Gypson of India and Epsom soon ousted her more sophisticated rivals. Maurice did go on seeing that actress, Rosemary, for a few months but then Colleen's histrionics and vicious references to her ("The Eyebrows") made him feel guilty.

Maurice joined the navy and was posted to Portsmouth, officially as an Ordinary Seaman although he also had a small unofficial role in Naval Intelligence. Later he joined the Film Unit as a "Leading Photographer". Not that Maurice has ever had a clue how cameras work, but he was supposed to use his media contacts to spread stories that might be of use to the navy. Handsome in his uniform, secure in his patriotic present and wealthy future, there was no reason why he should have missed Colleen. He smiles as he reads through the evidence that he did.

Finally, in July 1941, Maurice proposed by letter. Florence, who certainly would have liked her favourite son to marry into the aristocracy to consolidate their very new family fortune, was generous to Colleen. She undertook to improve her taste in clothes and furniture and "rub the typist off her". Aubrey had been born Abraham Samuell in Whitechapel. He'd refused a knighthood Lloyd George offered to sell him for ten thousand pounds, was genuinely not a snob and was delighted that Maurice had chosen a pretty, affectionate girl. But Edie, recently widowed, clung hysterically to her only child. She objected to Maurice's Jewishness and talked darkly about Hitler's coming invasion, the dangers of tainted blood and mixing the races.

Edie did, in the end, come to their wedding. Maurice stares into their wedding photographs which have already yellowed, dated, sidled into the absurdity of the past. He looks young and tall and shy in his Naval uniform, Colleen is tall and slender in a pill box hat, fitted jacket, pleated skirt, long legs, and a radiant smile. The two mothers wear fur coats, two sixtyish women.

Edie stands with grim, pinched smile, clutching her handbag defensively, like a moth-eaten ferret. Whereas Florence— Maurice's mouth falls open in admiration as he gazes back into his mother's elegance and joie de vivre.

They didn't see Edie at all during those early years of their marriage and enjoyed the sensation that they were still young lovers defying the world. He remembers Colleen's touching faith in fortune tellers, she was always consulting them and still gets a monthly magazine called Prediction. This reminds him of his encounter with the famous medium Helen Duncan.

In the early thirties Maurice used to hear of Helen and her nemesis, Harry Price, the founder of the National Laboratory of Psychical Research. Stories about these two were always good copy for the *Daily Sketch* when he was a journalist. Maurice recalls with a smile a story he wrote about Harry Price's investigation of the case of a talking mongoose on the Isle of Man who sang hymns in six languages and called Harry 'the man who put the kybosh on the spirits.' Harry insisted that Helen's ectoplasm was regurgitated muslin and referred to her clients as 'cheesecloth worshippers'. The battle between these two accomplished self-publicists was pure entertainment until the war turned it into something more dangerous.

Maurice has never told Colleen about all that because his Intelligence work was of course supposed to be secret and anyway he suspected Colleen would sympathise entirely with Helen and insist on meeting her. Even during the war, Colleen was far more interested in psychic matters than in national security. Maurice, who was chivalrous about women, wished he'd been asked to persecute a man instead of an overweight middle-aged woman with diabetes and angina. At one of her séances she materialised a sailor who had gone down with HMS Barham. That was six months before the sinking of the ship was officially reported and the Admiralty decided that Helen was a security risk.

Maurice remembers his visit to the Master Temple Psychic Centre, above a chemist's shop in the back streets of Portsmouth. Tickets cost 12s 6d, the temple was a seedy room given an ersatz religious aura by a cheap print of Leonardo's Last Supper and an altar with a wooden crucifix. A middle-aged woman led a prayer, then the audience of twenty, mainly women, sang 'South of the Border'. Chocolate brown curtains parted to reveal Helen, a hugely fat woman of about fifty. Snoring, her head on one side, she fell into a trance, out of which she made gnomic utterances in her own Glaswegian accent and various other voices.

Maurice felt the séance was more like an Ealing comedy than a national emergency, but the Admiralty was out to get Helen. In January 1941 Maurice, together with a group of journalists he'd invited, was at the Portsmouth séance at which Helen Duncan was arrested. *The Portsmouth Evening News* relished this: CONSTABLE GRABS 'SPIRIT' AT CITY SÉANCE: SHOCKING THINGS DIVULGED; Helen's arrest was announced on the BBC. She was accused of being an 'unmitigated humbug and pest', prosecuted under the 1735 Witchcraft Act and imprisoned in Holloway for nine months. At the time there were dark rumours that she'd put a curse on all her enemies, Maurice had to resist a shiver of fear when he realised his son was born on her birthday.

When Alex was born, they were living in a tiny bungalow in Ovingdean, near Brighton. Maurice was stationed at Roedean, where the Navy replaced adolescent girls, sleeping in dormitories.

'There's a sign above my bed saying, please ring for a mistress,' he told Colleen when he came home one weekend. He smiled at her as they stood with their arms around each other above the cot of their infant genius and she smiled back, sure of him at last.

Aubrey died, still hoping for a deathbed reconciliation with Benjamin who had quarrelled bitterly with his father just before he left to join the army. Aubrey was desperately hurt by his son's contempt for his father's lack of education and his cockney accent, also shocked by rumours that Benjamin was homosexual. I'm good enough to pay his bills, Aubrey used to complain. Florence and Benjamin both had uncontrollable tempers; they detested each other so much they couldn't bear to be in the same room whereas easy-going Maurice was always on affectionate terms with both his parents.

When Benjamin was lost at Dunkirk and Aubrey's will was read, Maurice realised he was going to be rich. Meanwhile, he and Colleen were still living very simply on his Navy salary. Colleen became pregnant again with the twins and Maurice's war ended in a blaze of optimism, fertility and domestic happiness.

A few months later Florence died of cancer, leaving Maurice a fortune tied up in trusts. He was such a devoted father that he slipped his disc giving rides to his three little sons. As he convalesced on his back, he considered his post-war career. He didn't want to rush into the wrong job and Colleen liked to have him at home. She couldn't of course look after three small children on her own, so they hired a succession of Dutch girls for thirty shillings a week. There were fewer separations, and so fewer letters.

Now the exclamation marks that littered Colleen's letters seem to have gone out of life, but not the bills that were so often enclosed. Yet Maurice feels a stir of contentment and desire at the thought of Colleen, warm and succulent. If only they could go to bed together right now.

In the corridor outside the children rampage, screaming and yelling. They must be standing right outside his door just to annoy him. Hard to believe there are only four of them, sounds like a cast of thousands. Maurice wishes he'd never invented the talking prize, wishes he he'd trained them all to be Trappist monks. Somewhere over the rooftops Boris, who he still hasn't phoned, is working away in his childless, wifeless eyrie. All right for some. But Rex, who has known Boris since the thirties, says it isn't all right; Boris drinks like a fish and the great novel is still in note form in dozens of box files.

Maurice struggles to return to Gertrude's autobiography. The most colourful of her three possible childhoods was the one in Smyrna so Maurice opts for that, elaborating on the belly dancing and the lecherous old goldsmith who seduced her and the mother who had to take in washing. As he types, he misses Gertrude. An impossible woman—but entertaining. Misses those cheques too, the bank manager is getting nasty again and the list of uniform and equipment Alex has to take to his new boarding school in the autumn is absurd. You'd think he was setting off in search of the Nile instead of going to Surrey. This book must be published, must do well. Maurice imagines a queue of old ladies with risqué pasts waiting to be ghosted. Dancing with skeletons in closets. Next time he'll find one so old that even Colleen won't be suspicious.

For God's sake what's going on out there? The door bursts open and Maurice turns blindly on the child.

'How dare you disturb me when I'm working? Get out of my study, you bloody little idiot!'

It's only when the words have boiled out of his mouth that Maurice looks at the child and sees it isn't one of his. Small, red hair, shocked expression. You're not supposed to lose your temper with other people's brats.

Before Maurice can apologise the door closes again and Stevie turns to Will. 'Does your father drink?'

'Oh no, it's my mother who's the alcoholic.' Will has already explained to Stevie that his entire family are mad; Daddy's outburst is a new humiliation.

'They're after us!' As Tom and Alex come thundering down the corridor Will and Stevie dart screaming into the twins' bedroom where Ben is sulking because he doesn't like Stevie. But when it comes to the crunch, the Alamo, the siege of Mafeking, he's always on Will's side against Alex.

Colleen, who overheard Will's remark, is indignant. Just because she likes a drink now and then—and she doesn't like the way the boys are always fighting, if she'd been lucky enough to have brothers and sisters, she's sure she never would have quarrelled with them. Will and Alex are like a pair of tomcats, forever spitting and scratching.

Twenty-Five

Now that they have a drawing room again, Maurice and Colleen decide to have a cocktail party. Nervously, Maurice invites Boris. Over the years they've occasionally written or phoned but vague protestations of wanting to see each other have replaced real feelings. They became old friends, then ex-friends.

Maurice remembers the power Boris once had over him, when he was a nineteen-year-old journalist and Boris, ten years older, was a lionised novelist of whom great things were expected. As he tries to explain this to his sons in anticipation of their meeting, he sees them snigger at each other. No, it wasn't homosexual, their friendship. Boris was the keeper at the gates of world culture when Maurice stood timidly shivering on the doorstep. He'd failed the entrance exam to Cambridge because his maths wasn't good enough and his parents had fixed him up with a job on a popular newspaper, *The Daily Sketch*. He interviewed film stars, authors and directors and his charming, slightly ingratiating manner and good looks made him successful at this job. He was immensely flattered when Boris, whose reviews compared him to Tolstoy, liked him enough to invite him to a party. Florence adored Boris (Maurice has never been sure exactly how far this adoration went) and he was often invited to her glamorous parties. Boris became a family friend, the clever older brother Maurice would have preferred to bad tempered, competitive young Benjamin. Maurice was flattered when Boris admitted he'd based a minor character in one of his novels, a good looking, ineffectual young journalist, on him.

Gradually the hero shrank while the worshipper expanded. In Boris's life there was more talking and drinking and complicated sex than writing; his tongue became sharper, his mind blunter, his cynicism about international affairs was not fashionable during the war. When Maurice introduced him to Colleen, Boris was most unpleasant and overplayed his hand as fraternal adviser: *If you marry that girl, you'll never write anything worthwhile. Such women eat one alive.*

Although Colleen didn't overhear this remark, she picked up his air of superiority and Boris was never invited again.

But now they're solidly married, ensconced in a comfortable flat, surrounded by bright children. At last, it's time to show Boris what he has missed and what Maurice has achieved over the last twenty years. Maurice's stage fright is visible to his children, they're all intrigued. The other guests, the boys observe, are the usual boring old farts. Fictive aunties and uncles have been dropped now the children are older; only Viola is still young enough to want to be liked and approved of by grown-ups.

As there are too many people to fit around the dining table Colleen and Gabriele, the current au pair (they never last long) have prepared vol-au-vents and canapés to pass around. Colleen greets them all warmly: Sally, Billy, Rex and his latest girlfriend, Eddie and Trish, Jim and Yvonne; these are her dearest, oldest friends, they all know each other and can be trusted to go through their party paces. She didn't want to invite Boris unpronounceable, Boris who-do-you-think-you-areski, but

Maurice insisted. Colleen smiles frostily at him and his girlfriend, Melanie (*quite young and attractive, can't think what she sees in the old soak*) and then avoids him for the rest of the evening.

Maurice is deeply moved to see Boris here, in his drawing room, in his life. He introduces his children as if he were presenting them to royalty. His affability is almost ecstatic as he says, 'And this is Alex, my eldest, who will be going off to school soon.'

Alex has prepared for this meeting by reading Boris's novels and tells Boris what they are about. Maurice steps back—and it's only then that he really sees his old hero.

Old is the word. Boris is in his sixties now, bald, with the broken veins and bloodshot eyes of an alcoholic. He wears a surgical collar and beneath his dinner jacket the stripes of his pyjama jacket can be seen. This fascinates Viola, who notes that he's the shabbiest person in the room, this living anecdote who is or was (Viola isn't sure of the distinction) a famous writer. Maurice is horrified by Boris's decay. Melanie has more the air of a nurse than a houri, her eyes are on Boris's glass of whisky, and she prevents Maurice from filling it up. Boris is still witty and articulate, but his voice is slow and constricted, as if squeezed by the surgical collar; for a second Maurice glimpses the brilliant young man who used to dominate any table he sat at, cracking jokes in English, Russian and French, absolutely sure of his own talent. That Boris has reigned in Maurice's memory for twenty years, judging him ruthlessly; this shambolic imposter is a shock.

Will has moved in, annoyed by the way Alex is monopolising Boris.

'My son the artist, very promising.' The two boys tower above Boris and compete to impress him although he doesn't seem to be listening. Maurice leaves them to take on Boris while he circulates among his other guests, filling glasses and emanating bonhomie.

He jokes with Rex about the clinches he's still illustrating for women's magazines which Ingrid, his latest girlfriend, models for. Rex is a landlord now, he owns a small block of flats in West Kensington. Maurice turns to Jacob and Trish, whose theatrical agency now finds actors for TV commercials. Billy and Sally are still together, her dress shop is flourishing and she has just opened a branch in Richmond, where they live. Billy is trying to get voiceover work from Jacob while Sally watches her husband's glass with exactly the same expression as Melanie watches Boris's. They all look so old—Maurice looks fondly across the room at Colleen, who is drinking less than she used to. Colleen and I don't look a day over forty, he thinks, and waits for one of his friends to notice. The richest people in the room are Jim and Yvonne, whose photographic business has expanded. When Jim mentions the hours he works Maurice looks queasy and changes the subject back to his children's achievements. Jim and Yvonne don't have any children.

'Great party, Maurice,' Jim says. 'Jacob and I were just saying, it doesn't seem like eight years since we all watched the coronation together.' He's careful not to mention Gertrude.

'Eight years! My God! And *The Mousetrap's* still running!'

'If only you'd backed that instead of *Murder at the Vicarage*.' Colleen never misses the chance of lamenting the money that ought to have come her way.

Boris is looking at his watch. Maurice rushes over and

throws in Ben. 'Will's twin, our late developer.'

Ben glowers at his father and glares at Boris. Maurice, remembering Boris was always more interested in women than men, turns to Viola, who has been staring at Boris, tongue-tied. She wants to ask if you have to stay in your pyjamas all day to be a famous writer but before she can form the question Boris shakes her hand politely, looks bored and announces he must go.

Maurice feels like a schoolboy who has been dreading an exam that has been cancelled. Forever. Boris the Magnificent has abdicated from his head. Benignly, he watches his family and friends. *Thank God I stayed with Colleen who's a good cook and loves me and the children who are amusing now that they're older.* Already his affair with Gertrude is fading, *just one of those things, she led me on.* The Roxenbrist lawyers have pounced on the libellous content of the ghosted autobiography; Gertrude claimed that the famous billionaire was a swindler who had repulsive sexual tastes involving small boys and goats—and now it seems the book will only appear in serial form in a Sunday newspaper. He still isn't rich but, as Colleen comes back into the room after putting Viola to bed, Maurice is satisfied with life as it is. She sees his happiness, feels it as a personal achievement, they stand with their arms around each other as their guests leave.

Twenty-Six

Viola sits in her favourite place, the top shelf of the airing cupboard, reading *The Magician's Nephew* and eating an apple. It's beautifully warm in here, she isn't disturbed by noisy smelly boys chasing each other and trying to hide in her room, there's a satisfying smell of clean sheets, towels, wooden shelves, and the dusty bulb that sheds just enough light to read by. It's secret, but someone will knock on the door to tell her when supper's ready. Her cupboard's a bit like the attic place where Polly finds Digby and Viola would like to find someone like him, shy and imaginative and friendly. Unfortunately, boys like that only seem to live in books.

In the kitchen the Spanish au pair, Juanita, helps Colleen prepare supper. She has only just arrived, Colleen chose her for her plainness after sacking a very attractive young girl from Brittany, Juliette. Alex and Viola spent far too much time in her room. Colleen didn't mind about Viola having a crush on her, but Alex's interest was suspect, particularly since his room was opposite Juliette's. Alex has always been precocious, Colleen is sure he and Tom exchange all kinds of smut. Just as well Alex is going off to public school soon, where nothing like that, Collen is quite sure, will be going on. Porky, as Colleen pronounces Juanita, is pleasingly fat and plain and only costs two guineas a week although she's inclined to be lazy and pretend to be ill.

But thanks to Porky and Mrs Jenks, who comes every weekday to clean, and Mr Hale, Colleen's little man, who is happy to come over to clean the windows or change light bulbs or do carpentry, this flat is now manageable. Maurice, her big man, is under control as well. He comes straight home after work and often brings her flowers. In fact, Maurice now treats Colleen with an apologetic devotion that makes her want to melt although she doesn't, of course, but instead reminds him about once a week that what he did was unforgivable and he's very lucky she didn't leave him.

The phone rings. Colleen leaves Porky to stuff the chicken and goes into the bedroom to answer it, hoping it won't be her mother, who is allowed to visit them again and has got into the habit of phoning every day.

'Sally! My dear, how are you?'

'Exhausted. I've been at the shop all day and just come home and Billy's gone off and left the house like a pigsty and Martin's coming home from school on Wednesday.'

'Gone off where?'

'Billy? God knows. The pub, London, Timbuktu for all I know.'

'But doesn't he tell you where he's going?'

'Billy's not Maurice, you know.' Amongst all their friends Maurice's husbandly virtues are still legendary, and Colleen isn't going to rock the boat. 'How is he?'

'Exhausted. He had to work so hard ghosting Gertrude's memoirs. They'll be serialised in the News of the World soon.'

'She must have had a fascinating life.'

'A different life every time she told it, apparently. Maurice says he still isn't sure if there were three husbands or four.'

'God! One's enough for me.'

'But you're not—'

'Divorcing him? My mother would turn in her grave. Probably come back and haunt me. I miss her so much.'

'She was a marvellous woman.'

'And how's your mother?'

'Oh fine, unfortunately. Seems to go on forever.'

'Colleen! You're so lucky to have her.'

'Why? She's an old misery. All she does is worry and nag.' She hears Sally gasp with shock and thinks defensively, well Mrs Taylor *was* marvellous; elegant and stylish and helpful and a good cook. If I'd had a mother like that, I could have loved her.

'We all have our crosses we must bear.'

Colleen feels nauseous, as she always does when Sally starts sounding Catholic. She wishes people would keep their religion to themselves, like picking their noses. 'Talking of crosses, I nearly won the football pools last week.'

'How exciting!' Sally is bewildered by the Samuells' approach to finances. They always seem to be spending money that isn't there and expecting vast sums to materialise. Billy calls them the Micawbers.

'If I'd had one more draw, I would have won a hundred thousand.'

Sally doesn't know whether to congratulate her or commiserate. 'How are the children?'

'Alex is going off to school in September. I think he's a bit nervous.'

'So good for them to get away from home and stand on their own two feet. Martin adores school, he's bored out of his mind in the holidays. I only wish the terms were longer.'

'So, he's stopped running away, then?'

'Oh of course, that was just a silly phase.'

'I don't know how you could bear to send him back.'

'As Billy said, children must get used to things they don't like. Martin got a jolly good beating.'

'But then he ran away again?'

'And we sent him straight back again! Twice!'

This is the closest the two women ever come to quarrelling. Spoilt brats, Sally thinks as she asks tenderly after Colleen's other children.

'Ben's fine, Will's getting a bit cheeky.' I'd rather he was cheeky than crushed and beaten. Colleen's heart stirs as she imagines the scene: the boy at the door, the police cars in pursuit, the heroic mother hiding him under the bed and barring the door to his persecutors.

'And Viola? Remember how nervous you were about having a little girl? The afterthought.'

'The afterthought's fine. She's going to stay with my mother next week. Rather her than me. The flat gets so impossibly crowded when they're all here during the holidays.'

'Whoever invented school holidays should be shot. They made the summer ones so long so that children could help with the harvest, apparently.'

'My children don't even help with the washing up.'

After she puts the phone down Colleen feels consolidated. She is, once again, that woman she wants to be: beloved wife, loving mother, good marriage, happy family, nice flat. This is the kind of thing she'd like on her tombstone, which she won't be requiring just yet, thank you very much.

As she sets off from Victoria in the Ladies Only compartment with her grandmother on Monday morning, Viola's happy. Ever since her friendship with Charlotte she has been disposed to like old ladies. Grandma isn't as interesting as Charlotte because she's always anxious, but she has plenty of time to talk to Viola, who basks in her undivided attention. Edie's worried there won't be enough food in her pantry to feed her Gargantuan granddaughter, so they stop at a shop near the station to stock up on sausages and baked beans and semolina, Viola's favourite foods, which she gets to eat at school but never at home. Then they get a taxi to the silent avenue where there's no traffic and nobody walks. Grandma talks about neighbours, so people do live here; Viola imagines them tiptoeing around their houses. To a London child these tranquil streets are ominous. Quetta sits like a dolls house, a green felt garden rolled out at the front and the back. After the noise and chaos of the Samuells' flat the silent, tidy rooms are puzzling, like a toy that's just been unwrapped and is still protected by cellophane. Viola has never been here without her family before. Usually, her father snoozes in the turquoise armchair while her mother glares out of the window as if the pear tree is about to attack.

Edie unlocks the rusty bolt in the scullery and Viola is sent into the garden while lunch is being cooked. She would prefer to read but she knows children are expected to play so she takes the quoit Grandma hands her. This is a kind of rubber doughnut left over from a pre-war P&O voyage, once dark blue but faded and time bitten. Clumsy Viola tries to throw it in the air and catch it, but she keeps missing it and chases it all over the lawn. Whenever she looks back at the house, she sees her grandmother watching her, a blur at the window.

'Don't run around in the sun like that, or you'll look like a native.'

'What's a native?'

'You should wear a hat. Lunch is nearly ready, darling.'

Viola doesn't look like Colleen, who was a skinny child. She's nearly as tall as Edie and considerably heavier but Edie still thinks of her as her dear little girlie and feels she's recovering some of that other distant childhood she missed, because she always seemed to be too busy or ill or unhappy to spend time with her daughter. That week Viola and Edie play out a little family idyll: the only child with her doting mother. They do nothing, companionably.

A trip to a department store in Kingston is the high point. They try on hats together. 'Does it suit me?' Edie asks coyly from under a shiny navy-blue straw pillbox decorated with cherries.

'You look—nice,' Viola says doubtfully. Grandma can't really look pretty because she's too old, but she *does* look nice as her brown eyes peer at her reflection. Like a turtle under a blue Brillo pad trying on a hat. After Edie buys the hat they walk arm in arm to the toy department, where Viola chooses a black toy poodle. Dandy won't play with her, but this dog will be more obliging.

As she climbs stiffly into the bed Carr died in, Edie feels how the terror has been extracted from the darkness. She won't need the cosh under her bed because no dacoits are going to break in tonight, she won't lose Colleen now because she has made friends with Colleen's daughter. Invisible wounds have started to heal.

Twenty-Seven

When Alex comes home from school at Christmas, he's as tall as Maurice and talks even more than he did before, using slang they don't understand: half and beak and fag. He rushes off to meet new friends.

The twins know they will soon have to disappear into the world Alex now inhabits. They've taken their Common Entrance exam: the exit from their common childhood, their entrance into alien sophistication. Ben is terrified of failing the exam, of being separated from Will, a terror so deep he has never admitted it to anyone. Will knows he will pass the exam, he longs to be part of that gothic monument in Surrey Alex has defected to; longs to shed this room he and Ben share, with its clutter of books and drawings and paintings and medals and clothes.

For Colleen the most alarming change in Alex is his religious fervour. Her father was an atheist who ran away from home to escape from his father, a strict Methodist and lay preacher. All Colleen's associations with religion are negative: cold churches her mother dragged her to on Sundays; depressing services at missionary schools; Edie's hysterical antisemitism when she and Maurice married—God causes nothing but trouble. She has never wanted her children baptised or christened or bar-mitzvahed or, as she says, any of that rubbish. But now Alex has come home determined to be both christened and confirmed; he has spoken to the local vicar who has suggested he paints the vestry as part of his religious education. Child labour, Colleen says indignantly, furious that Alex, who has never washed a plate at home, should be so ready to oblige a parson. Just before Christmas the vicar, who has few converts in this very Jewish area, rings their bell and asks for money. Colleen slams the door in his face and is equally rude to the local rabbi who calls a few days later. She imagines them plotting together, these sinister men in dark clothes, colluding over nasty rituals, passing on addresses and corrupting innocent heathens.

Viola has always thought Jesus is like Father Christmas and the Easter Bunny and the Tooth Fairy and conjurors at children's parties. You know they aren't real but humour grown-ups by pretending to be excited by their corny stories. She opens the book because it's the only one in the bookcase in her bedroom she hasn't read. The sugary pink and gold people in long dresses on the cover, rolling their eyes and hamming it up, have put her off.

Then she cuts out the room around her and lets the story carry her on its shoulders. He really happened, this man. He was born in a stable because they didn't have hospitals in those days and He wasn't just an ordinary baby, He was so important that He was born with a capital letter like a country or a city. All the animals and shepherds and even the stars knew He was special. His father was God, but he had another father too, a carpenter like Mr Hale, and His mother was a virgin. Viola doesn't know what a virgin is or whether her mother is one or not. He started to boss grown-ups around when he was twelve and when He grew up He told stories, wandering around in His long dress with a gold dinner plate stuck to his head. She reads and reads in the cold bedroom until her legs are covered with gooseflesh, but she can't stop, she knows something horrible is going to happen to Him. People loved His stories and the Romans, who had something to do with Julius Caesar, were jealous because they didn't know any good stories, so they put Him in prison and everyone was mean to Him and then they nailed Him to a wooden cross and killed Him.

She's sobbing over this picture of the crucifixion when Alex opens the door. He looks so old in his tweed jacket, with hair sprouting on his face and a tennis ball bulging in his throat, that she's sure he knows all about it.

'He isn't really dead, is He?'

'A lot of people would like to know the answer to that question.'

'But it's so sad!' she wails.

'No, not at all, you see Christians believe that he was resurrected and came back to us, that's why we celebrate Easter,' he says piously.

Alex tells Colleen that Viola has a religious nature and should come to midnight mass with him on Christmas Eve.

'Nonsense, she's far too young. I won't have you influencing her.'

'She can hardly be too young to be baptised.'

'Alex! I'm warning you. I don't like all this mumbo jumbo.'

Colleen begins to think there's an epidemic when Viola asks her to hear her prayers at bedtime. 'Not tonight. I'm busy.' She hugs her daughter brusquely and leaves the room.

Alone in the dark Viola mutters a bread-and-butter letter to God like the ones she's made to write to Grandma and Charlotte after Christmas: Dear Lord God and Dear Lord Jesus, thank you very much for the lovely day. She wants to ask Colleen if this is the sort of thing you're supposed to say to Jesus. She knows He's quite famous. That poem they all chant at school every morning, about art in heaven, is addressed to Him and so are all those songs. Hims. Before they broke up for the Christmas holidays a gramophone appeared at assembly and the children had to listen to thousands of people roaring Hallelujah. *Perhaps I should put a few hallelujahs into my prayers to make them more interesting as He must be awfully busy and can't possibly listen to everyone who prays.* Every night at bedtime she drags her mother into her bedroom. Colleen listens to her daughter's embarrassing prayers with a long-suffering expression.

This Christmas the Samuells enjoy each other's company. There aren't many relations, as Colleen was an only child and most of Maurice's relations are dead or in South Africa or alienated by Florence's will in his favour. Grandma comes to stay. Her presence is always good for them; she makes them feel clever and sophisticated and daring. In the afternoons the children play Monopoly with wild cheating and squabbles as they buy and sell London, galloping in and out of jail and past Go on a top hat or an iron. These games always end with paper money (opulent pink five-hundred-pound notes, orange one-hundreds, despicable blue fivers) being flung around the room as they squabble, and the board is overturned. The children are given the pillowcases full of presents that are, they all know, the real meaning of Christmas.

After dinner on Christmas night Colleen and Maurice get out Florence's old roulette wheel, cover the drawing room table with a green baize cloth and set up an impromptu casino in the firelit room. The children gamble their pocket money on Vingt-et-un and Hearts. Maurice appoints himself bank, enjoying his power as he claws in the heaps of round plastic chips, decides who goes bust and who's allowed to stay in the game. Tonight, at least, he understands money, controls it, wallows in it.

Grandma pretends to be shocked but joins in. At dinner on Boxing night, she washes down Colleen's rich food with several glasses of wine and between courses she demonstrates the lotus position. Long ago in India she studied yoga. Her brown silk skirt rises above the tops of her stockings and suspenders as she sits cross legged on the dining room floor. Her grandchildren roar with delight as Colleen watches in horror.

The evening's punctuated by Maurice's songs and the children's poems. They have a repertoire of nonsense poems by Edward Lear and Lewis Carroll, and Will and Viola have been pointedly encouraged by Maurice to learn Hilaire Belloc's Lord Lundy, who 'from his earliest years Was far too freely moved to Tears.'

One dark afternoon in February Will and Ben come home from school in their pink uniforms with their leather satchels full of homework. The cold has made them ravenously hungry; they run upstairs and ring the bell peremptorily. Colleen answers it—later Ben relives this moment again and again, unable to forgive that afternoon for pretending to be so normal. Colleen hands them two small buff envelopes addressed to Master William Samuell and Master Benjamin Samuell.

The twins stare at each other in the octagonal hall. Then they tear the envelopes open so that the printed results are jaggedly ripped but can still be read. Will doesn't need to see his brother's letter; he reads Ben's failure in the howl of pain as the stoical boy falls to his knees and buries his head in his arms on the leather armchair. Will cries in sympathy. Colleen goes to hug Ben, who pushes her away furiously. He doesn't want to be hugged or felt sorry for, he only wants the months to roll back so that he can go into the examination torture chamber again to write the lucid thoughts and accurate calculations that are buried in his mind. He only wants to go where Will goes.

The twins retreat into their room where Colleen brings them tea on a tray as if they're ill. Will feels treacherous currents of pride: *I really am clever, as clever as Alex perhaps, not just the Minister of Misinformation as Daddy calls me. I'll shine and make new friends…* yet he knows his twin's rejection is a terrible injustice. Late developer, a bit backward, not academic; he knows better than anybody that Ben isn't stupid, but he doesn't know how to defend his twin against this ruthless adult judgement. Will doesn't really want to go away to school without Ben. Who is going to laugh at his jokes and admire his drawings? Who is going to love him?

Twenty-Eight

Now that she has glasses, Viola finds the world manageable. The squiggles on the blackboard are words and numbers, the confusion on cinema screens is a story, the television in the hall becomes a rich source of entertainment. Playground games are no longer menacing, and she can see the ball at netball. Best of all, she can remember faces and names. She suddenly makes a lot of friends at school; at home she still lurks in the airing cupboard reading but also goes out on her bike or scooter to join a gang of children who live in the same block of flats and run screaming through the coal cellars trying to evade the uniformed porter, who hates them. At school Viola starts to enjoy lessons and at the end of term her report is enthusiastic. Schoolteachers are one of the groups of people Colleen dislikes, particularly women, who are only teaching because they can't get a husband. However, she's always pleased by her darlings' success although it is a pity Viola needs to wear those unfeminine glasses. Their blue plastic frames, usually patched together by Elastoplast or Sellotape, bounce up and down on her nose and stick out at the sides like an American car.

The first time Viola sees herself in the mirror she's devastated. Until now she has had only the vaguest idea of how she looks; she knows she's tall and fat and dark but because people have remarked on her eyes, she's always assumed they must be blue. Dolls, princesses, film stars and girls in books always have blue eyes, it seems to be impossible to get on without them. Dolefully, she stares at herself in Colleen's triple dressing table mirror. It throws back three reflections: sallow skin, greasy dark brown hair, bulging dark eyes that look even more froggy behind the heavy glasses. Her tears redden her eyes and nose, ravage her muddy features like hot wax dripping down a candle.

Colleen tries to comfort her. 'You'll be very attractive when you grow up,'

'How do you know?' Viola wails. 'I might just get fatter and fatter until I burst or get so yellow I'll turn into a banana or grow so fast I'll go through the ceiling. I'm never going to look at myself in the mirror again.'

Colleen knows about feeling ugly; she hugs her daughter tenderly and promises herself she will never destroy Viola's confidence by telling her, as her parents constantly told her while she was growing up, that she's too tall and gawky and looks like an old dishrag.

In bed, when she has taken off her glasses and returned to her dreamy inner life, Viola sees herself as she really is: fair and slender, the smallest girl in the class, she darts around the playground winning races and is so popular that the entire school has a tug of war over her. Whenever she draws, it is this elfin figure who appears on the paper, doing ballet and gymnastics and leaping on and off horses. At school she stares lugubriously at the girls who have stolen her true face and body, hardly able to speak to them for fear of the envy that will come boiling out.

Most of the conversations at school are about television programmes and although they only have BBC on their set—Maurice despises commercial television and somebody called

Low Grade—Viola is now able to boast about programmes she has watched. Her ambition is to watch a programme which is called, she thinks, Quake a Mask. It's so terrifying it makes you quake. Once a week, after supper, her parents and brothers gather in the hall to watch it and she is sent to bed. It will give her nightmares, Colleen says, she's too young. Every week Viola creeps out of bed to the corner of the corridor, outside her parents' room, and clings to the radiator, shivering with delighted terror as she tries to attach images to the horrible sound effects and the gasps of her assembled family. Every week Colleen shoos her back to bed. Viola hates being the youngest. Even when she's ninety-nine Alex will be a hundred and five and the twins will be a hundred and four; she can never catch up.

She falls asleep without prayers now; her religious fervour was short-lived. Jesus has joined the Little Match Girl, Beth in *Little Women* and Aslan in *The Lion, the Witch and the Wardrobe* on Viola's menu of delicious sadness. She can open the book at their deaths at any time, savour them and weep over them before returning to her own life, very relieved that she's not likely to be crucified or hacked to death by warlocks and werewolves or die of cold or scarlet fever.

Colleen's instinct to protect her children is so powerful that they dread it. In any quarrel she takes her own child's side. Colleen needs heroes and villains and it's quite obvious that she has produced three heroes and a heroine. Anyone who can't see this is malicious, and if her children's behaviour is less than perfect it must be because they're being led astray. She's convinced that Stevie, whose friendship with Will has intensified, is a bad influence.

One afternoon as Ben waits awkwardly to accompany them to the cinema Colleen overhears Stevie sneering, 'Mary had a little lamb and so did Will. And everywhere that Willie went his Ben was sure to go.' Colleen sees the pain in Ben's eyes; she explodes, screaming hysterically at Will and Stevie: 'How dare you leave Ben out?'

Colleen is fond of saying that she has rumbled people, as if she was an emotional detective and other people were criminals on her list of suspects. She has rumbled Stevie; she frowns and glares at him and is visibly displeased whenever Will sees him.

Will is furious that she has tried to interfere in his passionate friendship with Stevie. Ben is humiliated; he would rather be teased by his brother than fussed over by his mother. The twins start to mutter resentfully about her.

One Saturday morning Viola and Will are having breakfast in the kitchen, overlooking the fire escape down which Viola will soon gallop to play with her friends. Ben has just been sent to his room because he has been cheeky and Viola and Will sit opposite each other, buttering their toast and spreading it thickly with peanut butter.

'Why are you so cross?'

'Because she's a bloody beastly stupid fat old cow.'

'Do you mean Mummy?' Viola is shocked.

'You're too young to understand.'

'No, I'm not. Tell me.'

'She's always screaming and barging in and sticking her nose into other people's business. Well, me and Ben are fed up with her.'

'Are you going to run away?'

Will looks around the kitchen darkly, trying to think of a sufficiently impressive threat. 'If she doesn't stop going on and on at me, I'm going to—to—to do something.'

'But if you're mean to Mummy, she might run away.'

'I wish she would. I hate her. Bad tempered old bitch.'

Viola is shaken, as if these insults have been thrown at her. Colleen, listening outside the kitchen door, hears her son's words and rushes down the corridor to her bedroom, clutching her pink floral dressing gown tightly to her as if to stanch bleeding. She locks the bedroom door and falls onto the bed where Dandy the black poodle gives her a bloodshot look of sympathy. *The only one who loves me.* Dandy falls asleep again, snoring, and Colleen hears the tap of Maurice's typewriter in the dining room next door. It has a peevish, for God's sake keep those children quiet and don't disturb me until lunchtime, note. *Children say things they don't mean. In a few hours the twins will have forgotten, we'll all listen to the Goons together and get the giggles. All together.*

Colleen blows her nose, washes her face, puts on fresh powder and sits on the edge of the bed to dial Mary's number.

'Colleen! What a lovely surprise.'

'I expect you're busy.'

'You know I'm never too busy to talk to you. I'm so glad you phoned, I was feeling a bit down.'

'So was I! I was thinking about India. Where did we meet, Mary?'

'It was in Rawalpindi. I remember your family had just moved next door, I was six and you were seven. I was always complaining I had nobody to play with, so your father brought you over. I thought you were much older than me because you were so tall and skinny but then we played, and we were just like sisters.'

'I loved being at your bungalow. Your parents were so sweet to me, and to each other. How are they?'

'My father died last summer.' Mary hears genuine grief in the gasp at the other end of the phone. 'I'm sorry, Colleen, I meant to write but we've been so out of touch, and I've been so busy.'

'He was a lovely man. And your mother?'

'She had a stroke last month and she's living with us now. In fact, she's sitting here beside me, I was just feeding her when you phoned. She can't speak, unfortunately, otherwise she'd want to talk to you. I'll tell her all about your news later. I'm sure some of what I say to her goes in. We used to talk about you a lot, she was pleased you've done so well. And Edie?'

'Seems indestructible, unfortunately.'

'Colleen!'

'Well, you know what she was like. Stayed in bed for thirty years and now it looks as if she'll outlive us all.'

'Does she live with you now?'

'Over my dead body. She's got a horrible little house in Epsom, and she can damned well stay there.' Mary remembers Colleen's toughness, the way she always knew what she wanted and behaved as if she didn't have a mother. Colleen's thinking how desolate her childhood would have been without Mary and her family.

'Do you remember the mangoes?'

'I found a photograph of us eating mangoes just the other day, sitting on the veranda in Rawalpindi, or it might have been Quetta. I'll have it copied and send it to you.'

'I'd love that. I'll show the children.'

'How are they?'

'Fine. Alex is doing so well at his new school, he's made lots of friends, and Will's going there in September.'

'And Ben?'

'Well—we thought we might send Ben to a different school. How are your children?'

'They're both off at boarding school now—nowhere famous. Not like your boys. How's Maurice?'

'He's doing awfully well. Writing away, I can hear him next door.'

'And the naughty little one?'

'She's enormous, as a matter of fact. Only puppy fat. How's the farm?'

'Exhausting, but I love it. Pete does most of the heavy work, but I still have to be up at five most mornings. Colleen, do come and stay. Come in the summer, the countryside's so lovely then. You can all come if you like, there's plenty of room, I'd love to meet your children. Or you could come by yourself, just for a break. Please.'

'We're going to Italy this summer.'

'Italy! How wonderful! How long are you going for?'

'A month. We're renting a villa in Positano.'

'How glamorous! I haven't had a holiday for ten years, we can't leave the farm or my mother. Sometimes we drive the children to Scarborough for the day. Perhaps you could come when you get back from Italy?'

'Yes, we must get together some time, Mary.'

'I won't talk about India if you don't want me to.'

'What do you mean? Why shouldn't I want you to?'

'It's just that you always get cross if I mention India. But after all—'

'What?'

'After all, it was where we grew up, and your mother's family were there for generations. Do you ever see them now?'

I shouldn't have said that, Mary thinks, and sure enough there seems to be frost on the line between Yorkshire and London as Colleen drawls, 'Well, Mary, I must go and get my family some lunch.'

As she puts the receiver down Colleen knows she doesn't really want to see Mary although she's glad she exists. She doesn't want to be reminded of the sad lonely desperately shy child she used to be in India. Mary remembers, Colleen would see her in her old friend's eyes and couldn't bear it. The new Colleen, the real Colleen, is strong and confident, basking in the love of her attractive husband and wonderful children. *They do love me really. Maurice came back to me and Will's just going through a silly phase.* She runs a bath, dissolves a ruby coloured egg of perfumed oil into it and climbs in. *Not a bad body*, she thinks as she sees it in the mirror surrounding the bath. *Maurice still likes it and he's stopped seeing that horrible woman. Pete would never do that to Mary. But then how deadly to live on a farm in the middle of nowhere, in the depths of the country with all those smelly animals and get up at five and have your invalid mother to live with you.* By the time she's wriggled into her tight rubber girdle and put on her purple tweed dress Colleen feels tightly sealed once more inside the happy family she has made.

Maurice smiles up at Colleen when she knocks and comes in. He ran out of ideas forty minutes ago and is hungry. She presents her back to him flirtatiously; tenderly, he zips up the back of her dress over the oyster satin slip.

'What's for lunch?'

'Chicken and mushroom vol-au-vents with a salad and we can finish up the lemon meringue pie.'

He beams up at her. How right Florence was when she used to say, the way to a man's heart is through his stomach.

Twenty-Nine

Monsters are stacked on clattering shelves where they writhe and stir, thrusting claws and double heads up towards her. Giants rush past outside the window, some tall and thin, others curved and folded, studded with mysterious lights. Time is suspended between day and night, a silvery yellow pestilence that has trapped them forever here, nowhere. If she lets herself sleep, she will roll off her shelf and fall into the monstrous pit, so she must sit up here, floating above them, watching over the monsters in case they turn back into people. She waits for the terror that has always been in the dark, the flailing tentacle, the swooping shadow. Nothing is as it seems, she's being shown the real once upon a time.

Viola wakes with a start, finds to her surprise she's still on the top bunk, puts on her glasses and makes sense of the morning. There they all are, brothers and parents, only one head each. When they say they've slept badly she doesn't tell them just how badly.

They troop down long quivering corridors to the restaurant car, where baskets of fresh rolls and croissants and silver coffee pots wait on crisp white tablecloths. There are neat petals of butter, black cherry jam, honey and fruit—mountains of food to satisfy hungry Samuells while the Alps hurtle past; glimpses of meadows, streams and houses beneath a joyful sky, jewel colours so beautiful that you want to leap out of the window and chase them.

Maurice has been to Italy before, to pre-war Capri and Florence, in the pre-Colleen era of big houses, servants and obliging older women. He has paid the rent on the villa in Positano, but he's worried about how they're going to manage on their fifty pounds sterling allowance. They'll have to be careful; he will have to say no to Colleen and the children (how he hates saying no!); *make sure we don't miss the train from Rome to Naples, mustn't lose our luggage or tickets or passports, don't get cheated…* nobody seems to understand the French he learned in Deauville in 1928. Breakfast has cost thousands of somethings.

Colleen sees him looking anxious as he pays the bill and stuffs the bewildering notes back into his wallet. She's radiantly happy this morning. This long train journey reminds her of travelling across India but now at last she has attained the holiday she deserves; free of Edie, surrounded by her still handsome husband and beloved children, on her way to a fashionable resort for a whole month.

They manage to change to the right train in Rome and have lunch in another restaurant car, a rich meal of many courses. Soon the immaculate white tablecloth is buried under crumbs, tomato stains, wine, salt, and above it the six shining faces of the Samuells. The waiter brings a glass bowl of huge, rosy, succulent peaches bathing in water like beautiful women, distantly related to their shrivelled anaemic English cousins. Maurice has strict rules about table manners and insists that all fruit should be carefully peeled but Viola has already sunk her teeth into the velvet, her mouth is full of fragrant slithering flesh and her eyes are full of sun and colour.

At Naples that afternoon they hand the address of the villa to the driver of a vast old taxi and pile in. Maurice is too exhausted to worry about the fare. They all nod off, waking to glimpses of a dream landscape: corkscrew roads, sapphire sky and sea, white cliffs, suicidal driving, as if this really is paradise and all the cars are in a hurry to get there. The journey's easier with your eyes shut. Maurice, sitting beside the driver, wakes up in the dark to find the car has stopped.

'He's been driving round in circles!' Colleen says furiously. 'I'm not putting up with this. I'll find the blasted villa myself.'

Before anyone can stop her, she plunges out into the night.

'But darling,' Maurice says feebly, waiting for the villa to materialise.

The boys sigh because Mummy's being a bully and Daddy's being hopeless. Again. Viola, who until a few minutes ago was sleeping on her mother's knee, is terrified by her disappearance. Mummy has been swallowed by the foreign night, fallen down a cliff, been kidnapped by pirates, eaten by wolves—Viola howls and sobs, the driver shrugs and the three boys wish they'd stayed at home.

The warm night, crickets, bougainvillea; as soon as she's alone Colleen feels perfectly at home although she doesn't speak a word of Italian. *I'm going to find this bloody villa out of sheer willpower.* Sure enough, she crosses the road and sees the sign: Villa Margarita. When she appears again in the headlights, she's waving her arms triumphantly.

They carry their luggage up a flight of stone steps into a bare reception room where stale bread, cheese, mortadella, fruit and wine have been left on a table. Samuells take their food seriously, this isn't the meal they were looking forward to. The children run around the villa opening the doors of enormous rooms, laying claim to their new territory.

They've been abroad on family holidays before, to France and Germany and Switzerland. Those places seemed to happen behind glass, like waxworks, whereas this summer in Italy the Samuells are the wax, offering themselves to be stamped on by beauty and charm. Will and Viola feel this most. Will knows that Italy is where great art happened, although not in Positano, where creativity seems to be confined to the kitsch pottery animals his little sister collects with her pocket money. Still, you can feel it in the air, a vitality and grace and delight that can't be taught. The little town itself seems to have been designed by an inspired goat, with its plunging steps and alleys and houses trying to leap into the sea. There's always a view, it's always a surprise, as if the town reassembles itself whenever you turn your back.

The Villa Margarita is towards the top of the town, a crumbling pink house with terraced gardens full of vines and lemon trees. Voices and feet echo in the tiled rooms and the windows have rotting green shutters that bang in the frequent electric storms. Above the house, in all the hills between here and Naples, people are living in caves. You can see their silhouettes and sometimes their washing lines and fridges; they were bombed out of their homes in the war and now they stare down at the tourists.

Every morning after breakfast the Samuells put on their beach clothes—bright patterned shirts and shorts and huge straw hats that make them look, from above, like peripatetic mushrooms. The beach is tiny, so full of deckchairs, pedalos and fishing boats that there's hardly room to move. Maurice and the children swim and playfight for possession of the blue Lilo while Colleen sunbathes. After the cold slimy swimming baths in the Finchley Road the Mediterranean opens its arms; instead of pumping up and down in straight lines you can paddle, wallow, dive, float or explore the rocks and caves to the side of the beach where raw sewage flows picturesquely out. Whenever the sea is rough bathers look up at the mountains and mutter, *Vesuvio si arrabbia,* Vesuvius is angry. The threat of eruption hanging over the coast adds a frisson. When your legs are so tired from swimming that you think you'll never walk again you struggle through the swirling currents at the edge of the beach, where the sea sucks at you hungrily and wet pebbles slither away as you try to grab them.

Wrapped in towels, salted and boiled, they buy pistachio ice creams, iced fizzy drinks and crystallised strawberries and grapes from tanned little boys who carry trays like cinema usherettes. They also sell lurid artificial silk ties; shopping on a beach is such a novelty that Colleen buys dozens of them.

They have lunch on the beach, in an outdoor restaurant under a vine: huge plates of spaghetti, fritto misto di mare and melon with Parma ham, washed down with mineral water and wine. They're the padrone's favourite customers, they eat as much as possible at lunchtime because supper will be a picnic, whatever Colleen can buy in the shops. There was supposed to be a cook with the villa, but Colleen rumbled her after a few days of aubergines swimming in olive oil, tough meat and overripe fruit. Probably buying cheap supplies and pocketing the difference as cooks do. There's a scream up (Colleen doesn't really need words) and the cook disappears. But the money that should have been refunded hasn't been and Maurice is worried.

Italy is supposed to be cheap but nowhere is cheap when you're accompanied by a cloud of locusts.

After lunch the boys and Maurice go back to the villa to sleep and read while Colleen and Viola stay on the beach. Colleen soaks up the sun she has been starved of for twenty-five years. She feels as if she can never have enough, she loves the beach after lunch when it's empty and you can hear the sea breathing, slapping against the fishing boats. When she closes her eyes colours dance behind them, blue and ochre and yellow and green. She feels just as she did as a child when she lay down for her rest after lunch—only now she is happy. She opens her eyes; outside the circle of the beach umbrella the sand is spotted, clouds have rushed in as they do along this coast. Viola looks back at her mother, laughing because she's swimming in the tepid rain. Colleen puts on her towelling beach wrap, white with huge strawberries on it, and holds out a towel to envelop Viola as she comes running into her arms.

They climb the first of the hundreds of steps that will take them back to the villa. Viola leaps up but the stone steps are hard on middle aged legs and Colleen's gold sandals have heels. She despises sensible shoes, which are only worn by unattractive women, and looks forward to buying Viola her first pair of heels in a few years. They go into the steamy café on the tiny piazza to wait until the shops open again at four. Everyone's laughing at the rain, not moaning as they would in London. The waiter serves Colleen and Viola hot chocolate and rum babas with extravagant compliments.

One overcast afternoon, at the end of a long stuffy coach journey, they reach Pompeii. The Samuells are hot and grumpy, they stretch their long legs and gather their paraphernalia of cameras, books, sunglasses and hats as they stagger down from the coach to stand in the car park. The children have bickered all the way, Maurice is sick of their voices and of Colleen's demands: for a car instead of the coach, a restaurant meal instead of sandwiches, a night in a hotel instead of this long coach excursion. They trail around the ruins in single file, each of them sealed in a private envelope of discontent.

Pompeii is stony dead, not nearly as good as its own story. A furtive guide sidles up to Maurice and shows him photographs of writhing statues. In an expressive cocktail of Italian, English, French and sign language he explains that Vesuvius erupted just as a group of enterprising ancients were having an orgy, and their sexual antics have been preserved in a locked room. With a glimmer of interest behind his sunglasses, Maurice hands over the money and whispers to Colleen. They follow the guide.

The children, who a few minutes ago were desperate to get away from their parents and from each other, demand to know where they're going. Another note changes hands and Alex is admitted to the orgy viewing party. After all, his voice has broken and he shaves now. And so on. The twins and Viola are furious so Maurice, as usual, gives in. Only Viola is too young to be initiated into the mysteries of Pompeii, which turn out to be a group of lumpy and suspiciously plastery figures in a dark stuffy cellar that smells of pee.

Alone in the dazzling geometry of the ruins Viola tries to believe that this really was once a resort like Positano, where children played and grown-ups did boring things in locked rooms, where there were restaurants and schools and shops and ancient poodles and people wore sheets. She wonders if they took off their togas when they went swimming and if a little Roman girl was in the sea when they all said in Latin: Vesuvius is angry! Then there was smoke, and a thick heavy blanket, like the stuff that comes out of fire extinguishers, buried them for nearly two thousand years. Turned them to stone like the fauns and centaurs of Narnia. The boxlike ruins remind Viola of the air raid shelters that are still in the gardens of north London. She hopes the girl swam away in time.

It's late afternoon when the coach winds upwards past farms. Volcanic soil is particularly fertile, the guide explains; the optimistic Samuells admire the optimism of generations of farmers who have sowed and reaped, knowing they might be buried under lava at any minute. At the top of the angry mountain the guide leads them to the edge of the crater. Extinct or only dormant? Even the most jaded tourists are excited as they troop down the spiral path. They all hold hands and whisper about hell and Dante and horror films, giggling to keep out the whiff of sulphur and the end of the world.

Giuseppe, an artist who has a studio beneath the Villa Margarita, is painting Viola. Colleen was at first outraged by his suggestion. *Does he think we're made of money and we're going to pay him a fortune for the portrait? Is he so insatiable (you never know with these Italians) that he lusts after little girls?* The sittings have been allowed but only with Colleen in attendance, chaperoning her daughter who tries not to fidget as she sits on a low stool in her straw hat, pink and white striped shorts and shirt.

The door opens and Will slides in, fascinated by the mess and smells and stacked canvases. Sometimes he's allowed to visit Rex's studio. Rex paints soppy kisses, Giuseppe paints cheesy views of Positano; Will doesn't think either of them are any good but he's intrigued by these adult males who get away with it, who are allowed to draw and paint all day.

Ten days later the Samuells sit in a café in Rome, in Bernini's arcades. They've been stranded here for hours because Maurice has finally run out of money. They missed a train, had to pay a supplement and take a very expensive taxi—Maurice isn't sure exactly what happened but here they are, penniless, surrounded by luggage. Colleen is crimson with humiliation because Maurice has let her down. The children have devoured oceans of Coca-Cola, Antarcticas of ice cream, ziggurats of sandwiches. Maurice is too nervous to eat, he hasn't dared to look at the bill. Will they be seized by those musical comedy Swiss guards and forced to wash up in the papal kitchens?

He almost weeps with relief as a grey man in a white suit strides towards them. Bob runs the Rome branch of the company Maurice works for and in response to Maurice's panic-stricken telegram to London he has come to give Maurice fifty pounds in advance of his next salary cheque.

With money, Rome becomes an adventure; they decide to enjoy the hours before their train leaves for London, taking it in turns to stay with the luggage while the others wander off across the piazza to see San Pietro. The Samuells are still dressed in their beach clothes, Colleen wears a yellow low backed sleeveless sundress and the children and Maurice are wearing shorts. One by one, at the top of the steps, they are rejected at the magnificent door by a nun. Colleen rages at the tiny woman but the nun wins.

'Never seen legs before. Of course, all nuns are mad, they must be, fancy choosing to spend your life looking like an old penguin,' Colleen mutters as they pile into the taxi that is to take them to the station.

Viola has fallen hopelessly in love with Italy, nuns and all. On the long train journey back to Victoria she fantasises about her glorious return; one day she will explore these magical walled hill cities she glimpses from the train; grown up Viola, slim and elegantly dressed, will live in one of those ancient stone houses surrounded by olive trees and feast on giant peaches and pistachio ice cream.

Thirty

Three men carrying a four-poster bed march across her bedroom. Viola has always wanted a four-poster bed—but it does seem odd that they're delivering it in the middle of the night. They disappear. She gets up to investigate, barefoot in her red nightdress, opens the door of her bedroom and searches for them in the dark corridor. They aren't there, but in the toilet she meets an old lady in a hat and a long black coat holding a gun.

Maurice and Colleen aren't pleased at being woken up at four in the morning. 'It's Grandma Samuell. And she's going to shoot you, Mummy.'

Maurice laughs but superstitious Colleen questions her daughter anxiously.

'Don't go to the loo, Mummy. She'll kill you.'

'Now calm down. How do you know it was her? She died before you were born. Did she say anything?'

'No. I just knew.'

'She did have a black coat,' Colleen says nervously.

'Nonsense. The child's ill,' Maurice rationalises, although he can't help an atavistic twinge of fear that his formidable mother might be here, now, looking through his bank statements.

The cold glass thermometer presses against Viola's tongue. She has a temperature of a hundred and three. Colleen holds her hand as they go back down the corridor, switching on all the lights to reassure her there are no murderous ancestors in the toilet.

In the morning nice Doctor Lowndes comes. He says Viola has a mastoid which could burst at any minute unless it's controlled by penicillin. In between bouts of sleep and delirium Viola is fascinated by the idea that her ear, like Vesuvius or Mummy, could explode. After years of faking illness to avoid school she's rather proud that she has finally managed to achieve invalidism. Many friends send messages and cards and, to her surprise, she wishes she could go back to school as the weeks drag on. Too exhausted to read, she asks Colleen to put the huge blue plastic gramophone in her room and stack it with records: *Salad Days, Carousel, South Pacific, My Fair Lady, Tom Lehrer, Flanders and Swann.* Her room fills with the smell of hot plastic as she flatly chants along to the familiar songs: We're looking for a piano, some enchanted evening, gonna wash that man right outa my hair, I could have danced all night, just you wait 'Enry 'Iggins, everything seems all right on a Saturday night when we're poisoning pigeons in the park, I'm a gnu how do you do, no-one ever wants to court a warthog, though a warthog does her best…

Viola comes down from her cloud of lyrics to find herself in her bedroom again, surrounded by neglected toys. There are the board games and craft sets that arrived exquisitely arranged and cellophaned and have now spilled all over the room; the cuddly toys she's been too ill to cuddle; in the unlit fireplace sprawl her three puppets: the tennis girl in her short white dress clutching a tennis racket, the Scotsman in his kilt holding a handkerchief and a bottle of whisky and the witch with her broomstick. Their strings are hopelessly tangled, Viola has given up trying to make them do things. It would be easier to make up an interesting story about them if they didn't wear their characters on their sleeves like that; Viola has spent hours trying to detach them from their tennis racket, bottle and broomstick, but has only made them even more knotted. There's a puppet hospital you can post them to but Colleen has lost the address and meanwhile the puppets languish in the incurable chaos of Viola's room. She stares at them. If the witch couldn't fly and started to drink, if the Scotsman stopped drinking and went to live in Italy, if the girl stopped playing tennis all the time... is she their daughter or has the witch kidnapped her and if so, will the Scotsman rescue her... Of all her toys the puppets intrigue her the most. But she wants real people again.

'I want to go back to school,' she tells Colleen, who is so surprised she nearly drops her daughter's breakfast tray.

Alex and Will stand at the grey gates waiting for their parents, who are late as usual. The brothers don't exactly ignore each other but they don't talk much, either. Will is puzzled that Alex is regarded by most of the boys as a considerable personage. Everybody knows who he is, he's famously good at History and bad at games and rude to beaks. In Chapel the Church of England mystifies Will. He's not sure whether he's Jewish or not, there are lots of Jewish boys in his House. When they hold out their arms and mutter, 'What a way to spend Easter!' Will doesn't know if he should laugh. But Alex has wholeheartedly adopted Christianity, he genuflects and prays extravagantly and is annoyed by his brother's critical gaze. Alex wishes yet again that he'd been born an only child. And an orphan, he thinks as the shabby Humber drives up with its mortifying cargo. Alex looks round to make sure that nobody is looking (next time he must arrange to meet them further from the school) and the doors open on noise and mess as Viola is decanted onto Colleen's knee in the front and the three boys sit in the back.

Colleen turns her face up eagerly to be kissed and feels the chill in her sons' lips. They look so thin and middle aged in their tweed jackets and grey flannel trousers. She has lain awake night after night missing them, worrying that they aren't getting enough to eat. Maurice explains that emotional and actual starvation are privileges, she must not interfere in their good education, so she holds back her tears.

In the dining room of the Angel, Maurice feels a wave of satisfaction as the head waiter shows them to their table. He's proud of his tall sons as they demolish their lunch (the best, the ten shillings and sixpence set menu) and tell him about their new friendships, the books they've read, the beaks they like and the ones they hate, the cold cubicles where they sleep and the awful food they're expected to eat. Maurice beams, it sounds just like his own school, they're being made into men like him which is as it should be. But he will visit them more frequently than Florence and Aubrey, who had a habit of sending him the menus of delicious meals they'd eaten all over the world instead of turning up themselves. Now there's only Ben who must be stirred into the wonderful masculine pudding of England.

Will chatters, avoiding his twin's eyes. He's shell shocked by the last six weeks but thankful to have survived it; he can only bear to go back tonight if he keeps Ben out. It irritates him that his twin's so silent and gloomy, that Mummy looks as if she's going to cry, that he's being pulled both ways. Maurice's beams last until the bill arrives, when his face takes on its usual expression of baffled outrage. How has everything become so expensive? He hands over a five-pound note with a heavy sigh.

They go downstairs to the lounge where they sit around an open fire and drink coffee. Colleen and Viola look at copies of *Country Life*. Colleen loathes the country but lusts after the photographs of enormous houses. Perhaps Viola will marry one of them.

'Look at that, darling! Isn't it gorgeous? Queen Anne, twenty bedrooms, look at that library. Christ almighty, eighteen miles from Pontefract, why do these rich people always want to live in the middle of nowhere? Who needs twenty bedrooms anyway, seven is quite enough, now if I had all that money…'

It's dark when they drive back to the vast, bleak buildings to disgorge Alex and Will into the mud. Back to prison, Viola thinks, although she's careful to drop the name of their prison when she sits next to her headmistress at lunch the next day.

'That's a very famous school.'

'They've got a hundred acres,' Viola boasts. She imagines her tall brothers in their brown tweed jackets, wandering around their soggy domain.

At Easter Will's school report concludes, 'another one-legged Samuell'. Maurice shrugs off the sarcasm of schoolmasters. His children are not all-rounders (mediocrities in other words) but they will do great things.

Ben has been accepted at a school that's even more expensive than his brothers', although it isn't a 'proper' public school. The headmaster makes a fortune out of educating boys who for various reasons aren't accepted elsewhere. Despite the obvious jokes about Dotheboys Hall, Ben feels better now that he knows he's going somewhere in September. Staying at home has felt like a punishment. Maurice is relieved, too, and Viola thinks of brothers as fascinating but alien creatures who disappear for most of the year. Only Colleen protests that she likes having her children around and Maurice smiles because she doesn't understand the way things work.

Alone in their room for those few weeks of the holidays, the twins try to recreate their old intimacy. Will wants to admit how much he has missed Ben, how deeply he needs his twinship. But they can no longer talk to each other easily. One night after supper when they lie reading on their beds Will swears Ben to secrecy.

'I'm trying to read,' Ben says irritably.

'It's something Alex did, something really bad, Mummy and Daddy would be furious with him if they found out, I think perhaps he'd be expelled from school.'

'Don't be such an old ham. You always exaggerate everything.'

'No, honestly. Promise you won't tell.'

'Oh, all right then.'

'It happened just before the end of term. I was in the studio painting a scene of a washing line in a big garden and Stephens, this boy in Alex's class, came and looked over my shoulder and asked if that was the garden of my house in Derbyshire.'

'What house in Derbyshire?'

'Exactly. That's what I said. Then Stephens asked about my houses in Chester Square and Scotland and Cannes. And my pyaidaterror in New York.'

'What's a pyaidaterror?'

'I don't know. Something expensive. And I said there was just a flat in St John's Wood and he laughed, and I think he must have told everybody at school and now Alex is furious with me. Do you think I should tell Daddy?'

They think about this magnificent family Alex wants to belong to; they feel ashamed of his lies but also excluded because they don't think he'd want them turning up at one of his imaginary houses. They've always reluctantly admired their elder brother and believed he's cleverer than them, so they suspect his elaborate lies might be another manifestation of his cleverness.

'Perhaps Daddy would just laugh.'

Their father has never told them not to lie or cheat or steal. The moral message they've picked up from him is that if you go to the right schools, talk well, read a lot and inherit a bit of money you will be successful. Maurice is researching a book about famous swindlers. At mealtimes he entertains his children with tales of their heroic scams and deceptions: Horatio Bottomley, who posed as a noble patriot and cheated widows and orphans after the First World War; David Lamar, the Wolf of Wall Street; Charles Ponzi, whose scheme has passed into the language. Their exploits make their father weep with laughter. So the twins don't tell him about Alex.

Viola's happy to be back at school with her friends. Every day after school Colleen meets her daughter in the Finchley Road. Viola walks down the hill from the school with Mina, they buy sweets together, four for a penny, and talk. When they get to the bottom of the hill Viola turns somersaults on the railing (her only gymnastic feat) while they wait for Colleen. Mina stands in front of her protectively so that the world won't be able to see her grey flannel knickers. Last term Viola went to tea at Mina's house and met her parents, who were interested that Viola's mother had grown up in India and wanted to meet her. Ever since, Viola has been promising to invite Mina back. She knows this is important because Mina has no other friends at school. She's unpopular because she's the only Indian girl in the school and Viola, who at various times has been unpopular because she's fat, knows how horrible this feels. When invitations for a party are handed out and the whole class is invited except you; when they're picking games teams in the playground and you're always the last; when nobody wants to sit next to you at lunch because they all say you smell. Mina never cries and Viola, who is still a cry-baby, admires her strength.

'It won't last. They're just being silly. You don't smell and you're nice and I'd rather walk down with you than with anyone.'

'It's because I'm black.'

'You're not black, you're sort of yellow, the same colour as me.'

The two girls hold out their hands beneath their grey cardigans to compare them.

'I'm darker,'

'So what? You look nice, I think you're pretty.'

Mina looks dubiously at her enormous friend. 'I think you—you've got a nice chin. Oh look! Here comes your mother. Ask her, please! You promised.'

Colleen has stopped to talk to Emma's mother. 'Look at those two! They could be sisters. You'd think they were teenagers. Girls from that part of the world develop so early, don't they?'

'What part of the world?' Colleen asks furiously.

'Why, from India. '

'Viola isn't Indian, she was born in London,' Colleen hisses before going to hug her daughter and nod curtly at Mina.

'Mummy, can Mina come to tea with me?'

'When?'

'I'm free every day,' Mina says helpfully.

'Well. We'll have to see.'

'You always say that. I really really really want her to come to my house.'

'We're very busy this week.'

'No, we're not—'

'We have to go now. Goodbye.' Colleen pulls her daughter's arm and Mina turns sadly away.

This summer Viola has lots of friends at school and, at home, enjoys being in a smaller family. Her best friend this month is Ginny, whose mother is one of the two divorcees in the class, regarded with suspicion by the other mothers. Ginny's father is extremely rich and every Friday afternoon a huge black chauffeur-driven Rolls appears outside the school to take Ginny to tea with him. He's so kind that he likes his daughter to bring friends with her and there's competition to ride in the splendid car.

On sunny Friday afternoons the girls are allowed to spread rugs in the school gardens and read. Viola, who reads insatiably at home, always wants to talk instead. Talking is her latest discovery, so as Ginny doesn't like reading anyway, they lie on their tartan rug and whisper about the world. It seems well within their grasp now, the world, as they lie on their backs and stare up at the blue sky with fluffy white cloud boats scudding across it. Viola knows from lessons that the earth revolves but she has never felt it before. This afternoon she feels the warm soil and fragrant grass beneath her, the gentle arch of the sky above. Her stomach churns with excitement and happiness because she's here, now, part of the movement, going somewhere unknown and wondrous.

'Can I go to tea with your daddy?' she asks Ginny, as she does every Friday.

'Maybe next week.'

There's a long waiting list. Ginny is flattered but also aware that she isn't popular for herself. The word has got around that in addition to the amazing car you get shoes.

Thirty-One

The car has a cocktail cabinet facing the brown leather seats. Ginny opens it to reveal a mirrored interior full of little cans and bottles. She passes Viola a can of coke, presses a button and makes the roof slide off. The two girls stand on the seat, waving and screaming at the traffic all the way to Regents Park. Charles, the uniformed chauffeur, is tolerant even when they find the buttons that control the windows and send them whizzing up and down.

The car stops outside a very grand block of flats and their exuberance fades. Viola is intimidated by all the gilt and statues and mirrors in the lobby and Ginny's pale face inside its frame of wavy black hair looks anxious as they wait hand in hand for the door to open.

'Last week he was cross because I brought too many friends.'

'Perhaps he won't like me.'

Maurice, like the other daddies Viola knows, can't get away from children fast enough. But Ginny's father is different, he wants to play. He's fat and ugly like most grown-ups but smiles a lot and says to Ginny, 'Just one friend, that's good. And such a big girl.' He makes it sound as if being big is a good thing and Viola's delighted. 'Do you like to play?'

'Yes,' Viola says, expecting Monopoly or Scrabble.

'Shall we play our bear game?' he asks Ginny, who blinks nervously. 'Yes? Wouldn't that be fun? I am a great bear,' he explains to Viola. 'And I like to chase and tickle little girls.'

Viola wants to tell him she has advanced beyond such babyish games but remembers that this is his house, so he gets to choose what they play. He takes off his jacket and tie, as if playing is very hard work, then turns on them, red faced and shiny, growling in a silly way. The two girls run down the corridor into a dark room. Viola isn't sure if she's pretending to be frightened or if she really is frightened. She looks around to make sure Ginny's still here.

'On the bed,' he directs them from the door. 'Take off your shoes and socks, you can bounce on the bed.'

Soon they're leaping up and down on the huge pink satin bed, laughing self-consciously, aware that he's watching them be little girls. He comes closer and joins in the game, or at least his hands do.

'Are you ticklish?' he asks Viola, who nods. She's so ticklish that Colleen has only to brush her foot with her finger to make her dissolve into helpless giggles.

'Good. I like ticklish girls.' He rolls on top of her and tickles her vigorously while Ginny watches.

'Your tea is ready. You must eat now.' A thin woman with bright red hair stands in the doorway.

'Not yet,' Ginny's father grunts; his tickling is heavy and uncomfortable. Viola stops laughing.

'Yes, now! Come!'

The woman switches on the lights and bustles around the room, making the girls put on their shoes and socks and follow her into a vast kitchen. She looks angry as she serves the girls chocolate cake, sandwiches and orange juice, standing over them as if she wants them to go away. Viola is bewildered. If she's a friend or a relation, why doesn't she introduce herself? If she's a maid, why is she so rude and bossy?

'What's your name?'

'Elisabeta.'

'Elizabeth?'

'I am not English.' She has huge tragic dark eyes that don't match her gaudy hair and her face is like a ruined tower.

'Where are you from then?' Viola persists.

'From Vienna.' She glares at Viola as if it's her fault she has to live in a palatial flat in London instead.

Ginny's father appears in the doorway. He and Elisabeta look at each other angrily. 'These children are leaving now. I have telephoned to Charles.'

'No, not yet,' Ginny's father says rather pathetically. 'I have to give Viola her shoes.'

'I've got some shoes.' Viola shows him her shabby brown sandals. Perhaps he thinks she has to go barefoot, like Cinderella.

Elisabeta and Ginny follow them down the corridor back to the bedroom where Ginny's father asks Viola her shoe size and her favourite colour. The walls are lined with boxes, like a shop, and the boxes are full of shoes. 'Why have you got so many?' she asks as she tries on a pair of flat red slip-on shoes straight out of their tissue paper nest and inhales their delicious fresh leathery smell.

'They're not for me, they're for my friends.'

'You must have a lot of friends. Can I have a pair for my brother?'

'I only have ladies' shoes.'

Viola tucks the shoebox under her arm. 'Thank you for having me,' she says as she follows Charles and Ginny out to the car.

She and Ginny are subdued on the way home, but Colleen's delighted by the shoes and her glimpse of the car. Ginny is a suitable friend for Viola; her daddy owns a shoe factory and various other businesses, although the divorce has been a great misfortune for Ginny and her mother. Colleen asks lots of questions about the tea party and Viola starts to boast about her wonderful time. All week she brags about the cocktail cabinet and the bear game and the shoes. Ginny's her best friend for ever and ever, she says Viola can come to tea again next Friday.

Viola hopes the whole school is watching as she gets into the Rolls. Again, she and Ginny dance on the seats and help themselves to drinks. They poke their heads, in their school Panama hats, out of the open roof and sing and scream with laughter as London rushes past. This time Ginny's daddy is waiting at the door, smiling.

'He likes you,' Ginny mutters resentfully and Viola feels as if she has stolen something from her. 'I don't want to play that stupid tickling game,' she says as they stand in the lugubriously grand drawing room under a chandelier.

'Then we'll play something else. Shall we play hide-and-seek?' he asks Viola, ignoring his sulky daughter.

Viola's frightened of games that involve being chased, she has nightmares about them. But she smiles and agrees to hide, her heart thumping as she tries to think of somewhere clever to hide, listening to the voice of Ginny's father counting to two hundred. It shouldn't be a grown-up voice; it makes the game all wrong. Blundering through the enormous flat, her sense of direction even worse than usual because of her rising panic, she opens the door of the kitchen to find Elisabeta sitting at the table looking ferocious.

'You must not come here. You must go home.' Viola, who thinks this is a very rude thing to say to a guest, gapes. 'Come!'

Elisabeta makes her climb from a chair into the service lift at the back of the kitchen and closes the door. Viola crouches on a metal shelf with a bare wall lined with cables on one side and on her other the hidden flat she's hiding from. There's a smell of rotting garbage and damp bricks. She hears their voices calling her name. Perhaps Elisabeta is a witch, she looks like a witch, and Viola's in the food lift because she's going to be eaten like Hansel and Gretel. Perhaps someone will press a button and summon her to another, even stranger flat. She hears Elisabeta's voice say 'No, she is not here.'

Passive, stiff, frightened and cold, Viola stays in the lift for years, until Elisabeta opens the door and says it's time for tea.

Ginny sits at the table eating chocolate cake. She glares at Viola, who feels she has spoiled the party.

'There she is! She was in the lift all the time! What a funny place to hide.' His loud laughter makes Ginny's and Elisabeta's silence deafening.

After tea it's Ginny's turn to hide. Ginny's daddy takes Viola's hand and leads her into a small room, chanting loudly, 'One, two, three, four.' He closes the door of the room and stops counting, turning towards her. His hand is clammy, he smells of aftershave as he presses his body against hers and his wet soft lips slime into her mouth. One of his hands undoes the white buttons at the front of her school dress and the other gropes inside her white cotton knickers.

'There! Isn't that nice?' His voice sounds hoarse as he rubs something against her knickers.

Viola pulls away from the hot sucking mouth. 'I can't breathe.'

'I won't hurt you. I just want to kiss you.'

Ginny's voice calls plaintively, 'Have you finished counting?'

The mouth clamps down again, a swamp she can't climb out of.

'I bet you don't know where I am. I bet you can't find me.'

Ginny's voice sounds very near; Viola wants to call back, to go on being her friend, but the invading mouth and hands are so heavy that she can't speak. Just when she thinks she's never going to get rid of this enormous leech, Ginny stands in the doorway. Ginny's father leaps away.

'You were kissing!' She looks accusingly at Viola, who realises she has done something terrible. Ginny will hate her if she finds out.

'No. No, I wasn't. We were just playing.'

'I heard you.' Contemptuously she mimics the sound of squelchy kisses.

If Ginny didn't see anything there's just a chance Viola can make it unhappen. Behind her is a basin with a plug. 'It was this, it was the plug, it makes a funny noise,' she assures Ginny desperately.

Ginny's daddy backs her up, 'Yes, it was the plug.'

Ginny looks as if she's going to cry and Viola says, 'I think it's time to go home now.'

Ginny's daddy looks flustered and relieved. 'You will come again next Friday?' Viola and Ginny are silent. 'I do hope you had a nice time. And what about your shoes? You can't go home without your shoes.'

He goes into the shoe shop bedroom and Viola and Ginny stand in the doorway. 'My mummy says, can I have some black patent party shoes. Size five. Please.' He gets out a stepladder and climbs up, taking out boxes, puffing and sweating. Suddenly he looks old and sad. Viola takes off her sandals and he kneels as he puts the shining night on her feet. The aroma of fresh leather fills the room.

'There, that's a beautiful fit, your mummy will be pleased. Won't she? Let's put them back in their box and you can take them home. Let's call Charles and he can take you home in my car. You like my car, don't you? Would you like to come at the same time next week?' He talks them all the way out to the car.

This time the two girls sit in silence until Viola is dropped off.

Colleen's delighted with the shoes. 'And did you have a lovely time?'

'Yes.'

At school the next week Ginny and Viola avoid each other and on Friday Viola walks down the hill with Mina as usual. She passes the Rolls, with Ginny and two other girls climbing into it.

The two blubbery lumps on her chest that nobody else in the class has except Mina get bigger and embarrass her when one of the more naturist teachers suggests the girls should strip to their knickers and run around the gardens in the sun. Viola and Mina keep their vests on.

237

Just before the end of the summer term Ginny's mother comes to have a drink with Colleen and Maurice. She has never been invited before and Ginny hasn't been Viola's friend for ages, not for three weeks, so Viola is terrified they've found out about the kissing and she will be sent to prison or expelled from school. Viola hovers at the end of the corridor, staring at the drawing room door which is firmly shut against her. Colleen opens it and ushers her into a room full of serious adults, staring at her. The atmosphere quivers as Colleen says in a strangled voice that is supposed to sound casual, 'Now, darling, we just want to ask you a few questions.'

Viola has seen Perry Mason and has often wondered what she would say in court. She says no: nothing happened, he didn't do anything to me, I had a lovely time. As their questioning grows more intense, she bursts into tears and her tears work their usual magic: she's a child again, the grown-ups will have to look after her and feel sorry for her.

Maurice finds the scene painful. Gently, he tells his daughter to go to her room. Ginny's mother is very attractive, an ex-model. Maurice doesn't see why a man with perfectly normal taste in women would want to grope children. The whole thing is bizarre; he wonders if Ginny's mother has concocted this story to extract more alimony. They part frostily.

One evening a few weeks later Viola goes to the toilet and finds blood in her pants. Dark, sticky, fishy smelling, it makes her feel ashamed. For half an hour she sits there, staring down at it in disgust. She has lumps on her chest and now her wee wee has turned to blood. I'm turning into a monster, the only one in the world, nobody will want to be my friend.

When she doesn't come to supper Colleen bangs on the

door of the toilet and Viola whispers about the blood. Colleen says she has flu and should go to bed. When Maurice and Ben ask what the matter is Colleen looks embarrassed, which confirms Viola's worst fears that she's a freak. Flu doesn't happen in your bottom.

The next morning Viola stays at home and Doctor Lowndes comes to examine her. Afterwards she hears them murmuring outside her door and imagines the conversation.

Colleen: Is there any hope she'll turn into a human being again?

Doctor Lowndes (with charming and very expensive bedside manner): There is an operation, but she might die.

Colleen: Better dead than red and covered with lumps!

Just as Viola is imagining her beautiful funeral Colleen comes in with a box full of enormous nappies and a pink elastic belt with hooks on it.

'Am I going to get better, Mummy?' Viola asks in a brave voice borrowed from Beth in *Little Women*.

'Of course, darling. It's only the curse. You've started it early. I didn't get mine until I was fourteen.'

'What curse?'

'Don't sound so terrified. All women get it. It's so that you can have babies.'

'But I don't want babies!' Viola cries, thinking that letting Ginny's daddy kiss her has doomed her to have them anyway.

Colleen tries not to laugh, tries to remember back to her own gloomy initiation. Edie's joyless voice: *You'll soon find out what women have to go through.*

'Not now, darling. Later, when you *do* want them. Don't look so miserable! It just means that for a few days every month you won't be able to swim or play games.'

'Will you give me a note?'

'Yes, of course. You can get up now, you can go to school tomorrow, you'll just have to wear a sanitary pad.'

Viola tries one on and hobbles around the room. It feels as if she has a boat between her legs. The nappy bulges out of her pants.

'The other girls will see it and laugh at me.'

'Soon they'll all get the curse, everyone does. It just means you're a big girl.'

Viola, who has always been a big girl, isn't comforted.

Thirty-Two

For her tenth birthday Viola, who has hardly ever played with dolls before, insists on going to Hamley's to buy one. She stands with Colleen in front of the shelves of perfect little girls and chooses one with long golden curls and huge blue eyes. Belinda. At home she undresses her, checking the pink plastic flatness of her chest and her hairless, harmless bottom. She discovers another doll, Little Sister Susie, who comes with an enormous wardrobe which Viola collects with her pocket money. Again and again, she puts on and takes off the jodhpurs, the party dress, the nurse's uniform. Susie is so small that she seems even younger and safer than Belinda and her smooth brown hair is less annoying than Belinda's unattainable blonde curls.

Colleen and Maurice are delighted to have found a school for Ben, but Colleen misses her sons. Their detachment from her, their coolness when she does see them, feel like body blows although Maurice insists it's quite normal for boys to become independent. That's why you send them away, so that they won't turn into pansies, so that they won't need you.

Then what's the point of having children at all? Colleen wants to ask, but she knows he always wins these battles over education. Grieving for three of her children, she's delighted to be needed so much by the fourth. Her daughter moves into the space that used to be occupied by her brothers and basks in her parents' attention. The three brothers are mythologised, like the three bears, and she's reborn as an only child. In double figures, as Maurice says.

At school her new best friend is Lucy, a passionate child with a pale oval face, long straight black hair and a wild laugh. Lucy hasn't yet been cursed but she agrees that all things associated with growing up are horrible. They declare war on: pink, boys, frilly dresses, lipstick, personal hygiene, babies, jelly and liver. Lucy's an only child, adored by her parents, who are poor, according to Colleen. Her father's a teacher, they live in a small, shabby house and Viola loves staying there. The two girls are allowed to make as much noise as they like; in the bath they splash each other and scream with laughter; in bed they lie awake half the night, talking and giggling exuberantly. At school Viola annoys the teachers by imitating Billy Bunter, the only fat hero she has been able to find, and bellowing 'Yaroo!' She has always tried to please grown-ups but now she realises that being naughty is far more fun.

Lucy and Viola call themselves the twins and soon other girls want to join their gang. They become the triplets and then the quads; Viola and Lucy exercise their power during whispered meetings in the playground and long telephone conversations when they decide who is to be allowed in. You have to be an only child (or a virtual only child like Viola) with a proper contempt for pink et cetera and a dog. Lucy has two spaniels, Piddy and James, who live with Dandy in the girls' fantasy dogland. The real Dandy is neurotic, rheumaticky and growls whenever a child approaches, but his poodle alter ego is Viola's beloved companion, who talks to her secretly and sleeps in her room.

Colleen smiles as her daughter hogs the phone for hours, giggling and spouting nonsense about dogs. Innocent, childish nonsense; *Thank God nothing happened with Ginny's father*.

Alone in her room Viola plays with her dolls house which is, in her imagination, the Villa Margarita, with its roof garden and rosy crumbling walls. She opens it up to play out domestic dramas with people made out of pipe cleaners. Viola wants to shrink and live in the house herself, or for it to grow around her until she's embalmed in that Italian summer when all was well.

When she isn't trying to reinforce the bulwarks of childhood Viola shows off about her precocious reading. At school she ostentatiously reads an orange and white Penguin edition of PG Wodehouse and Lucy says admiringly, 'Viola's reading grown up books!' She loves Bertie Wooster because he isn't grown up, just wonderfully funny. His bumbling charm reminds her of Maurice and holds out the promise of children just pretending to be adults and getting away with it.

The boys have told her that dirty books are kept in a drawer in Mummy's dressing table. One evening when her parents are out Viola opens the drawer and sits on the floor. She tries to extract adult mysteries from the books. *Lady Chatterley's Lover* has no pictures, but she perseveres with it. She doesn't know what a gamekeeper is, she thinks it's probably like a goalkeeper and wonders why he wants to live in the woods, miles away from any shops or theatres. Anyway, Lady Whatsit loves him, which is nice, only what about her poor husband who has to sit in a wheelchair all day? Lady Whatsit likes kissing wet willies (this passage is marked in pencil) so she's obviously bonkers. Viola doesn't think it's nearly as good as Tom's Midnight Garden.

She turns to the Kama Sutra, which is even more puzzling. She thinks her parents are definitely an elephant man and woman, but the illustrations look improbably athletic. Daddy has a bad back and Mummy never walks anywhere if she can help it so they wouldn't be up to all those contortions. Her babysitter calls. Viola puts the Facts of Life back in their drawer and goes to supper. At school the next day she boasts in a world-weary tone about how boring sex is.

'I want to go and see Charlotte,' she says to Colleen in the Christmas holidays.

'Are you sure? She's awfully old now, constantly in and out of hospital.' Colleen finds Edie's declining years a great bore and can't imagine why a ten-year-old would choose to spend time with a decrepit old lady.

'You don't have to come. I want to go on my own.'

For the last few years their friendship has dwindled to occasional lunches, which Charlotte calls luncheons, and Christmas presents: a three-guinea gift voucher for Harrods. Viola enjoys striding around the vast halls, making friends with a monkey in the pet department before finally buying two Long Playing records or a carrier bag full of books. Colleen approves of this sign that her daughter might grow up to be a shopaholic.

Viola still thinks of Charlotte as her fairy godmother. It isn't money or food she wants, but something none of her other friends can give her. Nervously, Viola boards a number 19 bus at Sloane Square, where Colleen has seized the chance to visit her beloved Peter Jones (Never Knowingly Undersold). Alone, Viola is worried she will get off at the wrong bus stop. The King's Road has shrunk; when she gets off at Beaufort Street the glorious toy shop where she used to spend her pocket money and the post office where Ben used to hoard his running away money look small and shabby. The Green, the communal gardens where the children used to play, is overgrown and she notices for the first time the cruel broken glass on top of the walls, put there to discourage nasty children from playing with the nice children who lived in the houses. They weren't nice at all. Viola remembers being bullied by the older children, remembers Charlotte who was always happy to come down and rescue her when she pretended to fall over.

It's almost as if she has been allowed back into childhood. Charlotte is in her eighties now, crippled by arthritis, and spends most of her life in bed. Viola towers above the frail old lady in her richly coloured silk shawl and hugs her gently, afraid she might break. Letty, the maid who is almost as old as Charlotte, remembers Viola and greets her warmly. Being here alone with Charlotte, without Colleen who always talks about the weather and shopping, Viola feels again the direct stream of communication with Charlotte that comforted her when she was little.

They sit together on the creamy sofa and talk. Viola stares into Charlotte's clear blue eyes, like lunar pools you can dive into. Charlotte sees at once that the child is unhappy.

'How is school?'

'Awful. I get loads of homework now because I've got to take an exam next year and the teachers don't like me because they say I talk too much. You were so lucky to have a governess and not have to go to school.'

'I had lessons with my sisters.'

'But sisters are nice to each other, aren't they? Not like brothers.'

'I was the youngest, like you, and my two elder sisters, Emmy and Kitty, adored each other. I loved my brother Edward but he was sent away to school in England, so we three sisters were left alone in the wilds of Ireland with the servants.'

'Mummy wants servants; she had lots in India.'

'I don't think she would have wanted these ones. Mrs Bream, the cook, drank like a fish, a very cold fish. Nanny Conway would sit in the kitchen drinking with her and when all the servants were drunk, they would think up punishments for us. For me, usually, because Emmy and Kitty would tell tales and then I'd be locked in the cupboard in the nursery and in the pantry. The governesses were poor, frightened young women, just as terrified of the servants as we were, so they never stayed long.'

For a second Viola sees a little girl in a long white dress crying in a dark cupboard. 'But where were your parents?'

'Abroad, usually. My father gambled a great deal and my mother liked to dance and meet new people.'

'But when they came home didn't you tell them?'

'Adults didn't listen to children in those days. They believed I'd done all the bad things the servants and my sisters said I'd done.'

'I would have run away!'

'There was nowhere to run to. We were in the middle of the Irish countryside, ten miles from the nearest town.'

Viola stares at Charlotte, who has always seemed to inhabit a fairy tale, and sees that she's been a real person all along, with feelings of sadness and loneliness, a kind friend she might have talked to. But then she realises that they couldn't have had this conversation when she was five and Charlotte was an old lady, they can only have it now because she's no longer a child but an overgrown spotty monster; because Charlotte is no longer just old but, they both know, dying.

'And were your sisters always mean to you?'

'I think they forgot all about it when they grew up. But I never forgot.'

'I won't forget either,' Viola says savagely, plotting her revenge on Ginny's father and various teachers who pick on her. 'Alex says you were called the three beautiful sisters of England.' This phrase has danced across her imagination.

'That was a very long time ago. My father gambled away the house and we went to live in Paris.'

'Why?'

'It was cheaper, and nearer the casinos.'

'Didn't you like it?'

'I could never get my tongue around the language. And the men were—dreadful.'

Viola longs to hear more about the dreadful men but they go into lunch and the table puts distance between them. The dining room with French doors leading to the paved garden is just as it's always been. Letty has laid the table with a white cloth and piled it with cutlery, plates and glasses, as if the meal will last forever. Viola, who knows this is the last lunch she and Charlotte will eat together, wishes it could. There are the finger bowls, the fairy toast and butter, the bowl of sugar crystals she used to like to suck, the cushion she used to need to sit on so that she could reach the table—'I don't think we'll be needing that,' Charlotte says, laughing as she removes it. Viola tucks into tomato soup, chicken in white sauce with rice and peas and caramel custard. This was her favourite food when she was four and used to amuse Charlotte by drinking out of her finger bowl. After each lunch Viola used to go into the kitchen to thank the cook, who made a great fuss of her. But there's no longer a cook. Letty looks after Charlotte now.

Charlotte slowly eats a boiled egg. They smile at each other, but Charlotte grows paler and paler, fading until her face is just a transparent white circle floating above the deep reds, greens and blues of her richly embroidered silk shawl.

When Viola finishes her caramel custard Charlotte says, 'I'm sorry, darling, but I'm going to have to go and lie down. So silly.'

Viola stands over her, wanting to help, clumsily stroking Charlotte's frail arm and wondering what to do.

Letty comes, clucking and fussing, to lead Charlotte up to bed. In her black and white uniform, she looks like a penguin with a Fabergé egg tucked under its wing.

'Shall I go home?' Viola stands helplessly at the foot of the stairs as her oldest friend climbs them.

Charlotte clings to the banister with one hand and turns towards her. 'No, don't go. Later I might feel better. Wait here, if it's not too dull for you. Perhaps you'd like to look at those miniatures of my ghastly family. You used to like them; do you remember?'

Charlotte disappears and Viola knows she's being put to bed, as if all the years between Mrs Bream's tyranny and Letty's ministrations have been a dream. She has never been alone in these rooms before. They're dark at the end of the short afternoon, gleaming strangely from the snow that's falling on the communal gardens where Viola used to play.

In the small room that leads off the panelled hall she draws back the leather curtain that covers the cabinet of family miniatures. They have their own light, these faces from the past. Viola presses a button on top of the cabinet and the enamelled faces glow as they stare back at her from oval nests in their bed of threadbare green velvet. When she was little Viola thought they were Charlotte's brothers and sisters and aunts and uncles, who had just gone out to the shops and would be back soon to play with her; she was amazed that Charlotte didn't even know their names. Just beastly old ancestors, she used to say wearily as Viola stood on tiptoe to rub her nose against the glass that separated her from the pointy faced lady with the ruff, the little boy in blue velvet with long golden curls and the handsome, blue-eyed man in scarlet and gold uniform.

Now Viola sees that the thirty miniatures span four hundred years. Behind her the snow falls as she stoops to meet them, the first pictures that fascinated her. She wonders how anyone could paint in such exquisite detail; now it's the artists she admires, not their subjects who look haughty and conventional. If they're the tree that Charlotte grew on then she's even more wonderful than Viola has always thought her. Going to join her ancestors—she imagines her upstairs, shrinking until she's small enough to fit into the cabinet.

Letty asks if she wants to say goodbye. Viola follows her upstairs to the bedroom. Charlotte really has shrunk; she looks tiny without her shawl, her face and hair as white as the pillow.

'I don't want to go home. Can't I stay with you?'

'This house is so boring for you.'

'I feel safe here. Is it my fault you're ill? Did I make you talk too much?'

'I love talking to you. Of course it isn't your fault, I'm always ill now.'

Viola sits on the bed. Behind her is the bathroom where Charlotte used to put a plaster on her knee when Viola pretended to fall over to gain entry to the magical house. She wants to continue the conversation they were having before lunch, about the men in Paris, but she's afraid of exhausting Charlotte even more. On the pale bedspread her fingers touch Charlotte's swollen, papery hand and they smile at each other.

Out on the pavement Viola looks up at Charlotte's window and wonders if she will ever get old.

Acknowledgments

I would like to thank Martin Goodman, an inspirational publisher and editor, for his warm support of this novel. As always my beloved husband, Gordon, was kind and patient as I floated off each morning to write. Conversations with my brothers, Timothy and Nicholas Hyman, were invaluable and many of these memories of early childhood surfaced when I was talking to my daughter, Dr Rebecca Rohrer.

Researching my mother's Indian background was made possible by helpful librarians in the India Office which is now in the British Library. Their recordings of oral history vividly evoked the sad history of the Anglo-Indian community, despised by both Indians and by the British in India. A story by Kipling, *Kidnapped* (1887) describes the cruel racism of the Raj.

www.ingramcontent.com/pod-product-compliance
Ingram Content Group UK Ltd.
Pitfield, Milton Keynes, MK11 3LW, UK
UKHW040848010625
459141UK00007B/120